MONDAY
THE RABBI
TOOK OFF

by Harry Kemelman

FAWCETT CREST • NEW YORK

DEDICATION

TO FAMILY AND FRIENDS IN ISRAEL

MONDAY THE RABBI TOOK OFF

THIS BOOK CONTAINS THE COMPLETE TEXT OF THE
ORIGINAL HARDCOVER EDITION.

Published by Fawcett Crest Books, a unit of CBS Publications, the
Consumer Publishing Division of CBS Inc., by arrangement with
G. P. Putnam's Sons.

ISBN: 0-449-23872-5

Alternate Selection of the Literary Guild
Selection of the Mystery Guild

Printed in the United States of America

21   20   19   18   17   16   15   14   13

1

FROM the sofa in the living room where she was immersed in the Sunday paper, Miriam heard the door between the breezeway and the kitchen open and close. She called out, "David?" and when her husband came into the room, "Mr. Raymond called just after you left. It sounded important."

Rabbi David Small nodded, rubbing his hands from the cold. He crossed the room to stand in front of the radiator. "I saw him at the temple."

"You didn't wear your coat?" she said.

"I just had to walk from the car to the vestry door of the temple."

"And you've been having colds all winter."

"Just one cold—"

Although in good health, Rabbi Small was thin and pale and had a kind of nearsighted, scholarly stoop which made him seem older than his thirty-five years. His mother was always urging Miriam to coax him to eat.

"But it's lasted all winter. Was it about the contract he wanted to see you?"

He shook his head. "No, it was to tell me that the board had voted not to hold the congregational Seder this coming Passover."

She could see that he was disturbed. "But it's not for four months yet."

"Four and a half months," he corrected her. "But there's nothing like being beforehand. He told me so that as superintendent of the religious school I could inform the principal not to start coaching the children for their part in the service. That's called going through channels, like when I was a chaplain in the Army, I had to tell Pastor Bellson anything I wanted rather than talk to the colonel directly."

She could not fail to notice the bitterness in his tone. "Did he say why they decided not to hold it?"

"Not until I asked him. He said the last two years we lost money on the affair."

She looked up at him, "Does it bother you?"

"It bothers me that I wasn't invited to discuss it with the board. I've got over being bothered about not sitting in on board meetings. Although after six years where each new board invited me to attend, the failure of this board to ask me is rather pointed. But this question of the Passover is so peculiarly within the area of the rabbi's jurisdiction, you'd think they'd want to know my views. If I am not to pass on matters of this sort, then what is my function here? Am I just a functionary in charge of ceremonials? Do they think—"

"But are you sure it was intentional, David?" she asked anxiously. He was so irritable of late. She tried to mollify him. "They're new at the game; maybe they just don't realize—"

"New at the game! They've been in office for three months now. And if they are in doubt about what is proper, there are people they can ask. No, it's their entire attitude. They're in control, and I'm just an employee. Take the matter of my contract—"

"Did he mention it?" she asked quickly.

"He did not."

"And you didn't either?"

"I mentioned it when it was due to expire," he said stiffly, "and that should be sufficient. Do you expect me to keep asking them? Am I supposed to wheedle it out of them?"

"But you're working without a contract."

"So?"

"So they could fire you. They could give you a

month's notice telling you that your services were no longer required."

"I suppose they could. And I could do the same to them. I could notify them that I was leaving." He smiled impishly. "I'm rather tempted."

"Oh, you wouldn't."

He left the radiator to pace the floor.

"Why not? It might be a good idea, now I think of it. What would I lose? The few months to the end of the year? If they haven't given me a contract so far, it can only mean that they have no intention of re-appointing me next year. Why else haven't they talked to me about it? Why else haven't they asked me to attend board meetings? And this today—just telling me that they're not going to hold the community Seder. Yes, I'm sure that's what they have in mind. I am supposed to go through the motions for the rest of the year—marrying people, making little speeches at Bar Mitzvahs, giving my sermons on Friday night services—then they'll notify me that for next year they are planning to make a change. Well, why not beat them to the punch?"

"Oh, they wouldn't," Miriam protested. "They couldn't get away with it. Mr. Wasserman and all your friends would put up a fight—"

"Well, I'm not so sure that I want a fight. Why should I have to fight? How long before I am accepted? I've been here six years now. I'm on my seventh year, and there's been a crisis about my job almost every year. They've either tried to fire me or done something that left me no choice but to resign. I'm sick of it. It shouldn't be a condition of a man's employment that he should have to spend his time and energy just to keep his job. His energies should go into doing the work that the job involves."

"Well," Miriam pointed out, "the last board was planning to give you a life contract and a year's sabbatical leave as well."

"I heard rumors to that effect, and I suppose I would

have accepted it if they had," he said moodily. "And yet what good is a life contract? It binds me, but it doesn't bind them. Any time they want to get rid of me, they have only to propose something outrageous that I couldn't live with, and I'd resign. Isn't that what happened when I made a rabbinic decision on the matter of burying poor Isaac Hirsch, and Mort Schwarz, who was president at that time, overrode me and ordered the body exhumed? Well, if you remember, that was during the first year of my five-year contract. And I had no choice but to resign."

"But they didn't accept your resignation," Miriam said.

"Oh, they would have all right if it hadn't been for the Goralskys whom they were honeying up to. And only last year, didn't Ben Gorfinkle actually tell me he was going to pay me off for the few remaining months of my contract and fire me right in the middle of the year?"

"Yes, but he and his friends on the board thought you were turning their kids against them. It was just a power play. I'm sure they wouldn't have gone through with it. Your friends on the board, Wasserman and Becker and the others, would have stopped it."

"But Wasserman and Becker didn't stop it," he said. "The best they could do was to offer me a job in another congregation they were thinking of starting up. Only when those same kids got involved in a murder case did it save my job. And that same Becker, I might add, was the man who led the opposition to me the very first year I was here and was all for dropping me when not only my job but my neck was at stake."

"Oh, David," Miriam reproved him, "that's ancient history. Becker's been as strong a backer for you as Wasserman ever since. You surely don't hold his opposition the first year against him."

"I don't hold the opposition of any of them against them," he said, "neither Becker nor Schwarz nor Gorfinkle. They were all doing what they thought was for the best. Maybe the only one I should resent is Jacob Wasserman."

Miriam looked at him incredulously. "Wasserman! Why, he's been your friend from the beginning. He's the one who brought you here and kept you here against all opposition."

The rabbi nodded.

"Well, that's what I mean. He's been *too* good to me. Maybe if that first year he had gone along with the majority opinion, I would have left here and got another job with another congregation. Maybe I've had to fight for my job here because I don't really belong. If after six years, I still have to fight for my job, maybe it's the wrong job. Maybe another congregation—"

"But they're all like this, David," Miriam said, "all the suburban congregations."

"Then maybe it's me. Maybe I'm not flexible enough. Maybe I don't belong in the rabbinate at all, at least running a congregation. Maybe I ought to be in teaching or research or organizational work." He sat down on the sofa and faced her. "Do you remember last Passover, Miriam, when we were sure I was through here and we decided that instead of hunting around for another job right away, we'd go to Israel instead?"

"So?"

The hint of a smile crossed his face. "So why don't we do it? If they can send me packing with a month's notice, why can't I leave with the same notice to them?"

"You mean resign your job?" She was visibly shocked at the idea.

"Oh, not necessarily resign. I could ask for a leave of absence."

"And if they didn't grant it?"

"I'd take it just the same. I'm tired and fed up and sick of this place. Do you realize that we've been here six years and I haven't had a vacation in all that time. In the summer things slow down. The religious school is closed, and there are no holidays or Friday evening services, but there are weddings and Bar Mitzvahs, and people get sick and expect me to come to visit them, and people come to see me about things that are troubling them. But except for an occasional weekend, we haven't been away at all. I've got to get away where I can be with myself for a while." He smiled. "And in Israel it would be warm."

"I suppose we *could* take one of those three-week tours," she said, considering. "We could see the sights and—"

"I don't want to see the sights," he retorted. "They're either new buildings or the remains of old ones or holes in the ground. I want to live in Jerusalem for a while. We Jews have been yearning for Jerusalem for centuries. Every year at Passover and Yom Kippur we say, 'Next year in Jerusalem.' Last Passover when we said it, we really meant it. We really thought we would go. At least I did. All right, now is our chance. I have no contract binding me."

"But the board would regard it as the equivalent of resigning," she said, "and to give up one's job—"

"Well, suppose they do? We're young yet and can afford to take chances."

Miriam looked at him apprehensively. "But for how long?"

"Oh, I don't know," he said easily, "three, four months, longer maybe; long enough to feel we were living there, not just visiting."

"But what would you do there?" she asked.

"What do other people do there?"

"Well, the people that live there, work. And tourists are kept busy just sight-seeing—"

"Oh, if you're worried about how I'd keep busy, I could finish my Ibn Ezra paper for the *Quarterly*. I've done all the research; I've got all my notes. What I need now is lots of uninterrupted time to write it."

She looked at him, his face eager, so like little Jonathan pleading for some special privilege. More, she felt his desperate need. "This isn't something you've just thought of, David. You've been thinking about it for some time, haven't you?"

"All my life."

"No, but I mean—"

He faced her directly. "Last year, when it looked as though I were through here, I thought we could go before I started looking for another job. When else would we get the chance? Then when it turned out that this job was going to continue, I suppose I should have been glad that I was going to continue to draw a salary. But I wasn't. I'd had my heart set on going—and now I can't get it out of my mind."

"But to give up a job—"

"I'll be able to get another when we come back," he said. "And the chances are I won't have this one next year anyway."

She smiled. "All right, David. I'll write to my Aunt Gittel."

Now it was his turn to look surprised. "What's she got to do with it?"

Miriam put down the newspaper and folded it neatly beside her. "I've followed you, David, in every important decision. When you turned down that job in Chicago that paid so much money because you didn't like the kind of congregation it seemed to be, I agreed, although we were living on my salary as a typist and whatever you could pick up in the way of an occasional holiday job in some small town. And then there was the job in Louisiana that you didn't want. And the job of assistant rabbi in Cleveland that paid more than most regular jobs for rabbis just graduating because you said you didn't want to subordinate your thinking to another rabbi. And when you wanted to resign your jobs here during the Schwarz regime, I went along even though I was carrying Jonathan at the time and wasn't too keen on having to move to another town and find a place to live with a new infant. And now you want to take a chance on losing this job so you can go and live in Jerusalem for a while. Again I'll follow your lead. You're in charge of grand strategy. But you're not so good on tactics. If we're going to live in Jerusalem for several months, we'll have to have a place to stay. We can't live in a hotel for all that time. We can't afford it. Besides, in a hotel you're always a visitor rather than a resident. So I'll write my Aunt Gittel, who's been living in Israel since the days of the British occupation. I'll tell her what we're planning and see if she can find us an apartment to rent."

"But she lives in Tel Aviv and I want to stay in Jerusalem."

"You don't know my Aunt Gittel."

2

BERT Raymond rapped the meeting to order. "I think we can probably dispense with the reading of the minutes of the last meeting. We didn't do much as I recall."

Ben Gorfinkle raised his hand. "I'd like to hear the minutes, Mr. Chairman," he said evenly.

"Oh, well sure, Ben. Will you read the minutes, Barry?"

"Well, Bert, I mean Mr. Chairman, I didn't get around to writing them up. I mean I got my notes, but it's like in rough draft."

"Well, that's all right, Barry. I'm sure Ben will overlook any little mistakes in grammar—"

"What I was going to say is that not having it in final form, and since we didn't decide on anything special last meeting, I didn't think it worthwhile bringing my notes."

The president was a tall, nice-looking young man, a good guy that everyone liked and no one would think of embarrassing needlessly; he was obviously uncomfortable at the secretary's negligence. Gorfinkle shrugged his shoulders. "I guess if nothing happened, it doesn't make any difference." With this new board, there were so many major things to object to, it seemed fruitless to jib at a little matter like not reading the minutes.

"Okay," said the president gratefully, "then let's get on with the important business of this meeting. What's your pleasure on the rabbi's letter?"

Again Gorfinkle raised his hand. "I guess I must have missed something last meeting. I didn't hear about any letter from the rabbi."

The president was contrite. "Gee, that's right, Ben, you don't know about it. I got it during the week, and I talked to some of the boys about it, so I assumed everyone knew. I got this letter from the rabbi asking for a leave of absence for three months starting the first of the year."

"May I see the letter?"

"Actually, I don't have it with me, Ben. But there's nothing in it—just what I said. You know, 'Please regard this as a request for a three-month leave of absence.' That kind of thing, just a straight business letter."

"He gave no reason for his request?" Gorfinkle asked.

"No, just what I told you—"

"I tell you it's a ploy," interrupted Stanley Agranat. "He's not interested in a leave of absence. What he's interested in is a contract. He sends us this letter so we got to go to him and say, 'What gives, Rabbi?' Then he says he wants to take off for three months. So we say, 'But, Rabbi, you can't take off three months in the middle of the year like this. You got a job here.' So he plays Mickey the Dunce and says, 'Oh, have I? I don't have no contract.' Then we got to kind of make it up to him and explain how we haven't had a chance to get around to the matter of contract and how we're sorry and all that crap. And that's supposed to put us on the defensive, see? It's just a ploy."

"So what if we say no?" demanded Arnold Bookspan. "When you showed me that letter, Bert, I said right away it was an ultimatum. He's not asking us, he's telling us. Now, if he's a bona fide employee of the temple, he can't take off just like that. And if he can take off just like that, then as I see it, he's not a bona fide employee of the temple."

"Well, look, guys," said the president, "fair is fair. They always work on a contract, and we let his run out."

"We ought to go about this logically," said Paul Goodman, who, like the president, was a lawyer and had a methodical mind. "First we ought to decide if we need a rabbi at all, then—"

"What do you mean, do we need a rabbi at all? How are we going to get along without a rabbi?"

"Lots of places don't have them," Goodman replied. "I mean not regularly. They get a young punk down from the seminary every Friday evening and pay him maybe fifty or a hundred bucks and expenses."

"Sure, and you know what you get? You get a young punk."

"Not just a young punk," Goodman reproved, "a young rabbi punk."

"Yah, I've seen some of those guys from the seminary. A bunch of hippies, if you ask me."

"Look, fellows," Bert Raymond pleaded, "we can't do that. We got people who use the temple for their weddings and Bar Mitzvahs all year round. When they come to make arrangements, what do we tell them? Maybe we'll have a rabbi and maybe we won't? It's an all-year-round business with us, and we've got to have a rabbi full time."

"All right, so we go to the next step," said the

methodical Goodman. "Is it this rabbi that we want? Personally, if I've got to have some Holy Joe telling me what's right and what's wrong, I'd rather have an older man. It's a matter of sentiment with me."

"Well, to me it's a matter of business. And I don't let sentiment interfere with business," said Marty Drexler, the treasurer. "Now, when Bert told me about this letter, I did some checking around, and I can give you some hard facts to think about. The price of rabbis has been going up every year since World War II. Every class graduating from the seminary has been able to command a higher starting salary than the one before. You go out in the open market to hire a rabbi with five or six years' experience like ours, and you'll pay anywhere from three to five thousand bucks more than we're paying right now because he'll be somebody who's got a pulpit and we'll have to make it worth his while to leave. When you hire a rabbi, you're buying spiritual leadership. Now I say, why raise our spiritual leadership cost three thousand bucks if we don't have to?"

"That makes sense to me."

"Me too."

The president looked around the table. "All right, I think we have a consensus. I think we're all pretty much agreed that right now the best thing for us to do is to continue the services of our present rabbi. So that brings us right back where we started from. What do we do about this letter? My own feeling is that Stan Agranat is right and that what the rabbi is interested in is a contract. How about it? You all in agreement?" Again his glance swept around the table, halting momentarily at each of them for a confirmatory nod.

Only Ben Gorfinkle demurred. "It's my impression that the rabbi usually means what he says."

The president shrugged. "Maybe he did when he wrote it. He may have been a little sore. To tell the truth, I thought he acted kind of sore when I told him that we weren't going to have a community Seder.

That may have had something to do with it. But it's my opinion that if we offer him a contract, he'll decide right quick that he doesn't really want a leave of absence. It could be, you know, that what he wants leave for is to go job hunting."

"You got a point, Bert."

"All right, so what kind of contract do we offer him?"

Ben Gorfinkle, who was last year's president, felt constrained to speak once again. He was present at the meeting only because the by-laws made all past presidents life members of the board. The other former presidents, Becker and Wasserman and Schwarz, had stopped attending after the first few meetings. This particular board, all young men, none of them over thirty-five, consisted of close friends. They discussed temple business in the course of casual social get-togethers, so that the board meetings served little purpose beyond voting formally on what had already been decided between them. But Gorfinkle still persisted in attending, even though for the most part he kept his silence. But this was important. Slowly, deliberately, he explained to the board that at the end of the last season the rabbi had rounded out six years with the congregation and that the previous board had planned to offer him a life contract with a year's sabbatical leave for his seventh year. "But we felt that a contract like that should be negotiated by the new board rather than by the retiring board."

"I don't remember running across it in the minutes of last year's meetings," said the secretary.

"That's right," said Raymond. "I don't recall anything like that."

"Naturally," said Gorfinkle. "The rabbi attended board meetings in those days. We couldn't very well discuss it at the regular meetings."

"In that case," the president interjected, "we have to assume that it was just something that was talked about informally by some of the members. I don't feel that we're bound by it."

"I was just giving you the background," said Gorfinkle stiffly.

"All right, suppose we take that as a starting point," said the president. "How do you guys feel about Ben's idea of a lifetime contract and a year's sabbatical leave?"

"All I can say is it strikes me as a pretty sweet deal," said Agranat. "Mind you, I got nothing against the rabbi, but it's a sweet deal."

"On the contrary," said Gorfinkle, "it's the usual thing. The rabbi was on trial for a year, and then he was given a five-year contract. The next one is usually a still longer contract, and in most places it's for life."

"How do they work the salary on these contracts?" asked Marty Drexler. "Are there annual increments or—"

"I suppose," said Gorfinkle, "or some arrangement for cost of living adjustments. We didn't go into it at the time."

"Seems to me there's a lot of thinking we got to do about this," said Drexler. "If we give him a sabbatical, we're going to have to hire a replacement while he's gone. Think about that for a while."

"What are you getting at, Marty?" asked the president.

"I'll tell you what I'm getting at. This is a temple, and he is a rabbi. It's religion and all that. But a contract is a business deal, I don't care who it's between. Everything has to be spelled out, and each side has to make the best deal they can. Take, for instance, what I said before about the cost of rabbis going up from year to year. That's true, but you take when a rabbi gets to be around fifty, his chances of getting another job are not so good. He's like over the hill. So there he's a little weaker and we're in a little stronger position. He's what? Thirty-five or so now? So suppose we offer him a fifteen-year contract with the idea of negotiating again when that expires."

"Gee, I don't know. . . ."

"That's kind of dirty."

"What's dirty about it?" demanded Drexler.

Stanley Agranat waved his hand. "I want to make a motion."

"What's your motion?"

"Just a minute, Mr. Chairman, there's a motion on the floor."

"What motion?"

"There's no motion on the floor. We were just discussing, kind of chewing the fat."

Raymond rapped on the table with his gavel. "Just a minute, let's get organized. Nobody made a motion, so there's no reason why Stan can't make one. Go ahead, Stan."

"I move, Mr. Chairman, that you appoint a committee to go and see the rabbi and kind of feel him out and get the lay of the land——"

"You sure it's the rabbi you got in mind, Stan?"

The chairman rapped on the table. "C'mon, guys, get serious."

"Well, to be serious," said Goodman, "I'd like to amend Stan's motion and make it a committee of one, and I'd like to nominate Marty Drexler for the job."

"Yeah, that's right, let's have just one guy deal with him."

"How about it? You all in favor of having one guy do the negotiating?"

"Right."

"The only way."

"The only fair way—one against one."

"All right," said Bert Raymond. "All in favor say aye; all opposed, nay. The ayes have it. But I think maybe *I* ought to talk to him instead of Marty."

"No, let Marty."

"Why Marty? As the president of the congregation, it seems to me that I ought to talk to him."

None of them liked to say that they were afraid he might give away too much, but Paul Goodman offered to explain. "I suggested Marty in the first place because he's the treasurer and this is definitely a money matter. Besides, Marty is in the finance business and knows all about the angles that got to do with cost of living increases and that kind of thing. But if not Marty, then it seems to me that you'd be the last one we'd want, Bert, just because you *are* the president. Marty or somebody else can always say he's got to check with the board for further instructions or for approval of any deal he might arrange, but anything the president proposed, we'd feel we'd have to back him up on it. And if you promised something and then we didn't back you up, it would put you in a funny spot if you had to go back and say your board wouldn't go along."

"All right," said Raymond, "you see the rabbi, Marty, and work something out."

3

MIRIAM opened the door and ushered Marty Drexler into the living room where the rabbi was sitting. "Since it's temple business, Mr. Drexler, I'll leave you two—"

"Well, maybe you ought to sit in on this, Mrs. Small," said Marty. "In my own business when it's family finances like our family plan loan, I always tell the client to come in with his wife. You know what I mean?"

"Of course, Mr. Drexler, if you prefer."

The rabbi had risen, and he now motioned their guest to a chair and then sat down himself. "This has something to do with our family finances, Mr. Drexler?"

Marty Drexler smiled, a beaming loan company

smile. "I'd say it has. We voted in the board to give you a contract, and Bert Raymond appointed me like a committee of one to get all the little details ironed out with you."

"That's very kind of them," said the rabbi pleasantly. He leaned back in his chair and looked ceilingward. "Of course, I tend to think of a contract as an agreement between two equal parties since each has something that the other wants, rather than as something that one party confers on the other."

Drexler was determined not to be put out. He nodded. "Yeah, I guess you're right at that. I meant I'm here to negotiate it."

"And why at this time?" asked the rabbi.

Drexler looked at him reproachfully. "Rabbi," he said, "we're grown men. We're not a bunch of kids. We got the message. You send us a letter asking for a leave of absence; it didn't take us long to realize that you were tickling us on the contract. After all, we're all businessmen. All right, maybe we been a little remiss. Maybe we been sitting on our fannies— sorry, Mrs. Small—when we should've been tending to business. But to tell the truth, we're kind of new to the game. We figured it was just like a matter of form. All right, I'm sorry; we're all sorry. Now let's get down to business. Suppose you tell me what you have in mind, and I'll tell you what the boys figured was fair. Then if there's a gap between us, we'll chin about it. And you feel free to talk up, Mrs. Small, because you're as much concerned as the rabbi is, I guess. Maybe even more because I always say that it's the lady of the house that's the homemaker. She's the one who knows how much groceries the family needs and how much they're going to cost. So, you folks lay it right on me, and then I'll tell you how the board feels. We'll work out something, and if it's different from what we had in mind, I'll discuss it with the board and then come back here and see you about it again until we get it all straightened out. Fair enough?"

"It's fair enough, Mr. Drexler," said the rabbi. He hesitated and tapped the arm of his chair with his fingertips as he marshaled his sentences to explain. "You may find this hard to believe, Mr. Drexler, but when I sent that letter, all I was interested in was a leave of absence. That's still all I'm interested in. I haven't given any thought to the matter of a contract, and I don't think that I'm prepared to think about it right now. A leave of absence I asked for, and it's a leave of absence that I want."

Drexler was still not convinced. He could not help feeling a certain admiration for the rabbi's gifts at dickering. He tried another tack. "All right, you want to play it that way, I'll go along. Let's think about it and see where it leads. You say you want a leave of absence. In your letter you said three months. That's still what you want?"

The rabbi nodded.

"So you go away for three months. And you'll be expecting full pay, I suppose?"

"As a matter of fact, I hadn't thought about it." He considered. "No, I don't think I'd be entitled to any pay under the circumstances."

Drexler was annoyed. How do you dicker with someone who doesn't want anything from you? He had planned to point out that if the temple paid him three months' salary, a sizable sum, they would have to have some agreement that he would make it up to them. But if he didn't expect to be paid. . . .

"Suppose we refuse the leave of absence, Rabbi?"

The rabbi smiled faintly. "I'm afraid I'd take it anyway."

"You mean you'd resign?"

"You wouldn't be giving me any other choice."

"Then does that mean if we vote the leave of absence, you're definitely coming back?"

The rabbi was honestly troubled. "I don't know. I don't know how I'll feel or what I'll want three months from now." He smiled. "Who of us does?"

"But look here, that puts us in kind of a spot. I mean, we've got to hire somebody to take your place while you're gone, and if you're not sure you're coming back. . . ."

"I see your problem, Mr. Drexler. All right, why don't we just assume that I'm coming back? And when I do, we can then negotiate a contract that will be mutually acceptable." He smiled. "Of course, if I should not, then we wouldn't have to."

The telephone rang, and Miriam hastened to answer it. She listened for a moment and then said, "It's New York, David. Your mother, I suppose. Why don't you take it on the extension?"

The rabbi excused himself and hurried out of the room. On the phone, Miriam said, "Hello, Mother. Everything all right? . . . Yes, we're fine. . . . Yes, Jonathan is fine. . . . Yes, David's here, he's taking it on the other phone." She listened for the click that signaled that her husband had picked up the receiver and said, "I'll say good-bye now, Mother. We've got company." She hung up and came back to where she had been sitting.

She apologized to Marty Drexler for the interruption and then went on, "My husband has been in Barnard's Crossing over six years, Mr. Drexler. In all that time, he hasn't had a real vacation—just an occasional weekend. He's tired. He feels stale. He needs to get away from all his regular work so that he can get a chance to think. You think it's easy for me to pick up and leave for three months and live on our savings? You're right, I'm the homemaker. I'm the one who worries about expenses and this trip will be expensive—just the fares—"

"You're planning on a tour or something?"

"We're going to Israel, to Jerusalem."

"Oh, but look here, Mrs. Small, if it's Israel, well, I can understand that. I mean, him being a rabbi, naturally he's got to visit the place. He's probably the only rabbi around here who hasn't been yet. But look here, Don Jacobson, who's on the board, is in the travel business. I'll bet he can work out something, maybe a three-week tour where your husband will be the guide and it won't cost him a red cent. I'll talk to him."

The rabbi returned to the room while he was speaking. To Miriam he said, "Nothing important." To Drexler, he said, "It's kind of you to want to arrange something, but we're planning to go there to live for a while, in Jerusalem, not just to visit."

"You mean just in Jerusalem? You're not going touring to see the sights? And for three months? Why?"

The rabbi laughed shortly. "It might not strike you as compelling, Mr. Drexler, but I'll try to explain. The Passover is our basic holiday. We celebrate it not merely with a service but with an elaborate ritual so that its lesson, the philosophy on which our religion is based, will be engraved on our minds."

"Oh, you still bothered about our decision to drop the congregational Seder? Well, there were sound financial—"

"No, Mr. Drexler, I'm not bothered by the board's decision," the rabbi assured him. "There are good arguments on either side, although I might point out that it is a question on which the rabbi of the congregation would normally be consulted. No, I was going to say that the ritual ends with a devout wish 'Next year in Jerusalem.' Well, I've made that wish at the end of every Passover Seder, but last year it was for me not a wish but a promise, a religious commitment, if you like."

Drexler was impressed, and for the remaining few minutes of his visit he was subdued and respectful. But by the time he got home his natural cynicism had reasserted itself, and when his wife asked how he'd made out, he replied, "He says he wants to go and live in Jerusalem for a while; it's like a religious commitment with him. Who's he trying to kid? He's just lazy and wants to goof off for a while. He saves up a little money, and now he's going to blow it."

"Well, he'll be getting his salary—"

"He will not."

"You're not going to pay him his salary?" She was surprised.

"Look," said Marty, "he's taking a leave of absence. You don't pay a salary to somebody taking a leave of absence."

"That's kind of mean, isn't it? Is that what the board decided, or was it your idea, Marty?"

"Look, Ethel, it's not my money; it's the congregation's. As treasurer, I'm supposed to use it for their advantage. I can't just throw it away because it's the rabbi. Besides," he said, "he suggested it himself."

She did not answer then or during the remainder of the evening when he made sporadic remarks during the TV commercial to the effect that "Some guys sure have it soft if they can take off for three months and their wives go along with the crazy idea," and, "Of course, by paying his own way, he's got no obligation to us. He's probably writing to a bunch of congregations right now asking about jobs."

But later when they were lying in bed and he was on the point of dropping off to sleep, she said, "You know, Marty, it's crazy and all that, but it's kind of nice, too."

"What are you talking about?"

"I mean throwing up your job and just taking off—"

4

"HE asked for three months' leave of absence and they gave him three months' leave." Harvey Kanter threw one leg over the arm of his chair, ran a hand through his brush of iron-gray hair and focused protruding blue eyes on his brother-in-law, Ben Gorfinkle. "So how do you figure they done him dirty?" Harvey was a good ten years older than Gorfinkle, in his fifties, and was married to the elder of the two sisters. He tended to patronize him just as his wife did her younger sister. As editor of the Lynn *Times-Herald,* a local newspaper which might dismiss news of the gravest national or international importance with a paragraph while devoting two columns to the installation of officers of the local Dorcas Society, his editorials expressed the hidebound conservative Republicanism of the owners, but in private life, he was radical, agnostic and generally irreverent—especially when it came to his brother-in-law's connection with the temple in Barnard's Crossing which he found highly amusing.

"But it's without pay, and the guy can't have much money saved up."

"But you said that was what the rabbi said he wanted."

"I said that was what Marty Drexler *reported* he wanted," Ben remarked.

"And you think this Drexler lied? That's the money-lender, isn't it?"

"Great Atlantic Finance. No, I don't think he lied. He couldn't; it would be bound to come out. But a guy like Marty Drexler could maneuver the rabbi into a position where he'd pretty much have to say it. You know, 'Are you suggesting, rabbi, that you take off for three months and we hire a substitute and pay you, too, for not doing anything?' That kind of thing."

"Well," Kanter said, "the rabbi is a big boy and ought to be able to take care of himself."

"He's actually pretty naïve about money and business." Ben shook his head. "He could have had a life contract and a year's sabbatical. The board would have granted that if he had insisted."

"That's what you favored?" Harvey looked at his brother-in-law.

"That's what the board last year agreed to offer him," Ben said. "But it was at the end of the term, and on a lifetime contract we felt that the new board should pass on it. Naturally, we thought the new board wouldn't be much different from the old. You know, each year you drop some deadwood and pick up some new people, but from year to year it's pretty much the same. But the Raymond-Drexler crowd put up a full slate and they won."

"How'd they manage that?"

"Well," said Ben, "for one thing, the congregation was pretty much split down the middle last year. There was my bunch, and there was Meyer Paff's group. We had a majority, of course. That's how we got in. But it was a very slim majority, and after the trouble our kids got into, we were pretty disorganized, and frankly not too interested in campaigning for control of the temple. I guess a lot of us were feeling sort of disenchanted with the whole business. We didn't fight too hard."

Seeing his brother-in-law's skeptical look, Ben tried to explain more fully. "We figured we didn't have to fight too hard. We thought that since the Raymond-Drexler group were so young—under thirty-five—and since they were all relatively new to the temple—most of them had only been members two or three years— we figured they wouldn't get far. But over the years, that age group had been growing in numbers in the congregation, and right now, I guess there are more of them than there are of us older people. The kids grow up, people retire a lot earlier these days, there are a lot of reasons—"

Harvey still looked unconvinced. Ben elaborated:

"The temple was started by Jake Wasserman and Al Becker, people like that, well along in years. They had ties to the tradition which made a temple important to them. It certainly was to Wasserman, who is a deeply religious man. Besides, in those days, when the temple was just getting started, you needed men with money, and I mean a lot of money, like Wasserman and Becker, because they were expected to dig down every now and then to pay a fuel bill or a teacher's salary out of their own pocket when the treasury was empty. They took back notes from the temple organization, but I don't think they really expected that the temple would ever be able to make good on them. And I think some of them are still outstanding. Well, you had to be well along in years to accumulate that kind of money."

"That's true," acknowledged Harvey.

"And then when the temple began to stabilize, I mean when we were meeting current expenses, people like Mort Schwarz came into power. Somewhat younger men, but still pretty well-to-do, because in those days we were always having drives for funds and you couldn't urge someone to make a big donation or pledge if you hadn't made one yourself."

Harvey raised an eyebrow in exaggerated surprise. "Well, *you* don't have that kind of money. Or do you, Ben, and are keeping it secret?"

But Gorfinkle didn't react. "Oh, by the time my group came into power," he said seriously, "the temple was completely in the black. What they wanted was somebody who could run things efficiently, the administrative-executive type."

"What about Raymond and Drexler? Aren't they administrators, too?"

Ben shook his head. "No, they're different. They're younger, for one thing. And they're all either in the professions or in business for themselves, and they're all doing pretty well, I guess, but of course they're still on the make. And if you're a lawyer like Bert Raymond or Paul Goodman, being a big shot in an organization like the temple is helpful. People get to know you who otherwise wouldn't. And it helps an accountant like Stanley Agranat and the doctors and dentists who are part of the group."

"You mean they're in it just for the publicity?" Harvey needled him gently. "Not like the rest of you."

"Well, no," said Ben, ignoring the jibe at himself, "that wouldn't be entirely fair. Let's just say that they're mindful of it. For the rest, I imagine that they feel their oats and want to run things. They're in town politics, too, and for the same reason or reasons."

"All right," said Harvey, getting serious at last, "so what have they got against the rabbi that makes you think they want to do him dirty?"

Gorfinkle thought for a moment. "It's a little hard to explain. For one thing, he's the same age, thirty-five, and yet he doesn't think the way they do at all. He's not particularly interested in money or in getting a bigger pulpit with more prestige. He's done some pretty spectacular things in the time he's been here, but he's never courted any publicity for them, not because he's modest, because he isn't, but because he doesn't think such things are important. Maybe they'd tolerate that in an older man, but not in a man their own age. You understand?"

Harvey nodded. "I think so."

"There's another thing: He knows exactly what he thinks and he doesn't hesitate to say it."

"You mean he's dogmatic? Opinionated? Stubborn?"

"No, although it might seem that way sometimes and maybe some people might think so." Ben laughed dryly. "*I* thought so at one time."

"I remember."

"But it's something different," Ben went on. "Old Jake Wasserman once said of him that he had a kind of radar beam of the Jewish tradition in his mind. When the congregation went off to one side or the other, he heard a beep that told him we were straying and he'd chivy us back on course. The kids, the young high school and college kids like my Stuie, go for him in a big way. I asked Stuie about it, and he said it was because they know exactly where they stand with him. As I got it, he doesn't play up to them and he doesn't talk down to them."

"I think I get the picture. So what are you worried about?"

"Well," said Ben, "for one thing, these kids don't vote."

"Oh, you're worried that this Drexler and his friends will maneuver him out?" said Harvey, trying to see what his brother-in-law was driving at.

"That, and—well"—Ben looked away—"I wouldn't like to see him hurt."

"Is that all?" Harvey laughed and got up from the armchair. "Forget it, Ben. People like that, people with personal integrity, people like Drexler can't hurt."

5

THE young graduate of the seminary was eliminated from serious consideration almost immediately. Why would he want to come in the first place? With the demand so great for rabbis, why would he want a temporary job when he could get a full-time job?

"He said he wants some time to look around."

"So can't he look around in a regular job? If he should decide he wants to go someplace else, would they hold him there by force? I'll tell you why he wants this job: It must be because he *can't* get another one. And why should we want someone like that? Besides, he's got a beard. That's all we need is a rabbi with a beard."

"And his wife—did you get a load of her? With all that mascara junk on her eyes like a raccoon and her dress up to her *pupik?*"

Rabbi Harry Shindler, on the other hand, made quite a different impression. He was in his mid-forties and had an ingratiating and yet forceful personality. The main objection to him was that he had been out of the active rabbinate for several years. He explained it with disarming candor. "Well, I'll tell you. When I got out of the seminary, I was offered this job— associate to the rabbi of this large congregation in Ohio. Now I was told that the rabbi was going to retire in a year or two and that I would be given his job. Mind you, I wasn't just an assistant. I had the title Associate Rabbi. So in the middle of the second year I was there, the rabbi gets sick and I took over for the remainder of the year. Then when the next year begins and it's time to draw up a new contract, there's a group on the board that say they ought to have an older man but I could stay on as associate at the same salary. It's really a one-man operation, you understand, but they had me come in because the rabbi there was not in good health.

"Now a man's first duty is to his family—I mean, I had a wife and family—and the associate rabbi job, the salary I mean, just wasn't enough. Now one thing I want distinctly understood: It was not the fault of the congregation. And it wasn't the fault of the board. It was just one of those misunderstandings that happen. Maybe it was my fault for not getting everything down in black and white, but I'm not holding the congregation to blame."

This insistence that the congregation was not at fault made a great impression on the committee.

"So I took this selling job, and I'm not sorry I did. I sometimes think the seminary ought to require all their graduates to serve an apprenticeship of a year or two in business so they can get an idea of how their congregation thinks, what concerns them, what bothers them, what problems they have. I think most rabbis are out of touch with everyday life, and from where I stand that means out of touch with reality."

"How do you mean, Rabbi?"

"Well, take the business of our holidays. Mostly

they're two days, and most rabbis are pretty concerned about the observance of that second day. Now, having been in business myself, I know that sometimes it's almost impossible to take that second day off. So I can understand and sympathize when one of the congregants, who might be a big businessman, just can't make it to the temple on that second day. And I don't hold it against him. I don't take the point of view that because he's, say, an officer of the temple, he's simply got to show on both days."

There was a nodding of heads and thus encouraged, Rabbi Shindler went on, "Well, I made up my mind that I was going to give it the old college try, and if God called me to serve Him by engaging in business, I'd stick with it until I was successful. I worked hard, and I don't mind saying that there was many a time when I thought of going back to the safety and sanctuary of the rabbinate, but then I thought I'd be admitting defeat. Well, when I was made assistant general manager of the Northeast Ohio territory, I figured I'd served my time and then some, and that I could now go back to the rabbinate without feeling that I was doing it because I was a failure in business. And I don't mind telling you gentlemen that I could make a lot more money staying on with National Agrochemical Corporation than I could hope to make in the rabbinate. But the rabbinate is my real work. I feel it's what I'm called on to do, and that's why I'm interested in this position."

"But you're out of touch; you've been away—"

"Oh, no, I haven't. Sometimes I think I was more active after I left than while I was actively carrying on my official rabbinic duties. I was president of the local Zionist chapter. As a matter of fact, I helped start it. And I was vice-chairman of the Community Fund for three years. It's all in my résumé. I headed up the Ecumenical Committee—that's a group that was out to bring about better relations between Jews, Catholics and Protestants. I was on the Visiting Committee of

the Slocumbe General—that's the town hospital. And
for three years I was the panel chairman of the Kiwanis
Bible Study Class, which used to meet every other
Thursday right straight through the year, winter and
summer. And I guess you gentlemen can figure out
who did most of the talking in that class. And then I
don't need to tell you that whenever I had to go out
of town, the first thing that went into my overnight
bag was my *tallis* and *t'fillen,* because in resigning from
my job as rabbi, I wasn't resigning from being a good
Jew. And I wish I had a nickel for every time I led
the prayers in the minyan of some small town and
the number of times they asked me to give a little
sermon. In the small towns of Northeast Ohio I was
known as the Traveling Rabbi. And of course, through
natural inclination, I kept up with my studies all the
while," he added, to touch all rabbinic bases.

The committee was taken with Rabbi Shindler, but
as they discussed him, second thoughts began to develop. Not that they doubted his ability as a preacher;
they had been more than satisfied with the sample taped
sermons he had sent them, which had led to his being
called in the first place. Nor could they cavil at the
impression he had made during the interview. He
had been straightforward, self-possessed and sincere,
like a good salesman who believed in his product and
had gone to the trouble to make adequate preparation
for his presentation.

"Of course, we'd want to check with his congregation—"

"I don't know that we could get much out of them,
it's been eight years since he left. Chances are that
the same guys might not even be there."

"Well, at least we ought to try to get a line on him
from National Agrochemical," said Drexler.

"Gosh, we can't do that, Marty," said Raymond.
"He's still working for them. They might not like it
if they thought he was looking around for another job.
You know how these companies are."

"But we can't just take him on his own say-so. The whole story could be made up," Drexler insisted.

"Well, we know he's a rabbi because it was the seminary that gave us a line on him. Right? And we know he can preach because there's those sermons on the tapes. And we're all agreed he looked good to us."

"That's right, but there's something that bothers me," said Arnold Bookspan. "Those tapes, they were made right in the synagogue. Right? So, how come he made them?"

"What do you mean?"

"I mean why should a rabbi make a tape of his sermon?"

"Well, a lot of rabbis, they want to have a record."

"Yeah, but then they write them out first. I mean that if he was making tapes of his sermons, maybe he was already looking for a job back then and was making them to send out to congregations that might be interested in hiring."

"You got a point there, Arnold."

"Yeah, but that could've been toward the end," said Barry Meisner, who was in the insurance business, "when he was looking around, and that would be all right in my book. I tell you frankly, I'm sold on the guy. I can just see myself acting the same way he did. I've been in positions where I've had a deal going, and it's crapped out through some misunderstanding that was nobody's fault really, and I've had to rethink the whole business and start on a new tack. We all have. And then we go ahead on the new angle, and plenty of times it works out even better than if the original deal had gone through as planned. So I can see myself in the picture he painted. And I can see myself working up a presentation for this meeting, same way he did, and I'd plan it out pretty much the same way."

"Well, maybe that's what gets me," Bookspan insisted. "I mean, like you say, if I were going to sell a couple of gross of raincoats to some big outfit where

I'd never called before, I'd do it just this way. I think, I hope, I'd be as smooth as this guy."

"So?"

"So that's the trouble with him; he's just like us."

"So we're back where we started from. You know, all this takes time and we don't have too much time," Raymond observed. The boys were the salt of the earth, but sometimes it was hard to get them to come to a decision, especially when he tried to get complete agreement. Division, he felt, with one group voting down the other side just made for bad feelings.

"Yeah, but we can't just take anybody," said Book-span.

"I'm not so sure. It's only for three months."

"Or it could be a lot longer if the rabbi decides not to come back."

Geoff Winer was constrained to speak. He had only recently set up his business, Winer Electronics, in the area. Bert Raymond had done the necessary legal work for him and had got him to join the temple organiza-tion. "Look guys, I'm new in the area, and don't think I don't appreciate your asking me to serve on this committee. But I think, if you don't mind my saying so, being new and all that, that we're going about this in the wrong way. I mean, we're going after the wrong sort of guy. You take a young man, there's got to be something wrong with him or he wouldn't want to come here to take a substitute job where he don't even know how long he's going to last. And a middleaged man would be someone who has a job, and he wouldn't leave to take a temporary job unless he were pretty bad and thought he was going to be fired. So I think we ought to consider an older man.

"Now this rabbi that was the rabbi in the temple where I used to go in Connecticut where I came from— in fact, he married me—he's just retired after being rabbi in that same temple for thirty years. They made him like rabbi emeritus. Now, don't get the idea that Rabbi Deutch is some old geezer with a cane. He's sixty-five, but he's got a lower golf handicap than I have."

"Does he have an accent or something? I mean, does he speak good English, or is he one of those old-timers?" asked Drexler.

"Does he have an accent or something? I mean, does him. Look, he was born here, and so was his father, and I think even his grandfather, or maybe *he* came here when he was a little kid. He's related to the New York Deutch family, you know, the bankers."

"So why would he want to be a rabbi? Why didn't he go into the banking business?" Drexler asked the question, but it had occurred to most of them.

"Look, let's face it; there are guys like that. You know, it's like a crusade—"

"How about the *rebbitzin?*"

Winer made a circle of thumb and forefinger to indicate complete approval. "Believe me, the *rebbitzin* is real class, a Wellesley graduate, or maybe Vassar or Bryn Mawr—anyway, one of the top women's colleges. Matter of fact, if you want to know something, she's a Stedman."

"What's a Stedman?"

"Dan Stedman. Didn't you ever hear of him?"

"You mean the commentator guy? On TV?"

"That's right. That's her brother."

"Sounds pretty good," said Raymond. "Could you give him a ring and arrange to have him come down so we could get a look at him and see what he sounds like, maybe have him take a Friday evening service?"

"Unh-unh." Winer shook his head. "A man like Rabbi Deutch you don't ask him to come down for a tryout. If you guys are interested, I could sound him out. If he's interested, we could drive down to see him and talk to him."

6

SUDDENLY the Smalls found themselves popular. People they hardly knew found an occasion to drop in on them—to wish them a safe and pleasant flight, but especially a safe one. "We were planning to go about this time, but my wife thinks we ought to wait until things quiet down a bit—fella could get hurt when one of those bombs go off [self-conscious chuckle] —so we decided to take a trip to Bermuda instead."

To give them names and addresses of people they should look up. "I met him when I was there four years ago, and he's doing some very important research at the university. One of the outstanding men there. I'm writing to tell him you're coming. You call him as soon as you get settled."

To show them the itinerary of the trip they took last year together with colored slides and photographs of the places they had seen and to make sure that they wouldn't miss what they regarded as the highlights of their trip. "I took this on a kind of hazy day, so you don't get the full effect, Rabbi, but I tell you, the view is breathtaking. And be sure and see. . . ."

Meyer Paff, one of the pillars of the temple, came to see the Smalls. He was a huge tun of a man with large features. His sausagelike fingers closed over the rabbi's hand in greeting. "Take my advice, Rabbi, don't get sucked into the sight-seeing rat race. I been there four times already. The first time they had me going from early morning till night. After the first week I said I'm not moving from the hotel. And that's what I did all the other times we went. I'd stay in the hotel, sitting around the pool, *shmoosing*, playing cards. The missus, of course, she wanted to see things. She'd take one of these tours at the drop of a hat. So I told her to go and she could tell me about it afterward. You know, any other country I wouldn't think of letting her go alone, but in Israel, you feel it's safe. There's always Hadassah ladies that if she don't know them, she at least knows somebody they know. It's like family. And I'll tell you something: Just before coming home, I'd buy a bunch of slides of different places and when people asked me, 'You saw such a place, didn't you?' I'd say, 'You bet. Terrific. I got some swell shots of it.'"

Ben Gorfinkle came to see him. "I was talking to my brother-in-law. He's editor of the Lynn *Times-Herald* you know. He thought maybe you'd be interested in writing some pieces for the paper."

"But I'm no reporter," said the rabbi.

"I know, but what he had in mind was background stuff, personal impressions, local color. That kind of thing. All he could pay would be regular space rates. I don't know what it would come to—probably not much, and of course, he couldn't promise to run them until he'd seen them—but the way I look at it, it would keep your name in front of the public."

"I see," said Rabbi Small. "Well, thank him for me, and thank you."

"You'll do it?" Ben asked eagerly.

"I can't tell until I'm there."

"I really think you ought to try, Rabbi," said Gorfinkle, barely masking his disappointment.

"I understand, Mr. Gorfinkle."

Mr. Jacob Wasserman, the elderly founder of the temple, frail and with parchmentlike skin, came to see him. "You're wise to go now, Rabbi, while you're young and can enjoy it. All my life I've promised myself I'd go, and always something came up, so I couldn't. And now, when I'm under the doctor's care you could say every minute, it's too late."

The rabbi led him to a chair and eased him into it. "They've got doctors there too, Mr. Wasserman."

"I'm sure, but to go on a trip like this, it takes more than just wanting. The heart got to spring up at the idea, and with me, the way I am now, a little walk or maybe a ride in the car for an hour when my son drives me, or Becker comes, is already enough. But it makes me happy that you're going."

The rabbi smiled. "All right, I'll try to enjoy it for both of us."

"Good, you'll be my ambassador there. Tell me, Rabbi, this man who's coming to take your place, this Rabbi Deutch, you know him?"

"I've never met him, but I've heard about him. He has a very good reputation. From what I hear, the congregation is lucky to get him."

The old man nodded. "Maybe someone not so good would have been better."

"How do you mean, Mr. Wasserman?"

"Well, there are parties, cliques, I don't have to tell you."

"Yes, I know," said the rabbi softly.

"And you'll be gone how long?"

"Oh, three months anyway. Maybe more."

The old man put a blue-veined hand on the rabbi's forearm. "But you're coming back?"

The rabbi smiled. "Who can tell what will happen tomorrow, let alone in three months?"

"But right now you're planning to come back?"

His relationship with the old man was such that he could neither fence with him nor fib to him. "I don't know," he said. "I just don't know."

"Ah," said Wasserman, "that's what I was afraid of."

Hugh Lanigan, Barnard's Crossing chief of police, came to see him. "Gladys had a little gift for the missus that she asked me to drop off." He deposited a gift-wrapped package on the table.

"I'm sure Miriam will be very pleased."

"And look," he said, "if you're worried about the house being closed up all the time, I've given orders to have the man on the beat and the cruising car check the place regular."

"Why, thanks, Chief. I was meaning to drop down to the station to leave a key and tell them when we were going."

"I suppose you got to take this trip sometime."

"Got to?" The rabbi looked surprised.

"I mean, it's like a priest going to Rome."

"Oh, I see," said the rabbi. "Something like that, only more so. Actually it's a religious injunction with us, and for all Jews, not just for rabbis."

Lanigan still was trying to understand. "Like a Moslem going to Mecca?"

"No-o, not really. It doesn't confer any special grace, any special religious points." He considered how to answer. "I feel it like a kind of pull, like what I imagine draws a homing pigeon back to where it came from."

"I see," said the police chief. "Then I guess not every one of you has it, or a lot more of you would go."

"A lot of homing pigeons don't get back either, I suppose." He tried again. "You see, our religion is not just a system of belief or of ritual practices that anyone can assume. It's a way of life, but more than that, it's intertwined somehow with the people themselves, with the Jews as a nation. And the two, the religion and the people, are somehow tied in with the place, Israel, and more particularly Jerusalem. Our interest in the place is not accidentally historical. I mean, it is not significant merely because we happened to come from there, but rather because it is the particular place assigned to us by God."

"You believe that, Rabbi?"

The rabbi smiled. "I have to believe it. It's so large

a part of our religious beliefs that if I doubted it, I'd have to doubt the rest. And if the rest were in doubt, our whole history would have been pointless."

Chief Lanigan nodded. "I guess that makes sense." He offered his hand. "I hope you find what you're looking for there." At the door, he stopped. "Say, how are you getting to the airport?"

"Why, I expect we'll take a cab."

"A cab? Why that will cost you ten bucks or more. Look, I'll come down and drive you to the airport."

Telling Miriam about it afterward, he said, "It's curious that of all the people who came to see me, it should be the one Gentile who offered to take us to the airport."

"He's a dear, good friend," Miriam agreed, "but the others probably thought you had already made the necessary arrangements."

"But he was the one who thought to ask."

7

AS she hung his coat in the hall closet, his eyes flicked around the room for some sign of another occupant—a pipe in an ashtray, a pair of slippers beside the easy chair. After all these years, Dan Stedman told himself he was not jealous of his former wife, only curious. If she wanted to take a lover, it was no business of his. Certainly *he* had not been celibate since their divorce. He told himself that she meant nothing to him now, and yet although he had been in town for several days, as a kind of insurance he had held off coming to see her in response to her letter until today, his last day in the States. But as he had mounted the stairs to her apartment, he could not help feeling a quickening of interest, an excitement at the thought he was going to see her.

She joined him in the living room. She was still attractive, he noticed objectively. Tall and slender with her bobbed hair brushed back around her ears and her fresh complexion, she did not look her—he made a mental calculation—forty-five years. As she rounded a table to sit opposite him, he decided she was one of the few women who could wear slacks successfully. She got up again immediately to go to the sideboard.

"Drink?" she asked.

"A little gin."

"On the rocks, I believe?"

"That's right."

She regarded him covertly as she poured. He was still distinguished-looking, she thought, but he looked neglected. His trousers bagged at the knee—she would have seen to it that they were pressed—and his shirt cuffs looked frayed—she would have noticed and insisted he change to another shirt before going out.

"I called you and called you. I must have tried a dozen times. And then I decided to write."

"I was at Betty's in Connecticut for a few days. I just got back last night," he fibbed.

"And how is she? I should write to her."

"She's fine."

"And Hugo?"

"All right, I guess. He's retired from his congregation now, you know."

"Oh, yes, I remember you saying he was thinking about it the last time I saw you. Is he enjoying retirement?" She handed him his drink and then sat down in a straight-backed chair opposite him.

He grinned. "Not particularly. There was so much he was planning to do once he was retired and had the time. But you know how those things work. When he was busy at the temple, he had an excuse, and now that he isn't, he doesn't know how to begin all the projects he stored up all those years. It's even harder on Betty. He's underfoot."

"Poor Hugo."

"But he's getting another job, so it won't be bad. He's substituting for a rabbi in Massachusetts who's going to Israel for a few months. There's even a chance that he might be asked to stay on."

"Oh, that's good." She looked at him over her drink. "And how have you been?"

"All right," he said. "You know I left the network?"

"I heard. Trouble with Ryan again?"

"Not really." He got up and began pacing the room. "I was just fed up. What kind of life is it for a man, running around, sometimes halfway across the world, to broadcast news that his listeners have already read in their newspapers?"

"But you also made news," she pointed out. "You interviewed important people, high government officials."

"Sure," he said shortly, "and they never said anything that wasn't already well-known official government policy." He sat down again. "I've got a line on a job with educational TV. The same sort of thing, but there's a lot more freedom to comment and to give background information. And in the meantime, I'm doing a book for Dashiel and Stone."

"Wonderful. Did you get a good advance?"

It was typical of her, he thought, to ask about the financial arrangements before the subject. "Just barely enough to cover expenses."

"Oh."

"It's a book on public opinion," he went on, "what the man in the street really thinks."

"But you did all that on television," she said.

"No," he said, warming to the discussion. "There they knew they were being interviewed. But for the book I'm going to be using a lapel mike and a pocket tape recorder. Suppose I'm in a restaurant and a couple of people at the next table sound interesting. I just switch on the recorder and tape their conversation to play over and analyze at my leisure."

"I'm sure it will make an interesting book," she said politely.

He finished his drink and put the glass down on the end table beside his chair.

"Refill?" she asked.

"No, I guess not." He leaned back for the first time and looked about him, relaxed. "No need to ask you how you are. You're looking beautiful as ever."

She gave him a quick glance to see if there was anything more intended than the polite gallantry in the remark. "I'm working pretty hard," she said.

"Well, I must say it agrees with you, Laura." He nodded at the wall. "That painting is new, isn't it?"

"Uh-huh. It's a Josiah Redmond. He's doing a cover for us. I don't own it—yet. It's on loan. I want to live with it for a while first to see if I want to buy it."

He knew of Redmond by reputation. He was a chaser, and his work came high. He wanted to ask her jokingly if she was pursuing the same policy with the painter as with the painting, but he held back; he knew it would come out harsh and bitter. Besides, she could well afford to buy the painting in the usual way. As a senior editor at *Co-ed,* she must be making a good salary. So he merely nodded, and focused on the picture while he waited for her to tell him why she had written that she must see him.

"I *must* see you," the letter had said. "It is of the *utmost* importance that we discuss Roy's *future.* I am *extremely* worried . . ." for a couple of pages, every sentence containing at least one italicized word. Her speech was a little that way, too, and when they first went together, he had found it strangely attractive, giving a kind of breathless excitement to her discourse. Later he had found it a little trying.

"I got a letter from Roy," she began.

"Oh, he writes you, does he?" And this time the bitterness slipped out. "I haven't heard from him since he went to Israel."

"Perhaps if you wrote *him*—"

"I wrote him twice. Am I supposed to continue in the hope that he'll break down and answer?"

"Well," she said, "he's *unhappy*."

"That's nothing new. He was unhappy at college. His whole generation is unhappy."

"He wants to come home," she went on.

"So why doesn't he?"

"And lose a *year* in his studies? If he comes home now, he won't get any credit for the courses he's taking at the university."

"That doesn't bother these kids nowadays," Stedman said. "They switch from one major to another and from one college to another the way I change my shoes. And when they finish, they're not prepared to do anything, or willing to. What's he unhappy about?" he asked. "Something specific like a girl, or something general like the state of the world?"

Laura nervously lit a cigarette. "I don't see how you can be so flippant about it all when it's your son who's involved."

"My son!" he exploded. "I fathered him, I suppose, but I don't know that I had anything to do with him afterward."

"Daniel Stedman, you know I consulted with you on every step of his career, every school he went to, every—"

"All right, all right," he said. "Let's not get started on that again. What do you want me to do?"

"Well," she said, stubbing out the cigarette, "I think you could write him a strong letter, ordering him to stay until he finishes the year or you will cut his allowance."

"I see. I have to play the heavy."

"Discipline is a father's duty," she said primly.

"And this will make him happy?"

"At least it might keep him from doing something foolish."

"I'll do better than that," he said, getting up from the chair. "I'll go and see him."

"But you can't just pick yourself up and go halfway across the world." Then she saw that he was smiling. "Oh, you were planning to go to Israel?"

He nodded. "That's where I'm doing the book. It's a book on Israeli opinion."

"When are you going?"

"Tomorrow. I've got a flight to Zurich by Swissair."

"Not El Al? They say it's safer, that they're more careful."

"It's also a lot more crowded. And it's a long trip, and I like to break it up. This gives me a stopover in Zurich," he said, trying to keep his voice casual.

"Zurich?" She shot him a quick glance. "You're not involved in anything, are you?"

"Involved?" He laughed. "How do you mean involved?"

"I still worry about you, Dan," she said simply.

He shrugged his shoulders in a little gesture of annoyance. "Nothing to it. I go right on to Israel from there."

8

FROM her office on the fifth floor of the hospital, Gittel Schlossberg of the Social Service Department could see the rooftops of a considerable section of Tel Aviv, each with the black glass panels set at a forty-five-degree angle to catch the heat of the sun to supply warm water for the apartments below. A tall building blocked her view of the sea beyond, but she knew it was there, and sometimes she thought she caught the swish of the surf over the sounds of the traffic in the street below. She enjoyed the view from her window as she enjoyed driving to work through the narrow, crowded streets with their rows of houses in stained and crumbling stucco, not because it was a pretty view, but because it showed increase and growth.

She had lived in the city most of her adult life and could remember when there was space and gardens between the houses, but she preferred it cramped and crowded, with every bit of spare land put to use and pushing toward ever-increasing suburbs. It meant that more and more people were coming, to settle and work and make the city more prosperous and strong. And as she read Miriam's letter, teetering in her swivel chair, she daydreamed: Her niece was coming with her family; she was coming on a visit, but perhaps she could persuade her to remain.

Some of her colleagues on the staff were inclined to fault Gittel Schlossberg for being unprofessional in her methods. Hers was a purely pragmatic approach. If the problem, for example, was to get a job for a client, she was not above using a little genteel blackmail on a prospective employer to achieve it. And since she herself did not profit from the transaction, her conscience was clear. At the national game of *protectsia,* or influence, she was a past master. Needless to say, little of this ever appeared in her case records, which were spotty at best since she regarded them as a nuisance which agency directors forced on their subordinates in order to show their authority. Whatever was important about her clients she kept stored in the highly efficient record file of her memory.

All this was highly distasteful to her younger colleagues, who tended to be professionally objective in their approach and as scientific as the discipline permitted. On the other hand, the older members of the staff, those who knew her when she was a member of the Haganah in the days of the British occupation and remembered her numerous successes at wheedling food and medical supplies and even guns and ammunition out of the British soldiery, were devoted to her and ready to forgive her most outrageous breaches of standard operating procedure.

When her husband was killed in the terror that preceded the War of Independence, she was left with an infant on her hands. She could easily have elected to give up her activities with the underground and assume the passive role that her new motherhood justified; instead, she had chosen to bury her grief by throwing herself into the work of defending Jerusalem, where she was living at the time. She had even enlisted her infant son in the battle; many a time she had been able to cross the lines the British had established around the Jewish Quarter, to deliver an important message or even needed medicines, by approaching the guards with her babe in arms. Rather than turn back a mother and child, they had let her pass.

Although not a religious woman, she had a mystical faith in the old Yiddish proverb that for every pot there is a cover, that in every problem the good Lord presented her there was a matching problem which provided the solution to both. There had been plenty of men when she was younger who had offered the problem of their bachelorhood as a matching problem to her widowhood with the idea that marriage would solve both. But this one problem she had refused to solve. She had remained single, faithful to the memory of her husband, and had been both father and mother to her child.

A tiny woman, she was a shade over five feet, with a mass of gray hair not so much combed and set as piled on top of her head, which she would poke at periodically to keep from falling down. She was a dynamo of energy. Characteristically, no sooner had she finished reading Miriam's letter than she reached for the telephone and began calling real estate agencies.

It was in accordance with her system of keeping her desk clear of notes and memorandums by doing what had to be done, immediately.

"Shimshon? Gittel speaking." No need to announce which Gittel, even though it was a common name in Israel.

From Shimshon, a cautious, "*Shalom,* Gittel." Calls from Gittel frequently involved finding housing for one of her indigent clients and he would be expected to shave his commission to boot.

"I have a very special problem, Shimshon, and so I'm calling the best first. . . ."

"A furnished apartment at this time of year, Gittel? And for only three months? I'll look around, of course, but it's not going to be easy. I have nothing on my books right now."

Next she called Mair and then Itomar and then Shmuel, explaining to each why she was calling him first. Finally, she called Chaiah, who being a woman required a slightly different approach and tone. "I'm calling you, Chaiah, because it's a special problem that only a woman can really understand. You see, it's my own sister's daughter. . . ."

And it was Chaiah who voiced the difficulties that the others had hinted at. "Look, Gittel, you've got to be realistic. A furnished apartment like you want is not easy to get at any time, but right now, at this time of year, it's practically impossible. And you want it in Talbieh or Rehavia. The university men and the doctors who are going outside to teach or do research have already made their arrangements. If you had approached me in August, I could have given you your pick of half a dozen, but they'll be coming in January, you say. Who has a furnished apartment to rent at that time of year? I rented one last week, but it was for a whole year. And the kind of money they can pay, it's out of the question. My advice is to look around for a place in one of the hostels in the Old City or one of the convents that takes in travelers. Of course, if I hear of anything. . . ."

Gittel herself knew that Talbieh and Rehavia were the two most desirable sections of the city and as such, expensive, but she was certain that no other place was suitable. She did not even know her niece except through snapshots and photographs that her sister in New York had sent over the years, and Rabbi Small only from the wedding picture, but she was quite sure she knew the kind of place they would want. She knew her sister and brother-in-law, so her mind worked, and hence she knew the kind of person their daughter would be and the kind of man she would pick for a husband.

She tilted back in her swivel chair, closed her eyes, to let her mind play with the problem, and the thought of Mrs. Klopchuk, whom she had seen professionally only the day before, came to her. A few minutes later she left her office and headed for her car in the parking lot. It was a ten-year-old Renault that moved by prayers and imprecations if she remembered to fill the gas tank. This time the car started without difficulty, which she took as a good omen. By a sort of reverse magic, it was also a good omen if she had difficulty in starting. When Gittel was determined on a course of action, there were no bad omens.

A quarter of an hour later she was in the Klopchuk apartment sipping at a cup of coffee without which social intercourse in Israel is impossible. "I've been thinking of your problem and I am beginning to have doubts about your idea"—it had been her own idea—"of renting your spare room to a college girl. The money she will pay you—"

"But the money is not important, Mrs. Schlossberg," the woman protested. "I told you I was willing to offer her a room and board in exchange for companionship and help with the housework."

"Ah, but that's what bothers me," said Gittel. "What kind of companionship can you expect from a young college girl? And for that matter, how much help will you get? You'll end up working for her. One night she's got a date, and the next night she's got to study for an exam or she has a paper to write. And you'll say, 'All right, I'll do the dishes. You study.' And if you find out that she is not a very good housekeeper, are you going to send her away after she's moved in? You know you won't be able to."

"So what can I do? I can't afford to hire anyone."

"How about your sister in Jerusalem?"

Mrs. Klopchuk shook her head stubbornly.

"Why not?" Gittel persisted. "She's your sister. If you need help, she's the logical one."

"My sister, God bless her, on the New Year she calls me to wish me a good year. After my husband died and hers was still alive, I used to go there for the Passover. And that was all we ever had to do with each other."

"You are both getting on in years," said Gittel sternly. "These family quarrels, I know what they are. Someone said something and the other one answered, and you stop talking to each other except on the coldest and most formal basis. And most of the time neither party can remember what started the coldness in the first place. You have such a big family, you can afford to be on bad terms with a sister?"

Again Mrs. Klopchuk shook her head.

"Look what a wonderful arrangement it could be," Gittel said. "She could rent her apartment in Jerusalem and she could share living expenses with you here. It's a sister. You have so much in common. You're both of an age—"

"She's older."

"So if she should happen not to feel so good one day, you can help her. You can take care of each other and you're both alone now—"

"I'd cut out my tongue before I'd ask her."

"But if I arrange that you don't have to, that she'll come down and visit with you for a few months?"

"She won't come, I tell you. And she won't rent her apartment to a stranger. She's so fanatic that she wouldn't trust anyone not to mix up her meat dishes with her milk dishes—"

"But suppose I arrange to rent her apartment to someone she can trust absolutely?" Gittel asked. "A rabbi, for instance?"

9

"You are cordially invited to meet Rabbi and Mrs. Hugo Deutch and to wish godspeed to Rabbi and Mrs. David Small, who are leaving for an extended visit to the Holy Land. At the Temple Vestry. On Sunday, December 28. 4 to 6 P.M."

So ran the invitation sent out to all members of the congregation. The job of drawing it up and arranging for printing and mailing had been assigned to Malcolm Slotnik, who was in the advertising business (Creative Communications by Slotnik, Direct Advertising a Specialty) and presumably was expert in this kind of thing.

There were objections, of course, when he submitted his draft to the board.

Bert Raymond said, "Gee, Mal, I had in mind something like, 'You are cordially invited to a reception in honor of . . .' you know, something formal."

"Where you been, Bert? That's from the Middle Ages. Today everything is simple and informal. You send the other kind of invitation and people are apt to show up in tuxedo or something."

"Maybe you're right, Mal," said Marty Drexler, "but you don't say who Rabbi Deutch is. I mean you ought to say something like . . . 'ta-da, ta-da, ta-da to meet our *new* rabbi ta-da, ta-da, ta-da.'"

"Yeah, but then folks might get the idea that Rabbi Small was leaving for good."

"So?" Marty smiled and glanced at Bert Raymond.

"So, then there'd be a lot of questions and we might find ourselves having to do a lot of explaining. You take Al Becker, he's one of the rabbi's strongest supporters. Now, I got the Becker Ford-Lincoln account, and—"

"Yeah, I see your point," said Raymond. "As a matter of fact, I just started doing some of Meyer Paff's law work and I don't know how he'd take it either."

Stanley Agranat suggested that they ought to say, "our beloved rabbi."

"Since when is he your beloved rabbi?"

"Yeah, but they always say it."

"Only at funerals."

They stood at one end of the vestry, the two rabbis and their wives, waiting for the guests to arrive. It was early yet, and members of the Sisterhood were still busy with last-minute details, stacking cups and saucers, setting out plates of cookies and sliced cake, and arguing over the arrangement of the flowers and decorations. Every now and then one of the women would appeal to the rabbis' wives for an opinion, either because by virtue of their position, they constituted the court of highest authority or merely as an excuse to talk to the new *rebbitzin*.

The few members of the board who were present stood in a small group out of the way of the bustling women, casting occasional glances in the direction of the two rabbis, who were left to themselves on the assumption that they had professional matters to discuss. They could not help noting the difference between the two men. Whereas Rabbi Small was of medium height and thin and pale, Rabbi Deutch was tall and erect and ruddy with broad shoulders. And he was handsome, too, with a high forehead surmounted by white hair which appeared even whiter in contrast with his black silk yarmulke. He had an aquiline nose and sensitive mouth framed by an iron-gray mustache and imperial. When he spoke, his deep baritone voice came out in the measured tones of the professional speaker, quite unlike Rabbi Small's voice, which even in the pulpit was flat and matter-of-fact. None of them actually voiced their comparison of the two, but it was obvious from the enthusiastic agreement they gave when Bert Raymond remarked, "He certainly looks good." And it was plain they all concurred when Marty Drexler added, "Now, that's my idea of what a rabbi should look like."

The women were just as delighted with Mrs. Deutch as the men were with her husband. She, too, was tall with gray hair, which was brushed up in back and held in place by a comb. The effect was of a tiara, and it gave her an aristocratic, almost queenly appearance. And withal, she was so simple and democratic. When the president of the Sisterhood presented the officers of the organization to her, she said, "You know, girls, I'd never say it to Hugo, of course, but the plain fact is that it's the Sisterhood that runs the temple." They were enchanted.

They all liked Miriam Small, but in the way they might like the college girl in bobby socks and loafers next door who might occasionally baby-sit for them. Beside Betty Deutch she seemed not merely young, but immature.

When they came up to ask their advice about where the decorative candlesticks should be placed, Miriam said, "Oh, I'd put them near the middle of the table so they won't be in the way of the pourers at either end." Betty Deutch, on the other hand, stood back to get a better view of the table, came forward to move the candlesticks to the end of the table, went back to survey the effect, and then said, "This way they're far enough from the end so they won't bother the pourers too much, and the effect is to make the table seem longer. Don't you think so, girls?"

Their ready agreement carried the clear implication that it was Mrs. Deutch who was now the *rebbitzin*. Noticing it, Mrs. Deutch put her arm through Miriam's, and as they strolled back to where their husbands were standing, she whispered, "In matters that don't mean very much one way or another, I make it a point always to agree with the gals of the Sisterhood and to encourage them to do what they want to do."

"And how many do you get at a Friday evening service, Rabbi?" Rabbi Deutch was asking.

"Anywhere from fifty to seventy-five usually."

Rabbi Deutch pursed his lips. "Out of a membership of almost four hundred families? Hmm. Do you do any advertising?"

"Just the announcement in the press."

"Ah, well, in addition to the press release, we've always sent out postcards to arrive in Friday's mail. I've found that very effective. Also, I always try to pick an intriguing title for my sermon. That helps, believe me. Something topical—"

"Like sex?" asked Rabbi Small innocently.

"As a matter of fact, sex in the Talmud was the title of one of my sermons. We got quite a turnout on that one."

The women now joined them. "I suppose you're planning to do a lot of touring when you first arrive in Israel," said Mrs. Deutch.

"We haven't made any plans, to tell the truth," said Rabbi Small.

"David isn't much of a one for touring," Miriam explained.

"Rabbi Small is a scholar," said Rabbi Deutch. "It's my guess that he'll be spending most of his time at the university library."

"I hadn't thought of it," said Rabbi Small. "I'm working on a paper, but I've already done the research."

"You mean you have no special plans for your stay?" asked Deutch.

"Just to live there."

"Oh." It hardly seemed reasonable to Rabbi Deutch, and he concluded that his colleague was being secretive.

There was an awkward pause, and then Betty Deutch thought to ask, "Do you have family in Israel?"

"David has no one. I have an aunt there. She's the one who got us our apartment in Jerusalem, in Rehavia."

"Oh, that's a nice section. My brother Dan is in Jerusalem now. If you like, I could give him your address. He's been to Israel many times, lived there for about a year the last time. He knows the city well and could show you around."

"That's Dan Stedman, the journalist?"

"Yes. He's doing a book on the country. His son, Roy, is there, too, at the university."

"How nice. Is he doing graduate work?"

"Oh, no," said Betty Deutch, "he's quite young. He's at Rutgers and is taking his junior year abroad."

"By all means give your brother our address," said Rabbi Small. "We're at Five Victory Street, care of Blotner. Your brother and nephew might like a Sabbath meal family style once in a while."

"Oh, Dan will appreciate that." She jotted down the address. "I'll write him in the next day or two."

Bert Raymond came hurrying up. "They're beginning to arrive," he said. "Now I suggest that I stand here, and as they come in, I'll introduce them to you, Rabbi Small, and—"

"I think they know me," said Rabbi Small dryly. "Why don't you have Rabbi and Mrs. Deutch stand next to you and after you introduce the guests to them, they'll move on and perhaps say good-bye to us."

"Yeah, I guess you got a point there. Let's do it that way." The couples shifted places and just in time for Raymond to call out to the first people that came through the door: "Hyuh, Mike. Rabbi Deutch, I want to present Myer Feldman, one of the mainstays of the temple. And Rosalie. Rabbi Deutch, our new spiritual leader, and Mrs. Deutch."

For an hour Raymond presented the members of the congregation. Rabbi Small was amazed to learn how many were "mainstays" or "pillars" or at the very least, "terrific workers." They came in a steady stream for an hour, and then it slacked off, and the rabbis and their wives felt free to circulate among the guests. The Smalls soon found themselves at the opposite end of the room from the Deutches. People sought them out to wish them a safe journey, to suggest places that they should be sure to see, to give them travel tips they had found useful, to press on them the names of friends and relatives, all of whom seemed to be important people who would be overjoyed to entertain them.

Shortly before six, Miriam, mindful of her commitment to the baby-sitter who was taking care of Jonathan, suggested they ought to get started.

"I guess it's all right," said Rabbi Small. "They're really here to see Rabbi and Mrs. Deutch."

They made their way to the Deutches and shook hands and wished each other luck. "And when do you leave for Israel?" asked Rabbi Deutch.

"Thursday."

"Oh, I was hoping we might get to see each other again, but we'll be going back to Connecticut for a couple of days."

"We'll be busy, too," said Rabbi Small.

"And don't worry about your congregation," said Mrs. Deutch. "Hugo will take good care of them." She hesitated. "You're not worried about the bombings, are you?"

"Here or there?"

"Oh, that's good." She pulled at her husband's arm. "I just asked Rabbi Small if he were worried about the bombings, dear, and he said, 'Here or there?' "

Her husband looked at her expectantly.

"You know"—a hint of impatience in her voice— "the bombings on the campuses here."

"Haw-haw, of course. Very good, Rabbi. And a proper commentary on our society. A very good title for a sermon, too. Do you mind if I use it?"

Rabbi Small grinned. "With my compliments, Rabbi."

Rabbi Deutch offered his hand again. "Well, go in peace and come home in peace," he said in Hebrew. He chuckled. "Here or there. Very good."

As they drove home, Miriam asked, "Well, what do you think of them?"

"They seem to be all right. I didn't get much chance to talk to them."

"They're pros, David."

"Pros?"

"Professionals. I'll bet they won't have any trouble with the congregation or with the board. They know just what to say at all times and how to say it. They'll have the congregation eating out of their hand—and liking it."

Later, much later, for they had gone to the Raymonds for a bite of supper, when they were back in their hotel room and getting ready for bed, Betty Deutch asked, "Did you get the feeling, dear, that the Smalls might be having some trouble with their congregation or at least with some of the board members?"

Hugo Deutch neatly placed his jacket on a hanger. "I've been getting hints to that effect from the president and that close friend of his—what's his name? Drexler —ever since we've met. It's too bad. There's a technique to handling a congregation, and Rabbi Small hasn't learned it yet, I'm afraid. I'm not sure that he ever will." He unlaced his shoes and put on his house slippers. "He's a scholar, you know. He published a paper on Maimonides a few years back—I never read it, but I heard some complimentary remarks about it. Well, that kind frequently are not very good at leading a congregation. They're in the wrong business, and sometimes they realize it early enough and switch to their proper work—teaching, research—and sometimes they hang on, draining their energy doing something they cannot do well and probably don't even enjoy."

His wife smiled. "Perhaps he'll realize it after he's been in Israel away from it all for a few months."

10

AS Roy Stedman scrubbed his face dry with a towel, his friend Abdul walked around examining the large wall posters that were the principal decorations of the small room: the pig in a policeman's uniform standing on his hind trotters; the nun raising her skirt to her thigh to reach her purse concealed in her stocking; the nude couple facing each other, holding each other's sex organs, like two people gravely shaking hands on being introduced.

Over his shoulder, Abdul said, "The girls, when they see this, they do not object, they do not get angry?"

"No one's ever objected," said Roy with a leer. He didn't mention that so far he had not succeeded in persuading any girls to visit his room. "Maybe it gives them the right ideas."

"That's very clever. And if your papa, how do you say it, your daddy, comes to visit you, you will leave these in place?"

"Sure, why not?" Roy tossed the towel on a hook and then began to comb his long hair.

"He is rich, your daddy?"

"Rich? I wouldn't say he was rich. Comfortable, I guess, but I wouldn't call him rich."

"If he stays at the King David, he must be rich," said Abdul positively.

"Oh, yeah? Is it that expensive? Couple of times I was there, it didn't look so great."

"Believe me," said Abdul, "it is expensive. For one night, or for a week, maybe not; but to live there on a permanent basis. . . ."

"Well, he might get reduced rates being a TV personality. Or maybe he won't be staying there long. In his letter he said he'd be touring the country, that he'd rent or buy a car and move around—you know, a few days here, a few days there. This book he's writing will take him all over."

"And you will go with him on some of these trips?"

"If he's going somewhere I want to go."

"And the car, you will perhaps get to use it sometime on your own?"

Roy smiled. "Look, if my old man gets a car, I bet I'll use it more than he does."

"Then you won't have any time for Abdul. All the girls, how do you call them—chicks?—you'll have any you want."

"Nah." But Roy was obviously pleased at the idea. "The broads around here, they're like icicles."

"Icicles?"

"Yeah, you know, like cold."

"Ah, I see." Abdul nodded in wise understanding. Then he smiled. "Maybe I have you meet some different kind girls. Not cold. Hot ones."

"You mean the Arab girls around here? They're even worse than the Jewish ones. They're like on a rope and their old man's got a good grip on the other end."

"Ah, but there are other kinds—those who know how to act with a man. They know what a man wants. They make your blood boil." He patted his young friend on the shoulder. "You get a car and we get a couple of girls and we drive to a place that one of my relatives has for a couple of days, a weekend. I'll guarantee you a good time."

"Yeah? How about having me meet some right now?"

"You mean tonight?"

"No, not tonight, but you know. . . . Why do we have to take them to your relative's place? I mean what's wrong with right here?"

"Well, maybe. I'll think about it." He deliberately changed the subject. "He's a Zionist, your daddy?"

"Gosh, I don't know. I never talked to him about it."

"All Americans are Zionist." Abdul could not prevent some hint of indignation from showing in his voice.

"I'm an American, and I'm not a Zionist," said Roy mildly.

"I mean all American Jews."

"Well?"

"But you told me once that your mother was not Jewish. So even by the law of the Jewish rabbi, you are not Jewish."

"I don't know about that," said Roy. "I always thought of myself as Jewish, and that's how my friends thought of me. As a matter of fact, up until the time I went to college, all my friends were Jewish."

"And here."

Roy laughed. "That's right. In college and here, but this is college, too."

"That's right." Abdul glanced at his watch. "You're going to meet your father at eight; you don't have much time. You'd better get dressed."

Roy looked at his friend in surprise. "Why do I have to get dressed up to meet my own father? What's the matter with the way I'm dressed now?"

Abdul, who was twenty-six to Roy's eighteen, shook his head indulgently. Roy was dressed in a blue denim Eisenhower jacket and in faded blue jeans, frayed at the bottoms. His sockless feet were encased in open sandals. Abdul could not understand why the American students chose to dress like poor workingmen, like fellahin, when they had the money to buy proper

clothes. He had a smug satisfaction in the knowledge
that *he* was properly dressed, even well dressed, in a
tight-fitting suit of shiny black worsted with a shirt
with a long, pointed collar and a wide colorful tie.
Sitting with his legs stretched out in front of him, he
rotated his shoes on their heels and surveyed them
approvingly. They were Italian with large brass buckles
and brilliantly shined.

"You don't understand, Roy. You will come into
the King David where the women walk around the
lobby in mink stoles even on hot days. Your daddy is
probably planning to take you to the Grill for dinner.
I'm not even sure that they will seat you without a tie,
without socks. The hair, they will not like, but they
can do nothing about it. But the jacket and no tie—"

"Well, this is the way I dress," retorted Roy, "and
if they don't like it, they can lump it. As far as my
father is concerned, is it me he wants to see or a suit
of clothes? And as for the headwaiter, a man can't
let himself be pushed around by those types. I'll tell
you something, Abdul, a man has to be himself. That's
the main thing."

Abdul shrugged. He didn't want to argue with this
young American whose friendship he had gone out of
his way to cultivate. "Perhaps you are right, Roy.
Come, I'll walk you to the bus stop."

They stood in the lighted area of the bus stop until
Roy had boarded, and then Abdul strode off into the
darkness. Presently he heard footsteps behind him.
He stopped. "Is that you, Mahmoud?" he asked in
Arabic. "I thought I saw you behind us earlier. Are
you spying on me?"

The other fell in beside him. "I was not spying.
Who you want to be friends with is your business so
long as the rest of us don't get involved."

"I know what I'm doing," said Abdul shortly.

"All right. I won't argue with you, but if you think
you are fooling the Jews by being friendly with one of
them—"

"Let me tell you something, Mahmoud. We are all watched because the Israelis know that we will do anything to defeat them. But they hope that by treating us kindly, by encouraging us to attend the university, for example, some of us will be placated and resigned to the idea that they are in control and likely to remain for some time. Now," he said to his friend, "which will they watch more closely, the ones who are resigned or the ones who remain stubborn? And remember, they want so much to believe that they have won some of us over." He smiled in the darkness. "So I help them a little. Roy is young and not very bright, but he is good camouflage. Now if you were not following me to spy on me—"

"I have some news I wanted to tell you."

"Yes?"

"We heard from Jaffa. There has been a shake-up in the Shin Bet, and Adoumi has been transferred to Jerusalem. He's here now. He was seen."

"So?"

"So maybe we ought to go easy for a while and see what happens," the other said softly.

"How long has he been here?"

"Who knows? Perhaps months."

They walked in silence, and then Abdul said, "After all, what difference does it make?"

"Plenty. If he's in charge here, then we'll soon see the same harsh methods that were used in Jaffa and Tel Aviv."

"No," said Abdul. "That kind of thing can't be done here in Jerusalem. There are too many people from too many parts of the world—"

"There are even more in Tel Aviv."

"But they are all businessmen there," Abdul pointed out, "interested only in their big financial deals. Here, in Jerusalem, it is the religious and the learned and the scientific people and the diplomats and the writers and journalists, the people that the Jews try so hard to persuade of their liberalism and democracy. It is

here that you have the large Christian community with
their ties to Europe and America. And it's a smaller
town where everything that happens is immediately
known, and cannot be concealed. Believe me, the
methods he used in Tel Aviv and Jaffa—rounding up
hundreds of our people and holding them for questioning for days—he won't be able to get away with it
so easy here. Besides, if he's been transferred, he will
probably be here for some time. Does that mean that we
do nothing and just wait for the next shake-up when
someone else is sent in? Are we to be made women
by the reputation of one man? I for one am prepared
to go ahead. Get word to the Swiss. Have him prepare
the gadget. I'm ready to go ahead with the original
plan."

"And the rest of us?"

Abdul smiled. "Proceed as we arranged, or better,
get yourself a friendly Jew and arrange to be with
him when it happens."

11

JONATHAN, whether he was racing up and
down the length of the El Al lounge or just standing
in front of an elderly woman gravely watching her
transfer items from one bag to another, was obviously
enjoying the experience. Having flown from Boston's
Logan Airport to New York's Kennedy, he considered
himself a seasoned traveler.

Miriam, on whose shoulders the management and
logistics of the expedition devolved, had worried and
fretted, had made out lists—lists of things to be done,
of things to be taken, of things to be remembered. Now

at the airport, she realized it was too late to rectify any errors and was determined to relax and enjoy the trip. She sat quietly sipping coffee out of a paper cup, surrounded by the coats and bags that constituted their hand luggage. Curiously she was unconcerned about Jonathan's moment-to-moment whereabouts since all the people in the lounge waiting for the evening flight seemed strangely familiar almost as though it were a family gathering where others would keep an eye on him and see to it that he did not get into serious trouble. This effect of familiarity was heightened by an occasional nudge from her husband with an urging to "Look at that couple next to the counter. Doesn't he look just like Mark Rosenstein?"

Of the three, the rabbi alone showed impatience. The sooner they were aboard the plane, the sooner they would get to their destination, and he could not wait. He looked at his watch repeatedly and then would get up from his seat beside Miriam and stride up and down the lounge in an effort to make the time pass more quickly. When he came to the window, he stopped to look out anxiously at the driving snowstorm outside, fearful that it might prevent the plane from taking off and yet buoyed up by the thought that it had been no different at Logan and they had had no delay in take-off there.

At last came the announcement over the loudspeaker, like all the announcements first in Hebrew and then in English, that the plane was ready for boarding. Along with everyone else in the room, they hastily gathered their belongings and, with Jonathan securely in hand, hurried to join the line. They opened their handbags for inspection, and then the line divided into two, one for men and the other for women.

Each person was halted in a curtained cubicle where they were checked electronically for concealed metal and then manually frisked. The rabbi had seen the maneuver on television crime movies but had never been subjected to it himself. Jonathan began to whimper since he associated the frisking with an examination by a doctor which usually ended in something unpleasant like the jab of a needle, but his father reassured him. "See, it's nothing, Jonathan, nothing at all." When Miriam rejoined them, he said, "We were searched quite thoroughly, even intimately. How about you?"

She nodded. "The same, I expect. It's nice to know they're taking all possible precautions."

Although all had been assigned specific seats in the plane, there was nevertheless considerable pushing and shoving. "Why do they do it?" Miriam wailed as the crowd of passengers struggled along the aisle of the plane. "Don't they know we're not going to start until everyone is settled?"

The rabbi looked about at his fellow passengers. "I suppose for a number of them this is their first time in a plane. Or maybe they don't really believe that there is a seat for everyone. We've always been skeptics, I guess."

They had had only a light lunch and were now quite hungry. Fortunately, the stewards and stewardesses began to serve almost as soon as they were airborne. Here and there a passenger was skipped. The man sitting across the aisle from the rabbi pointed it out to one of the stewards. "Look, that man didn't get a tray."

"I know, I know," said the steward. "Are you his lawyer?" He hurried on down the aisle.

The man leaned over and confided to the rabbi. "Fresh. These young Israelis they're fresh—no respect."

The explanation for those who had been passed over was not long in coming. As soon as the stewards had finished with the trays, they began distributing flat cardboard boxes marked "Strictly Kosher."

"Aha, so why couldn't he say so?" the man demanded. "And isn't our dinner kosher? They told me that on El Al all meals were strictly kosher."

"Why don't you ask the steward?" the rabbi suggested.

"And get another fresh answer?"

"All right, I'll ask him. I'm curious myself."

When next the steward passed, he plucked at his sleeve and said, "Isn't our dinner kosher? In what way are those others more kosher?"

The steward shrugged and smiled. "Six years I've been with the airline and I haven't been able to find out."

The rabbi smiled and nodded his thanks, but his friend across the aisle shook his head slowly from side to side. "Fanatics, that's what they are. I understand the country is full of them."

Shortly after dinner the lights were turned out, and the passengers settled down for the night. Both Miriam and Jonathan slept, but the rabbi succeeded only in dozing fitfully. Nevertheless, when the sun came up, he was neither tired nor sleepy. Miriam was already awake, as were a good half of the passengers. In the aisle two or three men were standing facing the windows reciting the morning prayers in their prayer shawls and phylacteries.

"Are you awake, David?" asked Miriam. "The steward said they would be serving soon."

He nodded but did not answer, and seeing his lips move, she knew he was reciting the prayers. When he had finished, he said, "For this once, I said the prayers sitting down. At least I'm facing in the right direction. They"—nodding toward the men in the aisle—"are facing in the wrong direction."

"What do you mean?"

"The plane is heading east, and so am I. They are facing north and south."

Again the man across the aisle tapped him on the arm and nodded toward the men in the aisle. "What did I tell you? Fanatics!"

After breakfast, the passengers began to make ready for the landing, although it was still several hours ahead.

They shuffled in their bags for passports, for addresses; those who had left their seats to visit with friends returned to them; those who had made new acquaintances on the plane wrote out their intended itineraries or addresses at which they could be reached. Every now and then, the pilot announced points of interest that could be seen through the broken clouds—the Alps, the Greek coastline, the Greek islands—and dutifully, the passengers momentarily stopped what they were doing to look through the windows. Finally, he announced that they were approaching Israel and Lod Airport. For those on the right side of the aisle there was a glimpse of green fields and then the expanse of black tarmac. When, a few minutes later, the plane touched down lightly and taxied to a halt, there was a burst of applause from the passengers, whether at the pilot's skill or in relief that the long trip was over and they were safe on Israeli soil the rabbi could not tell. He noticed that Miriam's eyes were moist.

In Hebrew the pilot said, "Blessed be the coming to Israel," and then in English paraphrase, "Welcome to Israel."

It had evidently just rained, and there were puddles on the tarmac as they made their way to the lounge, clutching Jonathan firmly by the hand to ensure his walking around the puddles rather than through them. The air was as mild and clear as a May morning.

A large crowd waited beyond the customs barrier, to greet friends and relatives among the passengers. While they kept an eye on the baggage chute, Miriam and the rabbi scanned the sea of faces for someone who resembled the photograph of Gittel in the family album, taken years before. By the time they had reclaimed their bags and gone through the customs desk the crowd had thinned out considerably, but still they saw no one who might be Gittel. Only after they had repaired to a bench and Miriam was searching through her bag for her address book did Gittel arrive, inquiring anxiously, "The Small family? Miriam?"

"Oh, Gittel!"

Gittel hugged Miriam to her breast and then shyly offered her hand to the rabbi. He took it and then kissed her upturned cheek.

"And this is Jonathan!" She held him by the shoulders at arm's length and then clutched him to her ecstatically. She released him and stood back to look at the family as a whole. And now she was ready for business. "I had trouble getting my car started," she explained. "When it rains, the battery you know. And this morning it rained—the first time in weeks—the crops are thirsting for water, but you brought the rain. It is a good omen. You are hungry? You would like a coffee, perhaps? No? Then let us get started."

Waving her umbrella, she commandeered a porter with a luggage carrier, chivied them all out the front gate, and, planting the tip of her umbrella firmly on a spot on the sidewalk, ordered them to wait right there while she brought up her car from the parking lot. Before the rabbi could offer to accompany her in case she needed help with the car, she was gone. This time, however, the battery must have worked properly, for they did not have long to wait. She came chugging up the driveway, her horn blaring to warn away anyone who might have designs on the parking spot she had selected. She brought the car to a halt and jumped out. From the trunk, she brought out a knotted mass of rope, which she handed to the porter, and supervised him as he secured the bags on the luggage rack on the roof of the car.

The rabbi whispered to her, "How much do I pay him?"

"I will pay him," she said firmly, "and afterward you can reimburse me. He would take advantage of you."

As the rabbi waited on the sidewalk while the porter finished with the bags, he was approached by a youngish man in the long caftan and the broad-brimmed black felt hat of the Orthodox. He had a full beard and long, carefully curled ear ringlets. He sidled up to the rabbi and asked in Yiddish, "You are from America?"

"Yes."

"This is perhaps your first trip here?"

"It is."

"So I am sure you would like to have your first act on this holy land an act of charity. I am collecting for a yeshiva—"

Gittel, who had already paid off the porter, had overheard and exploded in Hebrew, "You ought to be ashamed of yourself. A stranger comes to the country, and he has barely landed, and you *shnorrers* descend on him. What sort of impression will he have of us?" She pushed the rabbi into the car and then got in herself behind the wheel. "Besides," she went on through the open window, "this man is a famous rabbi in America." And in a parting shot as she put the car in gear, "He's in the business himself."

As they pulled away, the rabbi remonstrated with her, "I'm not in the business of soliciting funds. Most rabbis in America are not."

She turned and patted him on the shoulder, almost colliding with another car in the process. "I know, I know, but that's the only argument that convinces that kind."

As they drove along, she kept up a rapid-fire comment on the passing scene. "That grove—ten years ago, there was nothing there but rocks and sand. . . . Over there, just beyond that house—it wasn't there then— a good friend of mine was ambushed by the Arabs and shot down in cold blood. . . . That road leads to a settlement. In forty-eight it was under attack. Three men with a machine gun stood off a whole company until they were able to get the children to safety. . . . We grow flowers for export. . . . Last year our agronomists tried a new fertilizer which doubled the yield per acre—fantastic! . . . Those are Arab fields. We taught them how to protect the seedlings with plastic.

It has quadrupled their production. . . . That's an Arab village back there. Primitive! You wouldn't believe the amount of dirt and disease. . . Trachoma and gastroenteritis were endemic. The children died like flies in the summer months. Then we opened a clinic there. At first they didn't trust us. Treatment had to be carried out in front of the whole family. And when we gave them pills, they would swap them among themselves—'I'll give you two white for a red'—that kind of thing. But they learned, and now the children don't die anymore. And some of the young people are taking advantage of government help and building modern houses when they get married instead of adding a room to the patriarchal compound. . . . A cement plant. They work around the clock—three shifts a day. . . ."

"A tent," exclaimed Jonathan, "and goats."

"Bedouins," she explained. "They lead their flocks to a bit of vacant land, pitch a tent, and stay for a couple of days or a week until they've exhausted whatever bit of green there is. Then they move on. The Bedouin sheep is one of the principal causes of the deterioration of the land over the years. They eat down to the root. . . . Those are tanks, Arab tanks and armored vehicles. We leave them there as a kind of reminder. We caught them in our crossfire. We were ready for them. Then we pushed them off the side of the road, and they've been there ever since. In the kibbutz just around the bend of the road, they have several, all painted in bright colors. The children play in them."

The scenery, except for an occasional palm or cactus which indicated that they were in a semitropical area, was unremarkable: a flat plain with small fields under cultivation. But soon the road began to climb in long, looping curves, and the scenery changed markedly. They were approaching Jerusalem, and all about them were the ancient hills, hill folding on hill, barren and covered with rocks except for small patches of green where the hillside had been cleared of rocks which were then used to construct terraces.

"The very stones look old and worn out," exclaimed the rabbi.

"It all looks so wasted and—and sterile," said Miriam.

"This was a land flowing with milk and honey once," said Gittel grimly, "and it will be again."

They had rather expected to come upon the city suddenly, dramatically, the walled city as it appeared in the pictures they had seen, but the road they had taken passed random clumps of houses, Arab settlements where the houses adjoined like pueblos and the more modern Jewish settlements of apartment houses, and gradually the settlements appeared closer and closer together until the row of buildings became almost continuous and they realized without Gittel's telling them that they were in the city.

They wound in and out of narrow streets lined with small, shabby stores, streets crowded with small European cars and sidewalks teeming with people. Disappointed with their first sight of the city, they looked eagerly at the passersby, calling each other's attention to whatever was novel and strange: the occasional Chassid in his broad-brimmed black hat and long caftan, his trousers tucked into his stockings; the groups of soldiers with their guns slung over a shoulder or dangling from their fingers by the trigger guards; the Arab in his black and white keffiyah held in place by a double black cord. Then they turned a corner and came out to a wider street with buildings on only one side; on the other, the land fell away in a broad valley, and beyond it, in the distance, was the ancient walled city, like a picture in a child's storybook.

Gittel stopped the car. "There, there is the Old City. Feast your eyes."

"It's beautiful," said Miriam.

The rabbi said nothing, but his eyes were shining.

"And will we be living far from here?" asked Miriam.

"Just around the corner. You will see this every day, and you will not tire of it."

12

THE two men, father and son, shook hands, patted each other on the back, and stood back to look at each other. Dan Stedman indeed had been thinking of dining in the Grill where he would be likely to point out important people to his son—the wife of the British consul, the American first secretary. He was no name-dropper, but he wanted so much to have his son think well of him. And he had then decided against it for the same reason: People who knew him might come over to talk, and he wanted to have his son all to himself tonight.

But when he saw how Roy was dressed, he was doubly glad he had made no reservation at the Grill; Avram, the headwaiter, would be certain to raise objections to the boy's attire. So he suggested the Artist's Club, which proved to be a happy choice since several of the young patrons were dressed much like his son.

Dan had given Roy news of his mother and of his Uncle Hugo and Aunt Betty; he had described conditions in the States; the weather there—"the worst winter they've had in years. You don't know how lucky you are to be here"—and his own immediate plans: "I'll spend some time in Jerusalem and then go on to some of the other cities—Haifa, Tel Aviv, and some of the smaller places, maybe even some of the moshavim and the kibbutzim." But transportation might be a problem. "Trouble is, buying a new car is a matter of a couple of months, and renting will cost me an arm and a leg."

"Whyn't you get a good secondhand?" Roy asked.

"Well, you know how it is with secondhand cars. You don't know what you're getting, and if you bring in an expert, how do you know he's not in cahoots with the seller?"

"There's this guy, Memavet, that advertises in the Jerusalem *Post,* maybe in the Hebrew papers, but I don't read them. He acts like an agent for buying and selling cars. And the way things are going right now, there's a good chance that when you go to sell it, you can get more than you paid for it."

"Memavet?" Dan repeated. "Funny name."

"Yeah, 'from death,' right? My Hebrew is not so hot, but I know that."

"That's right," his father said. "I might look in on him. I've already looked around a little—not here, but in Tel Aviv—and what I saw were a bunch of clunkers."

"Oh, yeah? How long you been here, Dad?"

Dan colored and then said lightly, "Oh, a couple of days. I decided to look up some people I knew in Tel Aviv, get that out of the way before coming up to Jerusalem and seeing you. You understand."

"Oh, sure." Roy did not really understand, but he saw no point in making an issue of it. It crossed his mind that "the people" his father might have looked up was a woman.

"Your mother said you were unhappy here," said Dan, to change the subject.

"Well, you know how it is," Roy said, sipping his coffee. "The guys here and the chicks, too, they're all such a bunch of bloody heroes. You know how Texans are supposed to be in the States? Well, that's what they are—Jewish Texans. You'd think that each and every one of them personally won the Six-Day War. They're always asking you how you like Israel. And if you fall all over yourself telling them how wonderful

it is and how wonderful they are, like some of the
American students do, they either smirk like they're
kind of embarrassed or look like you hit the nail right
smack on the head, although you get the impression
they're a little surprised a clod like you could be so
understanding. But if, God forbid, you should happen to
say anything the least bit critical of their precious country, like about people hanging out their bedding on the
front porches and beating their rugs right in the main
street, or take this begging that goes on all the time,
they land on you like a ton of bricks and explain how it
has to be that way, or it's something that's ordained in
the Bible. Like, take this business of the beggars. I was
saying something about somebody always putting the
bite on you, and this guy says that since the Bible
says you got to give charity, these guys are doing
an important service by being there to take it. They're
like enabling you to earn a blessing."

His father laughed. "Well, it's a new country—"

"Yeah, but it's not the only country, and the rest
of the world wasn't created just to help them. And
they're always challenging you. Why is America in
Vietnam? Why do we mistreat the blacks? Why don't
we do something about the poor? Why do we allow
our rivers and lakes to get polluted? You find yourself
on the defensive all the time."

His father looked at him quizzically. "Weren't you
always complaining of the same thing?"

Roy flushed. "Sure, but they put it in such a way
that if you agree with them, you feel like you're brown-
nosing them. And they exaggerate everything, so you
try to tell them how it really is, and pretty soon you
find yourself practically defending every thing American, even the things you object to yourself. And
cliquey! You can hardly get one of them to tell you
the right time. Especially the chicks. You try to get a
date and they're out to lunch."

"How about the other American students?"

"Well, they're not the kind I'd hack around with in

the States, I can tell you," Roy said. "Besides, they're in the same boat, so what's the point? It's like a bunch of wallflowers at a dance trying to make out with each other. It's even worse for the girls. The guys here act like they're doing them a favor if they say hello. Me, I hang around with the Arab students mostly," he added casually.

"The Arab students?"

"Yeah. Don't sweat it, Dad. It's the in thing right now. Make friends with an Arab. Matter of fact, a lot of the Israelis take the point of view that they're a lot closer to the Arabs than they are to us, since they're Israelis, too."

"I see," his father said. "So that's why you're unhappy."

"Well, you know, I was like on a kind of down cycle when I wrote Ma. I was homesick and dying for a hamburg or a pizza or a first-run movie, and I was alone here—"

Dan was glad of the opening. "But I'm here now," he said.

"Sure, and don't think it doesn't make a difference. And these trips you're planning, maybe I could go along and help out with the driving?"

"But your school—"

"Oh, everybody takes off, sometimes as much as a month. It's kind of expected. How about it, Dad?"

It was a tempting picture, the two of them taking long trips together, putting up at small hotels for the night, stopping at out-of-the-way places to eat, and talking, confiding in each other, making up for the years of separation. He might even be able to influence his son, reorient his thinking, mold his character, do for him what a father should do for a son. He smiled. "Roy, you've got a deal," he said, and in spite of his efforts to control it, his voice was tremulous.

13

BY the time they had unloaded the car and unpacked their bags, night had fallen. It came suddenly as it does in the tropics, and the air became chilly. They were tired and hungry, and Miriam suggested they go to a restaurant.

"A restaurant? It is an unnecessary extravagance," said Gittel. "There are stores—a grocery right across the street. We can buy what we need, prepare it, and serve it before a waiter in a restaurant would even take your order. Besides, what would we do with the child?"

Since the rabbi had carried Jonathan in from the car fast asleep, undressed and put him to bed still asleep, the point seemed well taken.

Gittel made further plans and arrangements for them. "Tomorrow morning we must go shopping for the Sabbath, Miriam—because on the Sabbath all places are closed," she added to indicate that her interest was secular rather than religious. "I will take you to a large market not far from here where you wheel a little cart around and pick whatever you wish, just like in America. But first, we will arrange for Jonathan to go to school. There is a kindergarten around the corner—"

"I hadn't thought of him going to school," Miriam objected.

"So what else would he do? All the children are in school. If he doesn't go, there will be no one for him to play with and you would be tied down all day. Certainly, you will want to be doing something while you are here. Now, I have a friend in the Social Service

Department of the Hadassah Hospital, and she is always crying for volunteers. It is work I am sure you will enjoy. I will arrange an appointment for you."

She told them that she wouldn't think of leaving until she had seen them properly settled, but she was sure she could manage everything in the morning. Fortunately, there was another bed in Jonathan's room, although she assured them it was no great matter. In Israel one could always make do; she could have bedded down on the sofa or even the floor, if necessary.

She told them of her work in Israel, of her son Uri, Miriam's cousin, who was in the Army. "Tall and handsome he is, like his father. The girls are all crazy over him, and when he comes home on leave, I hardly get to see him."

She noticed that the rabbi's eyes were half-closed. Instantly she was contrite. "Here I talk and you people are dying to go to sleep." And with a kind of wonder, "And you know, I am a little tired, too. We will all go to bed now, and tomorrow we will make our arrangements."

The rabbi got the feeling that only because he was a rabbi, and perhaps because he was not a direct relation, did she refrain from deciding what he was to do during their stay in the country. But he did not object to going to bed, and he had no sooner put his head to the pillow than he fell fast asleep.

He was awakened suddenly by a loud thud. It was dark, and he pawed for his watch on the night table and then for his glasses to see it by. He switched on the tiny bed lamp and saw it was twelve o'clock. Beside him, Miriam stirred uneasily, but she turned over and snuggled into the bedclothes, and presently he could hear her slow rhythmic breathing once again. He switched off the light and tried to get back to sleep, but after he had tossed about for a few minutes, he realized it was useless. He was wide awake. In bathrobe and slippers he padded into the living room, took a book from the bookcase, and settled down to read.

It was almost four o'clock before he returned to bed.

Miriam and Gittel were preparing to go shopping when he awoke the next morning. It was late, after ten. The women had already been out and dropped Jonathan off at the kindergarten and arranged for him to go every day.

As they were leaving, he called after them, "Don't forget to get wine for kiddush."

"We've got it on our list," said Miriam. "And what are you going to do?"

"I'll just walk around and look over the city."

By the time he had finished his morning prayers and eaten breakfast, the sun was already high in the heavens. It beat down in a hard glare on the white stone of the city so that he found himself squinting; he made a mental note that he must buy a pair of sunglasses. Still, there was a chill in the air as on a pleasant April morning at home, and he was glad he had thought to put on a light raincoat.

As he strolled along leisurely, he was strangely out of tempo with the others he saw walking along the street, mostly women returning from their morning's shopping, carrying their groceries in string bags. Even though the streets through which he walked were residential, some of them splendid with new apartment houses, here and there were tiny shops tucked away in semi-basements—a grocery, a coffee shop, a bakery, a laundry.

Ahead were a pair of civilian guards, middle-aged men, who, like him, were strolling leisurely. They were in a uniform of sorts: green armbands and berets and long military coats much the worse for wear. The trousers that showed beneath were obviously of civilian cut and material. One carried an old rifle and the other a steel rod about two feet long with which to prod suspicious packages left in trash barrels. Rabbi Small wondered idly if they took turns with the rifle. They were holding a heated discussion, gesticulating extravagantly. As he came near, he heard one say "So Agnon is not so much a Hebrew writer as a Yiddish writer who writes in Hebrew. There is a difference." The guard broke off when the rabbi stopped beside them and looked at him suspiciously.

"Can you tell me please if I am heading toward the center of the city?" the rabbi asked.

"Where do you want to go?"

"I am new here," the rabbi explained. "Where are the shops, the business district?"

"He wants Zion Square. What do you want to buy?"

"I don't want to buy anything. I just want to see the city."

"Ah, well, right ahead is King George Street. If you turn left, you'll come to Ben Yehuda Street. That is the business district."

The streets were narrow and crowded, and the stores along the route small and, compared to what he was used to in America, unattractive. They were like the stores he had seen in small New England factory towns, with merchandise in the windows that seemingly had not been changed since the stores were first opened. In narrow alleys or in the space between two buildings, and even spread out on the sidewalk where it widened slightly, there were men with stands, selling a large variety of small articles like pencils, combs, razors, wallets, umbrellas, cigarette lighters. At several points along the street, there were small kiosks where lottery tickets were sold. Here and there, in doorways and on the sidewalks, there were old men sitting, their backs resting against the wall of a building, selling newspapers. One or two had no papers to sell, nor anything else, but clinked a few coins in their hands at passersby.

Everywhere there were young men and women in uniform. Many of the men were carrying automatic rifles, short weapons with metal frame stocks. They carried them slung from their shoulders by straps, or under their arms like umbrellas, or dangling by the trigger guards like briefcases. It occurred to him that they did not look like soldiers, young and sturdy though they were. There was something civilian and matter-of-fact in their bearing, as though they were engaged in some civilian occupation that required a uniform, like a bus driver.

Here and there, too, he saw Chassidim, old and young, in their silk dressing-gown-like coats, their broad-brimmed felt hats, their pantaloons wrapped around their legs and stuck into their stocking tops, their ringlets jiggling as they walked. Once he was almost run over by a motorcycle that roared past him as he stepped off the curb at a crossing. On it were two young Chassidim, their beards and ringlets flying in the breeze, the one on the pillion clutching his broad-brimmed felt with one hand while he clung to his companion with the other.

The rabbi saw a hat store and thought to buy another yarmulke to keep in his jacket pocket. They were on sale in all the gift shops in red velvet and in blue, decorated with gold and silver braid, but he wanted a plain black one. The proprietor of the hat store was a tall man with a long beard. His son in khaki, home on leave, was helping out, his automatic rifle conspicuous on a shelf behind the counter. There were several men, evidently none of them customers, talking about Arab terrorists and what measures the government ought to take against them. They were talking in Yiddish, in which the rabbi was not fluent, but which he could follow. It was the son who broke off after a minute to ask him what he wanted, put two piles of black yarmulkes on the counter, indicated that one was two lira and the other four, and went back to rejoin the conversation, interrupting it again only long enough to take the rabbi's money and give him the necessary change.

It occurred to the rabbi that there was something curiously simple and, by American commercial standards, even primitive about the transaction; a transfer of money and merchandise with no formality; no wrapping, no sales slip. There was no cash register;

the young man had made change from a drawer under the counter. He had not even said the customary "Thank you," albeit when the rabbi did so, he answered automatically, "*Bevakasha*"—if you please.

Rabbi Small continued to stroll along the street, stopping to look in the store windows, automatically converting the prices in Israeli lira to American dollars. He followed the winding streets, none of which ever seemed to meet at right angles, and suddenly found himself in an open market district, an area of narrow lanes lined with stands of merchandise, largely fruits and vegetables, although here and there were fish or meat stalls and even an occasional dry goods or clothing store, all jammed together, presided over by Arabs, bearded Jews, women—shouting, dickering, gesticulating, prodding the merchandise. There were also stands, the precursors of the department store, where one could buy a comb or a notebook or a pack of needles or a box of facial tissues or an overcoat for that matter, if one of the half dozen hanging on a rack were the right size.

He wandered down a side lane and suddenly found himself in a residential district of old stone houses, one or two stories high, evidently occupied largely by Chassidim. The men were beginning to come home from their shops or their study halls to prepare for the Sabbath. In open courtyards children were playing, the little boys with heads shaved except for the ringlets that hung down the sides of their faces. They all wore skullcaps, which they were hard put not to lose as they ran or kicked at a soccer ball. The little girls played by themselves to one side, games like jump rope and hopscotch. Every now and then there was the drumming of the engine of a motorcycle, curiously out of keeping with the general atmosphere, and a dark, swarthy, truculent young man, clean-shaven, but with long hair in the mod style and dressed in flashy bell-bottomed trousers supported low on the hips by a

wide fancy belt, would roar by and disappear around
a corner.

The rabbi made his way through the district, uncertain of his direction but loath to ask any of the
women sitting on the steps of their houses, not knowing
if they would consider it improper for a strange man
to address them. But finally he came out to a wide
street with high modern apartment houses that looked
familiar. Sure enough, at the next corner he saw by
the sign that he was on Jaffa Road, which he knew
ultimately led to King George Street. He was tired
now and grateful when he spotted a small café where
he could sit for a while over a cup of coffee.

It was a pleasantly restful place, at least at that hour,
with a rack of newspapers and magazines in French
and German, as well as in Hebrew. Only a couple of
the tiny tables were occupied, and these by individuals
engrossed in their newspapers. He gave his order and
then selected from the rack a copy of the afternoon
paper.

The lead story concerned the latest terrorist outrage,
the explosion of a bomb in an apartment house in the
Rehavia section of Jerusalem the night before. A man
had been killed, a professor of agronomy at the university. Only because his wife and two children had spent
the night with relatives in Haifa had they been spared
his fate. The paper evidently had not had time to inquire
into the victim's background too deeply but gave a short
résumé of his life, the kind that is kept on file in an
administration office, together with a picture taken
from the same source.

On an inside page of the paper they ran a map of
the area. When the rabbi saw it, he sat up with a start.
The incident had occurred only one street over from
Victory Street. That must have been what had awakened
him in the middle of the night—the noise of the explosion!

A government authority admitted that it was probably the work of the CAT group—Committee for Arab

Triumph—which had exploded a bomb in the market-place in Jaffa a couple of weeks before, killing two people. In that case, CAT had called the police a few minutes prior to the explosion. On another occasion, their call had come early enough, or their device had not worked as planned, so that the police had been able to find the bomb and disarm it. This time there had been no warning call, however.

A photograph showed the device used, a small, oblong box of black plastic that looked like a pocket radio. Indeed, on one side was a dial which, when pulled out, actuated the mechanism, exploding the charge approximately an hour later. A notice in bold type accompanied the article, explaining that anyone who came across such a device could interrupt the action and prevent the explosion by depressing the plunger. Although this would not render it harmless, it could be reactivated by reversing the process and withdrawing the plunger again—it would make it safe enough to handle.

Most of the paper was devoted to the story, and the rabbi read it all avidly. An Army demolition expert was quoted as disparaging the device. "It is not a very powerful bomb," he said with the objectivity of the professional "and the thrust is only in one direction."

A neighbor who was interviewed said he understood the victim had been working on something that would have been of great value to Arab farmers.

An editorial heatedly attacked the psychology of the terrorist which led him to regard his nefarious attacks on innocent civilians as waging war.

The rabbi returned the newspaper to the rack, paid for his coffee, and left the café. He had overcome his momentary impulse to hurry home to search the apartment on the chance that a small black plastic box had been left there. He wondered if Miriam knew about the explosion and whether she was frightened or concerned. And if not, if he should tell her. But as he walked along, he realized that she was sure to know. She and Gittel had gone to the supermarket to shop. People would be talking about it, and even though the talk would be in Hebrew, Gittel would understand. And Gittel would tell her and, if necessary, calm her. It was two o'clock now, and on the streets people hurried as though they all were late for an important appointment. The stores were either closed or closing, the proprietors obviously also in a hurry. On one corner there was a booth where flowers were being sold; only here was the shopkeeper still doing business. But he, too, was busily trying to service the three or four customers who were waiting impatiently. The rabbi joined the group and bought a bunch of carnations. Then he too hurried home.

Miriam and Jonathan were there when he arrived, but Gittel had gone. "Uri usually gets a weekend pass," Miriam explained. "Naturally, she wants to be home to receive him. I suggested that she try to get word to him through the Army people to come to Jerusalem instead of Tel Aviv, but I guess even Gittel couldn't manage that."

"Did she try?" asked the rabbi.

"No, as a matter of fact, I gather she considers it unpatriotic to bother the Army with unimportant requests. The Army is sort of sacrosanct over here."

"It must be if she didn't try to manage it," he said dryly.

"Oh, but she's a good soul, David."

He looked surprised. "But of course. I think she's grand. I don't mind her managing. She comes of a long line of matriarchal managers, all the way from Devorah to Golda. It's a tradition with us. In the *shtetl*, while the men studied, the women ran things." He smiled. "You've got a little of it yourself, you know. I'm only sorry Gittel is not with us to celebrate our first Sabbath in Israel." He handed her the flowers and kissed her. "A happy Sabbath."

He wanted to ask if she had heard the news, but

Jonathan came running into the room. "I was in school, Daddy, and I'm going every day—with Shaouli from upstairs."

"That's fine, Jonathan." He touched his hair affectionately. "And how did you like school?"

"Oh, it was all right." Then with special excitement: "You know, the kids here, they don't know how to throw a ball. They kick it. With their feet."

"Well, that's mighty interesting." He wanted to say more. He wanted to question his son about the school. He wanted to ask Miriam how she had spent the day. But he could not; he was too tired.

"I walked all over the city," he began by way of explanation.

"Why don't you go and lie down for a while, David, and catch a nap? I did," Miriam said, "and I felt wonderful afterward."

"Yes, I think I will." He hesitated. "Did you hear about—"

She quickly turned to make sure Jonathan was out of earshot. "Yes, but let's not discuss it now. Go and lie down."

He had no sooner kicked off his shoes than he fell asleep. It seemed only a few minutes later when Miriam awakened him. "You'd better get up now, David. It's our first Sabbath in Jerusalem, and I think we should eat together. Besides, I don't want to keep Jonathan up too late."

He sat up with a jolt. "What time is it?"

"It's seven o'clock."

"But the evening service, it's over by now."

"I didn't have the heart to waken you. You were sleeping so soundly. It's the long plane ride. Our internal clocks are out of kilter."

He rose and washed, splashing cool water on his face. He felt refreshed as he came into the dining room and saw that the table was set, the candles lit, and his flowers in a vase in the center of the table. He sat down at the head of the table and filled the kiddush cup.

Then he rose and began the ancient prayer, "On the sixth day. . . ."

14

ALMOST from the day he arrived in Barnard's Crossing, Rabbi Hugo Deutch had been involved in a series of conferences with Cantor Zimbler and Henry Selig, the chairman of the Ritual Committee. The latter had been appointed to this important post by the president largely on the basis of the speed with which he read the prayers. Bert Raymond had gone to the minyan to say Kaddish on the anniversary of his father's death and there had noticed Selig. "He's the first one to sit down at Shemon Esrah. The first time I saw him, I figured he must be skipping like I do, but then I sat next to him, and he really reads the stuff. His lips practically vibrate. He must know it by heart."

As a matter of fact, he did know the daily prayers by heart, and that was the full extent of his knowledge of Jewish ritual. He interposed no objections, therefore, to Rabbi Deutch's plans. The cantor was a harder nut to crack. He was entirely agreeable to any suggestion that expanded his part in the service, but when Rabbi Deutch suggested that a particular prayer might be dispensed with, especially if it called for an extended musical rendition, he would say plaintively, "But, Rabbi, this prayer establishes the mood for the whole service." Or sometimes he pleaded on purely personal grounds—that it was the best solo in his repertoire: "I sing the first part of this falsetto, and then the next part in my regular voice, then falsetto again, then the regular voice again. It's just like a duet, and the folks here are crazy about it. There hasn't been a single Friday evening service when someone didn't come to me afterward to compliment me on that particular prayer."

But Rabbi Deutch knew his own mind and had had long experience in dealing with temperamental cantors. "Look, Cantor, there's one rule about running a successful Friday evening service program, and that is, keep it short and snappy. Remember, it's a week-in and week-out thing. If the service is long drawn out, the congregation gets tired, and first thing you know, they stop coming. It's got to be kept under an hour. Remember, they've had their evening meal, and they want to relax. So they hear you sing a little, and they sing a little; we have a couple of responsive readings to give them a feeling of the solemnity of the Sabbath; I give them a short sermon; the Amidah is a little interlude where they get a chance to get up and stretch their legs a bit; and then we close with a snappy Adon Olam and they go down to the vestry for tea and cake and general conversation. It's a nice evening's entertainment, and you'll find that the attendance will grow from week to week."

He had other ideas about improving the service, and on his first Friday night he managed to put them all together. As the congregation began to arrive and take their seats, they noticed that the high thronelike chairs on the dais on either side of the ark normally occupied by the rabbi and the cantor were empty. The service was scheduled to begin at eight o'clock and by a quarter of eight the congregation, anxious to see its new rabbi in action, had arrived and was seated. But still the seats on the dais remained empty.

The organ had been playing mood music, a series of mournful cadenzas in a minor key, but at ten minutes to eight the sound suddenly shifted to the major in a swelling diapason as the door of the enrobing room opened and the rabbi appeared, majestic in black gown and silken prayer shawl, a high velvet yarmulke like a cantor's on his head. He paused a moment and then moved slowly up the steps of the dais and stood in front of the ark, his back to the congregation. He stood thus for a minute or two, his head slightly bowed, and then straightened up and walked to his seat beside the ark.

Seated, he looked over the congregation, his face impassive, and what little murmuring of whispered conversation there had been stopped, as they felt his gaze rest upon them. At two minutes of eight he rose from his seat and approached the lectern. He did not face the congregation directly, but his body was turned slightly toward the door of the enrobing room. He stood thus expectantly waiting, and at eight o'clock exactly the door opened once again, and the cantor appeared and from the threshold began to chant *Ma Tovu*, How goodly are thy tents, O Jacob. Slowly, still chanting, the cantor mounted the steps to the dais while the rabbi remained standing, facing him. The chant ended just as he reached the lectern and only then did the rabbi retire to his seat beside the ark.

The cantor then sang the *L'Cha Dodie* with the congregation joining in on the refrain, after which the rabbi came forward to announce in his deep baritone, "We will now read responsively, the psalm on page twelve of your prayer books," and he read the first verse and then went on to join the congregation as they read the next verse, his rich voice plainly heard above the mumble of the congregation.

And the service *was* short and snappy. His sermon lasted only fifteen minutes, and at no time was any portion of the program permitted to drag. The congregation enjoyed the cantor's singing because there was not too much of it, and that their own portion of the service was largely confined to responsive reading where the rabbi did half the work gave them a pleasant sense of participation and yet was not onerous, and the Amidah, because it was recited while standing and in silence, was almost a kind of recess.

There were objections, of course. Some of the older members were not altogether pleased that their rabbi chose to wear a black robe, which to them was reminiscent of priests and ministers. And they also thought that the preliminaries were over-dramatic and hence smacked of theatricality and artificiality. But most approved.

"Look, what's the most stable religious organization in the world? The Catholic Church, right? And what's their stock-in-trade if not drama and ceremonial? They know what brings them back week after week—a good show, and they put one on."

These same dissidents found some objection to the sermon. "To me, he really didn't say anything."

"Yeah, but he didn't take forty minutes to do it."

But even the most antagonistic were forced to admit that the service was marked by great decorum, that favorite shibboleth of Conservative Judaism.

By far the great majority, however, thought it was a wonderful service and made a point of coming over to the rabbi to tell him so.

"I really enjoyed it, Rabbi. I haven't come to Friday evening service much in the past, but you'll be seeing me every week from now on."

"That sermon of yours, Rabbi, it struck a responsive chord if you know what I mean. I'll be thinking about it for a long time."

"You know, tonight for the first time I felt like I was taking part in something—well—holy. That's the only way I can put it."

"Me too, Rabbi. It was the best Sabbath I can remember."

Bert Raymond, standing beside Rabbi Deutch, beamed.

15

THE effects of their journey on their internal time clocks had not yet worn off, and the Smalls slept through the early hours of the morning—the rabbi, and Miriam since there was no Gittel to awaken her to the duties of the day, and even Jonathan. The bright sun shining directly into their faces awakened them; it was after ten o'clock and too late to go to the synagogue.

Miriam was remorseful. "I know you wanted to go to the synagogue on your first Sabbath in Jerusalem," she said.

"I had planned to," he said lightly, "but there'll be other Sabbaths. Why don't we all take a walk? There's a park bordering King George Street."

As they walked through the streets of the city, they realized that they were experiencing something new— a whole city observing the Sabbath. All the stores were closed—that was to be expected—but it was more than that. There were no buses running and almost no automobiles on the streets. The traffic lights were operating on flashing yellow instead of alternating red and green. And people were strolling along the streets as they were doing; men with their wives and children, all in their Sabbath best, walking three and four abreast, not going anywhere, just enjoying the weather.

Others, on their way home from the synagogue, were walking more purposefully, some of them still wearing their prayer shawls draped over their shoulders to avoid carrying them, which would of course be work of a kind and hence a breach of the Sabbath.

Now and again they saw a Chassid, brave in his Sabbath finery, the broad-brimmed black felt replaced by a fur *streimal*, the short knickerlike pantaloons gathered just below the knee, the legs encased in white stockings. Some were garbed in the long black silk robe kept closed by a sash. Others, the younger ones for the most part, favored a Prince Albert, which because it was warm, they kept open, thereby displaying the fringes of the *tallis katon*, the small prayer shawl they wore all the time, showing beneath their vests; around their waists the braided girdle they put on for prayer and that served to separate the lower and more earthy portions of the body from the upper and presumably more spiritual portions.

"Why do they dress like that, David?" asked Miriam.

He grinned. "Strictly speaking, pure conservatism. That's the costume of the well-to-do Polish and Russian merchant of the eighteenth century, presumably what Baal Shem Tov, the founder of the movement in the eighteenth century, wore, and in emulation of the *rebbe,* they wear it, too. I guess the Amish in Pennsylvania do the same thing and for the same reason. We tend to associate clothes with attitudes. That may be why people nowadays object to the new mod clothes; they consider them indicative of a rebellion and a break not only with traditional styles but with traditional morals and values."

"I don't mind it in the old ones," said Miriam, "but the young ones—that they should adhere so closely to the tradition—that one there, he can't be more than thirteen or fourteen."

The rabbi followed her gaze. "He's something of a dandy, isn't he? That *streimal*—it's mink isn't it?—must have cost his folks a pretty penny." His voice took on a melancholy note. "It's a sad paradox that while they adhere so strongly to the fashion in clothes, they have largely departed from the spirit of the movement. Chassidism was originally a kind of romantic mysticism, a movement of joy and laughter, of singing and dancing, that involved a kind of direct confrontation with God. It was a useful and necessary reaction to the meticulous observance of religious regulations that was characteristic of the time. But now it has come full circle, and this group is the most pedantic in its strict adherence to the letter of the law."

In the park, boys ranging in age from ten to twenty and more were playing football. The games were informal, with teams chosen at random; it was a vigorous game, and frequently players came crashing together, but no one seemed to get hurt.

The Smalls sat down on a park bench and watched. Other spectators were sitting on the grass on the edge of the improvised playing field, and although every now and then the ball would come sailing over their heads or players would race around them to get at it, no one seemed to mind.

They sat there on the park bench in the bright sunlight, reluctant to move on. Jonathan after a few minutes had wandered off and stood watching a group of younger boys playing with a smaller and lighter ball. Once it flew toward him and came to rest in front of his feet. "Kick it back," one of the children shouted in Hebrew. He did not understand, but automatically he kicked at it and was surprised and delighted to see it sail in an arc for some distance. Overjoyed at his success as well as a little fearful that he should not have kicked it so far, he ran to his parents, shouting, "I kicked it, I kicked it. Did you see me? Did you see me kick the ball?"

His mother gave him a hug.

"That was a fine kick," said the rabbi. "Maybe if you go back, you'll get a chance to kick it again, or maybe they'll let you play."

"David!" cried Miriam. "Those boys are two or three years older than Jonathan. He'd get hurt."

"Oh, I don't know, nobody seems to get hurt. And there doesn't seem to be any fighting among the kids. Look around you."

But Jonathan was unwilling to venture and snuggled against his mother. Presently, the games began to break up as the noon hour approached. The Smalls, too, decided to leave, walking at the leisurely pace that seemed in keeping with the spirit of the day.

"This is the first Sabbath in a long time that you haven't gone to the synagogue, David," said Miriam as they neared their house.

"So it is, but I don't feel that I missed anything," he said. "I've always gone, not only because it was expected of me as a rabbi and before that as a rabbinical student and before that as the son of a rabbi, but because I always had the feeling that it was the way to impose the Sabbath on my week. I'd dress a little differently, and I'd walk to the temple, leaving the house in good time so as not to have to hurry. And I'd walk back the same way because I knew there was no pressing business I had to come back to. I suppose I did it as much in an effort to establish as to celebrate the Sabbath. Well, here you don't have to establish the Sabbath. You don't have to impose it on your work-week. It's done for you. The whole city is keeping the Sabbath. You know, although I didn't get to go to the synagogue, it was the best Sabbath I can remember."

She looked at him curiously. "That's a funny thing for a rabbi to say."

"Yes, I suppose it is. But it's the way I feel."

16

THE assistant, dark, swarthy, diffident, sidled into the office of his chief, Police Inspector Ish-Kosher. He cleared his throat to attract attention. Ish-Kosher, a mild, square man, very neat in his uniform, looked up and said pleasantly, "Yes, Aaron?"

"There's a man outside," he said apologetically. "He is a civilian guard and was on duty in the area, you know up at Alfont Street—"

"He saw something? He knows something? Speak up, man." The police inspector fingered the little yarmulke that was kept in place by a bobby pin fastened to his thinning hair. It was not so much a sign of piety on his part as of allegiance to his party, which considered religious orthodoxy important. It also concealed the bald spot on top of his head.

"Well. . . ."

Ish-Kosher sighed. His assistant was typical Sephardi, he decided. While very good in the lower ranks, on foot patrol, traffic work, that sort of thing, in the more executive responsibilities they tended to freeze up, to vacillate. But of course, one had to persevere with them and be patient. In a few years there would be lots more of them in the headquarters building; already they were a majority on the force. "Sit down, Aaron," he said kindly. "Now, what's the story?"

"Well, I didn't know whether to bother you with it or not. It's really nothing, except that the time checks, and we don't have much of anything else."

"So bring him in. We'll talk to him. As you say, we don't have anything else."

"There's two of them, but one does most of the talking."

"So bring them both in. We don't have enough chairs?"

Both men were in their forties, and by their dress and general appearance Ish-Kosher assumed they were small businessmen, storekeepers, perhaps. Shmuel, the one who did most of the talking, was a little neater than his friend. His suit was pressed, and his shoes were shined. Moshe also wore a business suit; but he also wore a sweater, and it was spotted. Ish-Kosher thought most likely he worked out of doors; he might be the proprietor of a stall.

"We are on guard duty," said Shmuel.

"Night duty," Moshe amended.

"You want to talk, Moshe, or shall I?" Shmuel demanded.

"You talk."

"All right. We're on *night* guard duty," Shmuel went on, "and it's maybe a few minutes before eleven. We're up near the end of Alfont Street. The explosion was at number ninety-eight, so we were a couple of houses down, say at eighty-six. We stopped to light a cigarette—"

"You lit the cigarette," said Moshe.

"So I lit the cigarette. You're afraid the inspector is going to report me? So a man came up and he says very nice, very polite, do we know where is Victory Street."

"He spoke in Hebrew?" asked Ish-Kosher.

"He spoke in Hebrew, but he was not an Israeli. A foreigner, an American, I think."

"All right, go on."

"So you know how Victory Street goes, it curves around. So I ask him what number he wants, because if it's a high number, he's got to go back the other way, and if it's a low number, it was in the direction we were walking, down Alfont Street and over to the right." He gestured with his hand.

"He said number Five," said Moshe.

"I was just going to tell the inspector," said Shmuel indignantly.

"All right," said Ish-Kosher, "so he wanted Victory Street, number Five. So then what happened?"

"Nothing," said Shmuel triumphantly.

"Nothing happened?" Ish-Kosher stared at the two men and then questioningly at his assistant.

Shmuel held up a hand either in placation or perhaps to indicate that there was more to come. "Then I read in the paper how when the bomb is activated, it takes an hour before it goes off. So the bomb went off just about midnight, and this man approached us just around eleven. So I spoke to my friend Moshe here and—"

"I see. Did you get a good look at him?" asked Ish-Kosher. "Can you describe him?"

"Describe?" He looked uncertainly at Moshe. "He was a big man. Right, Moshe?"

Moshe nodded.

"Maybe six feet, Moshe?"

"Six feet sure."

"What color hair, what color eyes?" asked Ish-Kosher.

"It was dark. It was late at night. You saw his eyes, Moshe?"

Moshe shook his head.

"How old was he?"

"He was a regular man. I mean, not a boy, not a youngster. Maybe fifty. Would you say fifty, Moshe?"

"Fifty sure. Maybe fifty-five even."

"How was he dressed?"

"In a coat and hat. That's why I couldn't tell the color hair. He was wearing a hat."

"And he was an American? How could you tell? His Hebrew?"

"His Hebrew was good, but it was not the way we talk. It was like he learned it, you know what I mean?"

"All right. So he asked you how to get to Victory Street, and you told him, and he went off?"

"No-o, not exactly. He wanted number Five, and we were going that way, so we walked along and talked."

"You talked," said Moshe.

"So I talked. Did I give away some special secrets?"

"What did you talk about?" asked the inspector.

"We talked the way people talk. We talked about the regime, about taxes, about the war—you know, like you talk."

"And you walked him to where he was going?"

"No, we walked down to the cross street and I told him he should go down there and that would be the the second or third house from the corner."

"And he walked down the cross street—" Ish-Kosher prompted.

"No." Shmuel smiled, pleased that he had trapped the inspector in error. "He looked at his watch and said maybe it was too late to go visiting. He thanked us and continued down Alfont Street."

Ish-Kosher looked quizzically at his assistant when he returned from escorting the two out. "I told you," said Aaron, "that I didn't think there was much there, but—"

"But we have nothing else," said his chief. "And yet, when you come to think about it a little, it is curious. Eleven o'clock—that's pretty late to be going visiting, just as late as the few minutes later when he decided it was too late. It might be worthwhile making a few inquiries. I don't expect much, you understand, and probably Adoumi's way of rounding up a bunch of Arabs and questioning them in the hope that one will get nervous and admit something is the correct one. Still, a man was killed in my area. That he was killed by a bomb is beside the point. It was murder, and I am charged to investigate murders. So, it might be worthwhile going to Victoria, number Five, and inquiring if any of the residents were expecting a visitor that night, quite late."

17

SUNDAY the Smalls set out to see the city. They were free for the morning at least, since Jonathan would be kept in school until two, and the school would give him his lunch at noon.

"And don't worry about hurrying back exactly on time," said Mrs. Rosen, their neighbor. "He can play with Shaouli until you get home."

"We want to go to the Old City and the Wall," said Miriam. "Will we be able to get back in time?"

"Of course." And she gave them directions on what bus to take to get to the Jaffa Gate. "You'll see signs directing you to the Wall. It's not far. You could even walk it. But this first time, better take a bus."

So they took a bus. No sooner had they paid their fares than the driver swung his vehicle away from the curb and they lurched to their seats. But a car zoomed ahead of the bus, and their driver had to put on his brakes in a hurry. He poked his head out the window and shouted at the driver of the car, "May no harm befall you, but you are a great fool." Then fuming and red-faced with indignation, he put his bus in gear again, and they zoomed forward.

They rode for some minutes, the rabbi and Miriam, eagerly watching the scene as it fled past their window. One of the passengers, a middle-aged woman with a couple of string bags full of groceries on the vacant seat beside her and parcels on her capacious lap, pulled the signal cord and then, for fear that the driver had not heard, pulled it again.

He looked up in his rearview mirror and shouted, "It's all right. I heard you, I heard you. Or do you think you're playing a musical instrument?" He pulled over to the curb and came to a stop.

The woman gathered up her bags and her parcels and headed for the door. "He acts like his father built the road," she complained. "And how many times do you pull the cord and he doesn't stop? And how many times when it's raining and you're waiting at the stop, they ride right by?"

"Lady, lady, we've all got places to go, and if you don't hurry, you won't have time to cook your husband's dinner before he comes home. You'll finish the story the next trip."

"Bus drivers are all the same," said Miriam.

Her husband smiled. "This one is the same, but with a difference."

The bus deposited them in front of the Jaffa Gate, and before entering, they turned back to look at the portion of the new city that they had left.

"It's all so white, David," Miriam exclaimed.

"It's built of Jerusalem stone. If I remember rightly, during the British Mandate there was a law requiring it. Maybe there still is. But it's quite an effect, isn't it?"

They passed through the gate, crossed a wide-open plaza and, following the other visitors, entered a narrow corridor less than ten feet wide, the main street of the Old City. It was covered over like a tunnel, and on either side were stalls and shops with their Arab proprietors sitting outside on low stools, gesturing the passersby inside.

The street sloped precipitously; every few feet there were two or three steps so that they seemed to be descending constantly deeper and deeper into the bowels of the earth. The street was crowded with Arabs, tourists, clerics of various orders, and everywhere children. Side streets led off the main street and, like it, were covered over and lined with shops. Here and there, however, they caught glimpses of squares or courtyards that were obviously residential. As they paused at one corner, a small boy of eleven or twelve approached them. The lad was clean and dressed in Western jacket and trousers.

"Do you need a guide, lady and gentleman? I can direct you anywhere. Do you wish to go to the Western Wall? Are you from America?"

"Yes, we are from America," said Miriam.

"Perhaps from Chicago? Or Pennsylvania? I have many friends in Chicago and Pennsylvania. Perhaps you know some of them. Dr. Goldstein of Pennsylvania is a very good friend of mine."

"No, I don't know Dr. Goldstein of Pennsylvania," said Miriam, amused in spite of herself.

"Perhaps it is the Via Doloroso you wish to see? I can show it to you and arrange for you to go inside the monastery. Father Benedict is a very good friend of mine."

Miriam shook her head.

"Perhaps you are interested in buying rugs or jewelry? I can direct you to the best shops. As my friend you will be given the best prices. Or Persian enamels— I know a shop where the proprietor is planning to give up his business and everything is being sold very cheap."

"We don't want to buy anything," said Miriam.

"My brother can get you leather goods at wholesale—"

Miriam shook her head and hurried after her husband, who had marched straight ahead, refusing to be drawn. As they turned a corner, they saw the young man approach someone else.

"You mustn't encourage them," said the rabbi, "or you'll never get rid of them."

"That one must be rather special. He'll probably be mayor of the city someday."

The rabbi grinned. "Not he. He'll be a merchant, the proprietor of a small store like one of these, and sit on a stool in front of his shop smoking his water pipe and drinking cups of coffee all day long. He'll own half the city, and the mayor will be on his payroll."

As they penetrated deeper into the ancient city, always descending, they noticed a change in the character of the street. The stores were no longer intended for the tourist trade, but rather for residents of the town. There were shops where radios and clocks were being repaired and others where pots and pans were being mended. There were butcher shops with whole carcasses of sheep hanging by their heels and stores where strange foods were sold. There were shoe repair shops and barbershops. There were small cafés in which radios were turned up so that the eerie, piercing Arab music to which they were tuned could be heard yards away. And the proprietors who sat in front of their shops were no longer smiling and ingratiating; they gazed at the passersby indifferently, knowing it unlikely that they would be interested in their wares.

Once Miriam and David had to flatten themselves against the wall as two donkeys, each loaded with a huge arch of empty wooden fruit boxes, came mincing down the street, urged along by the shouting of a small boy. On another occasion, they had to retreat into a convenient doorway to avoid being jostled by a flock of sheep that were being herded through the narrow corridorlike street.

At one point the street widened unaccountably into a kind of square where some little girls of five or six were playing a street game similar to hopscotch. As soon as they saw the Smalls, they came running up, their grimy little hands held out in supplication, crying, "Money, money."

"Pay no attention to them," said the rabbi and shook his head sternly at them. One little girl clutched her belly to indicate hunger, and when even this brought no response, she staggered and fell to the ground. Miriam was tempted to stop; but her husband was striding right along, and she was afraid she might lose sight of him. When she looked back a minute later, she was glad to see that the little girl had picked herself up and was once again playing with the other children.

"Do you suppose she might have been hungry, David?"

"Not that one certainly. They all seem to be well fed, and she's wearing new shoes."

There was a sign that directed them to a narrow flight of stairs, and they followed the crowd. When they had mounted, they saw a wide plaza and beyond it, the Wall. A soldier was stationed on either side of the pathway, and the women had to open their handbags for inspection.

The Smalls found themselves on a stone balcony

looking down on the scene. A fence at right angles to the Wall separated the women's portion on the right from the men's on the left. A couple of dozen women were standing close to the Wall on the women's side, touching it. On the men's side, there were many more, most of them praying, rocking and swaying in their ecstasy.

Miriam looked up at him. "Does it do something for you, David?" she asked softly.

He shook his head slowly, considering. "Not the Wall itself. To me, it's just a wall. Although probably part of the temple, it was probably built by Herod, and he is no great favorite of mine. I find the people praying there affecting, though. Maybe a particular holy place *is* necessary for a people."

"Shall we go down?" They separated at the barrier. "I'll meet you here in about twenty minutes," he said.

He strolled about and then approached the Wall, not to pray but to stand in silent meditation for a few minutes. Then he began walking again, stopping occasionally to inspect the massive stones, passing his hand over them to feel the texture. He went through the archway that adjoined the Wall where excavation was in progress and inspected a shaft that had been sunk to what was supposed to be the original level of the temple. Then he made his way back to wait for Miriam.

When she rejoined him, he asked, "Well, did you pray?"

"I did. But I won't tell you about what."

"I don't think you should."

"Well, I won't then. There was a woman who tried to get me to put on a long skirt she had with her. I refused."

He looked down at her legs. "She was probably just jealous."

"There were all kinds of little bits of paper stuck in the cracks between the stones on my side."

"On mine too. I looked at some of them."

"You didn't!"

He nodded. "Sure I did. Why not? I put them back afterward."

"What did they say?"

"Well," said the rabbi, "one wanted God to cause an earthquake in Egypt. I was tempted not to put that one back, but then I thought God could probably take care of Himself. And there was one that asked for a winning number in the lottery. And one asked to be cured of a sickness."

Noting his tone of voice, she said, "You don't approve, do you?"

"No, but it was rather touching. I think at home, I might voice my disapproval but here. . . ."

Miriam put her arm through his. "There is a difference, isn't there?"

He nodded soberly. "So many different types, and all coming here to seek something. See that tall blond man? He looks just like a fellow I knew in college. He's a little stockier, but then he would be, I suppose." He knitted his brows, straining to remember. "Abbot, William—no, Willard Abbot. He came from one of those fashionable, exclusive private schools where all the teachers are very British and they go in for games. The rest of us were largely from city high schools. He was Jewish, but very few knew it. He was totally assimilated."

"One seems to know so many people here. Everyone looks like someone you know."

"That's to be expected, I suppose. There are a number of definite types of characteristic Jewish faces. But that wouldn't apply to Billy Abbot. In this case the old cliché was true: He didn't look Jewish."

They were turning to go when the rabbi heard his name called. "Small! Dave Small!"

They stopped, and the tall blond man came striding toward them, his hand outstretched.

"Billy Abbot! It's really you."

"In the flesh. You're touring, of course. You have the look."

"That's right." He introduced Miriam. "And you? Are you here on business?"

"I live here, up near Caesarea. I'm an Israeli citizen. I'm what's called a chartered accountant here. I get up to Jerusalem about once a month on business, and when I do, I make a point of coming to have a look at the Old City and the Wall. Most of my clients are in Tel Aviv and Haifa, so I live halfway between the two and get a chance to play some golf."

"And is there a Mrs. Abbot?" David asked.

"Oh, yes. And three little Abbots, two boys and a girl. And you? Do you have children?"

"One boy, Jonathan," said Miriam. "He's here in Israel with us."

"I seem to remember that you were planning to go on to the rabbinical seminary, Dave—"

"I went. I have a pulpit in Massachusetts, Barnard's Crossing—"

"Right," said Billy Abbot. "I know the place. A friend of mine used to go down for the boat races. I went along once to crew for him. Nice town, as I recall."

"We like it," said Miriam.

"It's curious, your coming here to settle," the rabbi offered.

"Well, I lived in London for a while and in Rome," said Abbot. "My folks were in the music world—my father was a concert pianist—and we traveled around a bit. After the Six-Day War I decided to come and settle here."

"But why here?" the rabbi persisted.

"I had no religious instruction and no sense of national or religious affiliation, if that's what you mean. My parents thought of themselves as citizens of the world. And that's how I was brought up. They never denied the fact that they were Jewish, but they never advertised it either. But the world isn't ready to have citizens of its own. Jews are everywhere, and the Jew as a subject of conversation—and discrimination—keeps coming up. An insulting remark about Jews, on the assumption that you're not one—your pride, your manhood, doesn't permit you to let it go unchallenged. There was a girl I was interested in—well, never mind; it's not important." He grinned. "Anyway, I finally decided that if I was going to escape the bloody Jews, I had to come here."

The rabbi grinned back. "You certainly chose a funny place to escape Jews."

"Ah, but here I don't feel like a Jew."

The rabbi nodded. "I think I know what you mean."

It was after two when they got home, and Mrs. Rosen greeted them with, "Jonathan is playing with Shaouli. You could have stayed away all afternoon."

"The morning is enough for the first day," said the rabbi.

"By the way, were you expecting anyone the other night, Friday night?" asked Mrs. Rosen.

"Friday night? We had only just arrived. And we know no one here. Why?"

"The police were here making inquiries," Mrs. Rosen said. "They spoke to each of the neighbors. They wanted to know if anyone here in the building was expecting someone late Friday night."

The rabbi looked at Miriam inquiringly and then shook his head.

18

ISH-KOSHER studied the list in front of him. "You questioned each of them personally?" he asked.

"Everyone except the . . . Smalls," said Aaron, consulting his notes. "They weren't home. I could go back and speak to them if you think it's worthwhile. But they just arrived from America. It's not likely they'd be expecting anyone the first day."

"And what does the family consist of?"

"There's a husband and wife. He's a sort of rabbi. And they have a little boy. Oh, yes, and according to the neighbor, they arrived with an aunt of Mrs. Small's, a citizen who lives in Tel Aviv who drove up to the city with them to see them settled in."

"Aha!"

"You think the aunt—"

"No, but she's already not someone who just arrived."

"She's no longer there. She left the next morning."

"On the Sabbath?"

Aaron nodded.

Ish-Kosher shook his head—in annoyance, in disapproval. Then he sat back squarely in his chair and said, "Listen Aaron. There's probably nothing there, but it might be worth your while to check. In the next couple of days if you're in the vicinity, you might look in on them."

Aaron nodded. Then he shifted in his seat and cleared his throat. "You don't think that maybe Adoumi is on the right track—"

"Of course he's on the right track. There's no doubt it's terrorists. The type of bomb shows that. But which terrorists? Was it Al Fatah, or the Palestine Liberationers, or the Committee for Arab Nationalism, or the Arab Commando Battalion? They've all claimed responsibility. They always do, as you know. So Adoumi pulls in all whose names he has in his files and questions them. Most of them are young and inexperienced —and nervous and let something drop. That's the Army and the Shin Bet method. And it works because it's based on the assumption that the terrorists attack blindly, anyone—women, children. The purpose is to strike terror, not to achieve some definite military objective. On that assumption, their method is probably the only logical procedure."

The inspector leaned back in his chair. "But suppose one of the terrorists has a grudge against a particular Israeli citizen. Then their attack can be directed just as easily against him. Do you see? Now this time the victim was a professor at the university. Suppose they were after him in particular. That suggests the possibility that it was an Arab student group. And the Shin Bet system doesn't work so well with Arabs at the university. They tend to treat them with gloves—government policy. So, if we can pinpoint the group or the individual, we might be able to do what perhaps the Shin Bet can't."

"But we questioned his colleagues and his students, and they all were agreed he was a mild, inoffensive old man who never harmed anyone, who never failed a student."

"Just a minute, Aaron. You're quoting. Wasn't that in one of the reports—'mild, inoffensive old man'?" He shuffled papers on his desk. "Ah, here it is: Professor Robinson's statement. 'Yacov Carmi was a mild, inoffensive old man who never harmed anyone, Arab no more than Jew. Why, just the other day, he told me of some project he was engaged in for the Arab farmers in the Jericho area, something that could increase their yield fourfold.' What do you think of that?"

"Well, sure I read the statement, but—"

"But what does it mean, Aaron?"

"Well, it means that he was a mild, inoffensive old man—"

"*Tcha*," said the inspector. "It means that Yacov Carmi had an idea that would perhaps mean extra income to the Arab farmers. And there has been no formal announcement of it, but it was known around the university. And that means, Aaron"—he held up a forefinger to emphasize the significance of what he was about to say—"that if what he was planning to do

was contrary to the policy of the terrorists, only somebody at the university was apt to know about it."

"But if it was to help the Arab farmers—"

"This is precisely what the terrorists *don't* want. Who
has suffered most at their hands? Not the Jews. We've
been able to protect ourselves. It's been the Arabs,
ten to one, twenty to one. Those poor devils in Gaza—
they're the ones that have got most of it. And why?
Because the terrorists don't want their people to cooperate with us. They don't want them to be prosperous
because then they might decide that they are better off
with us than with Arab masters."

He sat back and teetered in his chair as he studied
the swarthy face of his assistant. He came to a decision.
"Look, Aaron, that American couple at Five Victory
Street, you can forget about them for a while. Or let
one of your men check them out. For the next few
days, I want you to hang around the university. No
uniform. Talk to some of the Sephardi students; they're
closer to the Arabs. At least, they speak Arabic and
may have overheard something. Do you know any of
them?"

"My sister's boy."

"Excellent. See him and get him to introduce you
around. And you might see Professor Robinson and
find out all you can about this project Carmi was working on."

19

THE formula of short and snappy Friday evening services proved to be successful in Barnard's
Crossing, and within two months Rabbi Deutch suc-

ceeded in doubling the attendance. The direct mail campaign helped some, but as Malcolm Slotnick pointed out, "If the product hadn't come up to its billing, there wouldn't have been any repeat business." With the large majority of those who attended it had become a habit.

"Friday night? Oh, I'm afraid Friday night is out. Friday nights we go to temple. . . . Well, we're not religious either, but it makes for a pleasant evening for one thing. You get out of the house . . . and of course, the rabbi is a dear, and Betty Deutch—well, we've become such good friends, I'd feel I was letting her down if I missed a Friday evening service. She's such a lovely person. She's a Stedman, you know— the TV Dan Stedman. . . ."

There were critics, of course. Meyer Paff, for example. "I'm not saying the new rabbi ain't good. I'm just saying maybe he's too good. Me, when a guy starts speaking, I look at my watch. Makes no difference if it's a political speech or some highbrow lecture the missus dragged me to or a rabbi giving a sermon—I look at my watch when he starts, and I look at my watch when he stops. Now Rabbi Deutch averages about fifteen minutes. Sometimes he goes seventeen minutes, or eighteen minutes, but usually from start to finish it's fifteen minutes. Now the delivery is good, I'll give him that, but it's still fifteen minutes. Now me, I figure. I can't help it; I figure all the time maybe because I been doing it all my life. So you take fifteen minutes and you multiply by the number of Fridays— say, thirty-five because in the summer, of course, there's no Friday evening services—and that comes out to a little less than nine hours. Then you divide that into what we're paying the guy, and let me tell you that works out to a helluva lot per hour. So that's what I mean about him being good. I mean, anybody that can make that kind of dough per hour is not only good, he's damn good. But then I start wondering about another thing: Can the guy make a long speech? Has he got enough stuff for a long speech?"

At the Purim service, Rabbi Deutch proved at least that he could make a long speech. His sermon ran fifty minutes by Meyer Paff's watch. It was the first holiday since he had taken over, and the greater portion of the sanctuary was filled. The title of his sermon was "The Purim Story; Fact or Fable?" It went well. Dozens of the congregation came over to tell him that they had never really understood the significance of the holiday until just now. And Bert Raymond called him the next evening to say, "I just had to call, Rabbi. I've got so many wonderful comments on your sermon, I just had to let you know that we're grateful."

Rabbi Deutch was immensely pleased, and when he hung up, he could not help philosophizing to his wife on the success of his sermon. "You see, all I really do is tell the story of Purim, but it happens to be a corking story. Of course, the congregation has a recollection of the general outline of the story, but that only adds to their enjoyment. Still, if I were to do nothing but tell the story, they'd feel they were being treated like children and would be indignant. Justifiably so. So I embellish it with all sorts of speculations to give it plausibility in a modern context, such as suggesting that the Persian king feared a palace revolution by Haman and plotted with Esther to bring about his ruin." He chuckled. "I could tell it was going over well as I gave it."

She smiled sympathetically. "Yes, dear. You like it here, don't you?"

"Very much," he said without hesitation. "It's a nice town and convenient to Boston and Cambridge. I've enjoyed being able to go to a symphony concert now and then—which is gratifying the way I feel about music."

Betty Deutch shook her head to indicate he was missing the point. "I mean you like this temple, the congregation, the work you're doing."

"That's the best part of all. No problems with the

board, everyone going out of their way to be agreeable, and I only do whatever work I care to do. That sermon now, you know when I wrote that?"

"Of course. You used it in your first pulpit in Coventry, Michigan, and again when you first came to Darlington, Connecticut. And I didn't really have to ask if you were happy here," she said with a smile. "I can see that you like it. Have you thought that it might be a good idea to stay on?"

"Oh, that's out of the question, Betty. This is just a temporary job. Rabbi Small will be back in another month. Besides," he said, "I've retired. Remember?"

"Yes, I remember, dear. And I also remember that you weren't very happy in your retirement. A man like you, a man in good health and vigorous, you've got to have something to do. You can't just spend your time moping around."

"I wasn't aware that I was moping around," he said stiffly. "I was planning to do some writing, some scholarly work that I've had in mind for some time now—"

"Oh, Hugo, face reality. If you had writing to do, you would have started right in doing it. You would have done it while you were still the rabbi of the congregation in Darlington. You certainly wouldn't have spent those months just hanging around."

"I was mulling over in my mind a number of projects," he said.

"No, Hugo. If you really want to write, you write." She shook her head. "Don't you see? The work you're doing here, running a temple and a congregation, that's your work. And you're awfully good at it. So why not continue?"

He turned away, hurt. "Well, I'm sorry you think that my writing plans were just so much make-believe—"

"But they were, Hugo, dear. Don't you remember when you thought the congregation in Darlington was sure to ask you to stay on, and you wondered what you'd do if they didn't. Then you said at least it would give you time to put your papers in order and that you might edit your sermons for publication. But that just meant that you weren't ready to face the thought of retirement. But they *didn't* ask you to stay on, and you *had* a few months of retirement—"

"I was sure they were going to ask me to stay on," he said quietly. "They hadn't picked a replacement yet. At least, they hadn't been able to agree on one. But," he said resignedly, "I guess after thirty years, they get tired of you."

"The congregation changed, Hugo," she said in a tone that suggested they had had this discussion many times before. "A different class of people came into power and began running things." She smiled. "Besides, you were getting tired of them, too."

"Yes, that's true."

"But here," she went on, "everyone respects you. If you were to stay on—"

"It would be the same," he said. "Everyone is kind and courteous and pleasant because they know I'm here for only a short while. If I had a regular long-term contract, it would be the same here as it was in Darlington."

"Don't you believe it, Hugo," she said quickly. "You were a young man when you came to Darlington. You had nothing—no money, no reputation. They were in a position to push you around, and they did, until over the years you gained strength and won their respect. But here, they know you don't need them. Your pension is almost what they're paying you. Nobody here can push you around, and they know it, so they won't try. Oh, Hugo," she pleaded with him, "you could stay on for another five years or seven years, and then we'd move to Florida or perhaps go to Israel."

"Well, it's not a bad idea, I mean taking another pulpit," he conceded, "but of course, this one is out of the question. You seem to forget that Rabbi Small will be back in another month."

"How do you know?" she said sharply.

"Well, that was the—the general agreement. I was

hired for three months because Rabbi Small was due back in three months."

"It's not quite like that, Hugo." Even though they were alone, Betty Deutch lowered her voice. "There are a couple of girls in the Sisterhood that I'm really friendly with, and they let down their hair. Did you know, for example, that Rabbi Small is not being paid while he's on leave?"

"Not being paid?" He was horrified. "You mean they stopped his salary?"

"As I understand it, he refused it. He refused to talk about a contract and even refused to promise that he was coming back here."

Rabbi Deutch found that hard to believe. "He seemed like a very level-headed young man. It seems quixotic for a young man with a family to refuse to take his salary. Of course, it could be the way it was offered."

"But it also could suggest—"

"Let's say, it makes one think about possibilities." He nodded. "Yes, it makes one think."

20

THE Small family settled into a regular routine, and within a few weeks they felt as though they had lived in Jerusalem for years. In spite of her meager Hebrew, Miriam was perhaps the most acclimated, by reason of her busy schedule. After she had got Jonathan off to school, she went to the Hadassah Hospital, where she did volunteer work five mornings a week. She would get home by one o'clock, giving her an hour before the stores closed for the afternoon, to do her shopping. Previously, she had decided what she wanted to buy and had asked her husband for the Hebrew words for the articles or looked up the unfamiliar words in a dictionary. Sometimes she would practice the sentences she might have to use and recite them to the rabbi so that he could correct her if necessary. "How much are these a kilo?" "Do you have larger ones?" "Will you please deliver these to Victory Street, number Five? You may leave them outside the door if I am not at home. The milk and butter I will take with me."

Afternoons, while Jonathan returned from school, played with Shaouli, she went to the Ulpan, the special school that gave an accelerated course in Hebrew. In the evenings, after supper, she would prepare her Ulpan lessons for the next day. Sometimes, she and David would go for a stroll in the evening or, on rare occasions, get a baby-sitter so that they could go to a movie or spend an evening with friends they had made.

For Jonathan, there was the happiness of having a number of children of his own age living in the immediate vicinity, quite different from the situation in Barnard's Crossing. And he was picking up the language, more rapidly than his mother for all her lessons and homework. Within a few days he had begun to call her *Eemoleh* and his father *Abbele,* the diminutives of *Emah* and *Abba,* the Hebrew for "Mother" and "Father." He spoke in English to his parents, even when he knew the Hebrew for what he wanted to say, but more and more Hebrew words crept in, and the common short sentences—"I want a glass of milk," or "I want to go outside to play"—were apt to be entirely in Hebrew.

Gittel had chosen wisely in the matter of a school. There were three or four nurseries and kindergartens in the area since practically all the mothers worked, but the one she had selected fortunately had several children who were English-speaking—their parents either were on extended visits from the States or the English countries or were new settlers. So the transition to Hebrew was made easier for him. At first he played with the English-speaking children exclusively, but as he began to gain knowledge of the language, he played with the others as well. Shaouli, the little boy from the upstairs apartment, was of course his most constant companion and his best friend.

As for the rabbi, even though he had no routine to adhere to, time did not hang heavy on his hands. In a sense, he had been master of his time all the years he had been in Barnard's Crossing, too. There had been meetings to attend, committees to consult with, counseling to give, but none of them came at regular hours. He kept no regular office hours and was not subject to a daily routine. So here, his day was not too much different from that at home. In the morning he went to one of the nearby synagogues for morning services, and afterward he might linger on to talk with some of the other worshipers, perhaps even breakfast with them at a handy café. He explored the city. And he read much, finding the many bookstores and the completeness of their stocks a constant source of surprise. And of course, he worked on his Ibn Ezra paper.

They both made friends, the rabbi and Miriam, she at the hospital and at her Ulpan, and he at the synagogue. These they entertained occasionally in the evening and were entertained by them, after the manner of the country with tea and coffee, cookies, and conversation. Once the rabbi overcame his misgivings of traffic conditions and rented a car; they toured the Galilee and spent a few days at a kibbutz. They had met the *chaver,* comrade, at a party when he had come up to the city to transact some kibbutz business. His name was Itzical. They never found out his surname.

"Come and visit us for a few days and see how the real Israel lives. My next-door neighbor is going on holiday and you can use his cottage."

"But who shall I ask for when I arrive?"

"Ask for Itzical—they'll know."

His child, a youngster of Jonathan's age, had been given permission to stay with his parents rather than at the Children's House, where the children of the same age lived together communally, so that Jonathan might have someone to play with. He came with his father the next day, Friday, to take them to the community dining hall for breakfast. The rabbi was reciting the morning prayers when they entered. The little boy watched, his eyes wide with astonished interest.

"What is he doing, Father?"

"Sh—he's praying."

"But those things he's wearing, the shawl and those straps?"

"Those are his *tallis* and *t'fillen*. You remember in your picture book of the war, there were some soldiers at the Wall wearing the same things."

"Why do they wear them?"

"They think it helps in their prayers."

"But why do they pray?"

The rabbi had finished. He smiled at the youngster. "Because we are grateful and wish to give thanks," he said.

Itzical smiled, too. "We are a nonreligious kibbutz," he said. "Maybe even antireligious."

"You don't observe any of the holidays or the Sabbath?"

"Not the religious holidays, and the others in our own way."

"But none of our holidays are purely religious, except perhaps the Day of Atonement," the rabbi said.

"So that's the one we don't observe."

"You go out of your way not to observe it, or you disregard it—which?"

Itzical shrugged. "You know how it is. Most of us just disregard it, but some of the enlightened ones tend to be doctrinaire, and you could say they go out of their way to disregard it."

Nevertheless, the evening meal, the Sabbath dinner, was festive. All the kibbutz members had spruced up, the women wearing dresses instead of jeans and the men in white shirts open at the throat. The meal was the traditional meal of gefilte fish and chicken, and there were even candles and wine on the table.

The Smalls sat at the same table as Itzical and his family, and the rabbi looked around the large room. Over in one corner he saw several couples at a table, and all the men wore yarmulkes.

He nodded. "Who are they? Are they members of the kibbutz?"

"Yes, they are members. They are religious. No one minds; we even have a separate kitchen for them. They joined us a few years ago. We were glad to have them. It was a little dangerous in those days. Would you feel more comfortable eating with them?"

"No, I'm completely comfortable right here," the rabbi said. "But would you mind if I put on my yarmulke? It's a matter of habit as much as anything with me. And it will save Jonathan asking questions."

"By all means."

"And do you mind if I say the blessing for wine and for bread?"

"Go right ahead, Rabbi. I understand. Of course, I don't believe in it myself—"

"It's showing gratitude for the food one receives." He smiled. "The ability to express gratitude is one of the ways in which man differs from the lower animals, and it's good to manifest the difference occasionally."

Itzical shook his head. "I can see you don't know much about animals, Rabbi. Believe me, they can express gratitude, too."

The rabbi considered, and then he nodded and smiled. "Well, it's also good to show the similarity with the lower animals now and then."

Itzical laughed. "You're all right, Rabbi. I see that no matter what, you'll find an excuse for saying the blessing. Go ahead. I'll even stand while you say it."

As they started on the long drive back to Jerusalem several days later, Miriam asked, "Do you think you would like living on a kibbutz, David?"

"Yes, I think I might. If we were to stay on here,

I'd give it serious consideration. It used to be a kind of heroic thing to join a kibbutz, and I guess it still is in some parts of the country. But for most of them, it seems to be the best deal in the country on a purely economic basis."

"How do you mean?"

"Well, you know things are not cheap here."

"Food is—at least certain things are cheaper than in the States."

"Yes, but everything else is apt to be more expensive —housing, clothes, a car, electrical appliances. Most people seem to have them, even though it would seem impossible on the salaries that are paid." He shook his head. "How people live on their salaries—that's the big miracle of Israel! I keep asking people, but I haven't got a convincing explanation yet. As far as I can make out, you borrow to buy the things you need, like an apartment, and then if you don't keep up your payments, it's almost impossible to evict you. So they just add the missed payments to your debt, and you just sweat it out until the currency is devalued or the government passes some sort of relief law. Well, in the kibbutz, you don't have to worry about such things. Everything, all expenses are taken care of. And it appears to be a good life. Yes, if we decided to settle here, I'd give it a lot of thought."

"A religious kibbutz, of course," Miriam pointed out.

"I'm not so sure. Or perhaps I should say that I'm not so sure that the nonreligious ones aren't really religious. You know, the Sabbath we just spent, it could be that was the way it was supposed to be celebrated. And I imagine that it's quite possible that in Biblical times, they celebrated the various holidays the way they celebrate them in the nonreligious kibbutz. Some of them are nature festivals like Shavuoth and Sukkoth. Well, the people who live close to the earth, as the kibbutzniks do, probably celebrate them the way those primitive people of Biblical times did and for the same reason—because it's natural."

They had left the irrigated fields of the kibbutz and were now traveling through desert, the land parched and dry, stony and barren, save for an occasional clump of low, dusty bushes that marked the path of a wadi. The bright sun was reflected off the hard-baked ground in a yellow glare. The oppressiveness of the lifeless scene silenced him. And then, in an effort to throw it off, he began talking again.

"As a rabbi, I'm a professionally religious person. I pray at stated times and in specific ways. Some of it is a matter of habit, like brushing my teeth. And some of it I have consciously practiced because I thought it important for the preservation of the religion and the people, like the Englishman who was supposed to dress for dinner in the jungle. But things are different here. You don't have to follow strict observances here because you don't have to make the point. I imagine that same Englishman was a lot less meticulous about dressing for dinner when he was back in London. It may be all that we've added over the years, the prayers, the special ceremonials, were done to make that same kind of point and were necessary for that reason. But now it may be that the reason is gone and they are no longer necessary."

"It's funny," Miriam said softly.

"What's funny?" He looked at her out of the corner of his eye, remembering always to watch the road.

"That you should come to the Holy Land and find that all the holy things aren't really holy."

"I see what you mean." He smiled. "But it could be like my friend Bill Abbot who doesn't feel like a Jew because he's among Jews. Maybe holy things are out of place in the Holy Land. I don't think I'd be very comfortable if it were a holy land in the strict sense of the phrase. You remember how shocked you were when you read your first Israeli newspaper and saw stories of burglaries, and thieves and prostitutes.

It didn't seem right that there should be theft and prostitution in the Holy Land."

"It wasn't so much that," she said, "so much as it was that the prostitute was named Rachel and the thief Baruch."

"And yet, if there weren't a prostitute named Rachel and a thief named Baruch, it would not be a society that had been established here but rather a museum like Colonial Williamsburg where people are paid to parade around in Colonial costumes. Like a museum, it's all right for a brief visit, but you couldn't live there. Now, here it is just the opposite. I don't think I'd care to come here for a brief visit, but I think I might like to live here."

"You're really thinking seriously of it then?"

"Yes, I am."

"And the rabbinate?" she asked quietly. "Are you thinking of giving that up?"

He did not answer immediately, and they rode for some little while in silence. Then he said, "I'm not afraid to face up to the possibility that I might have made a mistake."

21

REGULARLY, every Sunday afternoon when the weather and road conditions made it at all possible, Al Becker stopped by at the home of his old friend Jacob Wasserman to take him for a drive. Wasserman was the first president of the temple, indeed its founder, and Becker had backed him during the trying period when the organization was aborning and had then succeeded him in the presidency. They used to meet at the Sunday board meetings, but since neither of them now attended, the drive was by way of substitute. They talked of temple affairs largely; it was the one interest they had in common.

It was a mild day, the occasional mild day in March that was a forerunner of the lovely spring weather that sometimes comes to New England, and Wasserman was already in his overcoat, waiting on the porch when Becker drove up.

"I got a card from the rabbi," Becker greeted him.

"Me too."

"What did yours say?" Becker was a short, stocky man with a deep, gravelly voice that always carried a note of belligerence, an effect heightened by his tendency to twist his face forward when he spoke, as if to challenge the listener.

"What you say on a picture postcard. It was a picture of the Wall. On the back it said he was having a nice time. To tell the truth, I think it was the *rebbitzin* that wrote it and he signed it."

"Same here. You know, sometimes I don't understand the rabbi, Jacob. Now we're his strongest backers in the temple, and we've gone to bat for him I don't know how many times, and yet all he can think to send us is a lousy postcard which his wife wrote at that."

"So? When you go on vacation, do you write letters?" Wasserman's English was not so much accented as it showed a special effort to pronounce each word correctly.

"That's different."

"You send postcards, like when you went to California last summer. And it was Mrs. Becker that wrote them. Am I right?"

"Sure, but this is different. With me, it was just a matter of friendship. But with him, it's business. He goes away for three months, which in itself is not such a good idea, not when you've got a board and a bunch of officers that are trying to screw you. When you're in that position, you should stick around so you can fight back. Then he goes away without any contract. Now that ain't smart, especially when you see them putting in a real hotshot as your replacement. Of course, we only got Marty Drexler's say-so that that was what he wanted. I wouldn't put it past that little bastard to maneuver the rabbi into a position where to save his self-respect he had to refuse a contract. And having agreed, he'd be too proud to come to us and tell us that Drexler had played him for a Mickey. So you'd think he'd be writing to us, to the guys who've been backing him, asking questions—what's going on? What's happening? Making suggestions on strategy. At least letting us know when he's coming back so we can make preparations."

"Ah, Becker, you're a smart man, but not smart enough to understand the rabbi." He rose slowly to his feet, and Becker held out a hand to help him down the stairs. "You've never understood him. The rabbi never plays tricks, and usually he says just what he means. He said he wanted a leave of absence; he was tired and wanted a rest. So that's what it was—like a vacation. For people like us, when we take a vacation, what does it mean? It means if it's the winter, we go to Florida to get a little sunshine. If it's the summer, we go to the mountains maybe to get away from the heat. We see new people. We get away from business maybe. The wife doesn't have to do any housekeeping or bother with meals. It's a little rest. But with a man like the rabbi, it's something more. A rest like me and you need, he don't need. When he stops working, it's because he wants to take stock."

"Take stock? What kind of stock has he got?"

"You're thinking like in a warehouse? No. Or maybe yes. His stock is himself. So when he takes stock, he is asking himself how much of himself he's used up. Did he get a good price for it? How much he's got it left? And should he go on peddling it like before, or should he change his method of operation?"

Becker, helping the older man to the car, stopped

and faced him. "Honest to God, Jacob, I don't know what the hell you're talking about."

"No? Tell me, would you want to be a rabbi?"

"A rabbi? Hell, no."

"Why not?"

"Why not? Well, for one thing I like to be in business for myself. From the time I was a kid peddling papers, I been working for myself. I don't want to have to take any crap from some boss. And if it had to be from some of the guys we've had on the board, and yes, as president, there ain't enough money in Fort Knox to pay me."

"And for the money we pay Rabbi Small?"

Becker, his hand under the other's arm, urged him forward again. "You'd have to tie me hand and foot."

"So you think you're smarter than the rabbi? In the old country, it used to be different. There the rabbi was the biggest man in town In the *shul* there was a president, but the rabbi was like president of the whole community. In some places he was rich; in some places he could barely make a living. But it didn't make any difference; he was the headman. If the rabbi made a decision, who would dare go against him? Not even the richest man in town." Wasserman eased himself onto the car seat. "So here's a young man, and he feels capable he should run the operation. So he goes into the rabbinate. But here it's different. Here, a rabbi is not such an important person. Here, he has a bunch of bosses like Marty Drexler or Stanley Agranat or Bert Raymond. He sees right away it's not like what he thought, but he keeps on because he keeps thinking maybe it's improving a little, maybe he's beginning to get control. Comes a time when he thinks maybe it's always going to be this way—one year a little better maybe, the next year a little worse. Then he's got to decide what to do. Of course, if he's a rabbi like Rabbi Deutch—"

"What's wrong with Rabbi Deutch? I'm sold on

Rabbi Small, but I got to admit Rabbi Deutch is a good man." He leaned forward to start the motor.

"Rabbi Deutch is a good American rabbi. For doing what an American rabbi does, he's one of the best I've seen around. He looks nice, he talks nice, and he don't get into any trouble with the important people. Maybe when he was the same age as Rabbi Small, he had the same questions in his mind and decided it wasn't worthwhile fighting, that by bending a little here and there he could have a peaceful life." Wasserman waved a blue-veined hand to illustrate Deutch's probable flexibility. "But Rabbi Small is a little different. So that's what I'm afraid of, that he might decide that it isn't worth it."

"How do you know all this, Jacob? Did the rabbi confide in you?"

"No, he didn't confide in me, and he didn't ask my advice. But I know it just the same. I knew it when I heard that he wasn't taking any money from the temple while he's on his vacation. Because if he took his salary while he wasn't working, like you might say if he took money for nothing, then he would feel obliged to come back. So when he wouldn't take the money or a contract or anything, that meant he wasn't sure he was coming back. Not sure, you understand. Because if he *was* sure he wasn't coming back, he would just have resigned. And that's why he didn't write us yet. Because so far he hasn't yet made up his mind." He looked at Becker. "Now, how do you put that on a postcard?"

22

THE voice was so loud that the rabbi held the receiver a little away from his ear. "Rabbi? *Shalom.* I'll bet you'll never guess who's speaking. Well, it's V. S. Markevitch, that's who."

In his mind's eye, the rabbi could see the speaker at the other end of the wire, beaming with satisfaction at the pleasant surprise he had been able to confer on him. V. S. Markevitch was always conferring pleasant surprises on his friends and acquaintances. Back in Barnard's Crossing, he would drop in on someone of an evening without bothering to call in advance, and even when he found they were preparing to go out, he was never put out of countenance, but would talk, raising his voice so that the lady of the house, who was in the bedroom putting on her makeup, would not miss anything he was saying to her husband, who was forced by politeness to remain in the room and zigzag his tie on there without the aid of the bedroom mirror. He was always sure people were glad to see him.

He usually referred to himself in the third person, rarely using the pronoun, preferring to repeat the mouth-filling name as often as necessary. He was not a member of the board of directors of the temple, but he did not hesitate to get up at general meetings and Brotherhood get-togethers to give his opinions. Rising to his feet, his round bald head gleaming, his mouth wide in a perpetual smile, he would say, "Mr. Chairman, V. S. Markevitch would like to comment on the motion on the floor." When recognized, he would bombard his listeners with, "V. S. Markevitch feels that . . ."

and "In the humble opinion of V. S. Markevitch. . . ."

"When did you arrive, Mr. Markevitch?" said the rabbi.

"Just got in." The voice sounded surprised as if to convey the idea that it was unthinkable for V. S. Markevitch to come to Israel for whatever reason and not call his rabbi the very first thing.

"Are you alone, Mr. Markevitch? Or is Mrs. Markevitch with you? Are you on a tour?"

"I'm here with just Katz, my partner. We're here on business, Rabbi. We got a bunch of meetings scheduled, one with the Minister of Industrial Development for sure, and then we join a group that will meet with the Prime Minister, but that's later on in the week. It's probably nothing very much to you. I guess by this time you've met all the big shots—"

"I'm afraid not."

"Well, maybe I'll be able to introduce you to them— after I've met them. Now here's what I'd like. We got a cab, and they're just loading our things on, and we're taking off for Jerusalem in a couple of minutes. We'll be staying at the King David tonight and tomorrow. Then we go off to Haifa. So how's about us getting together, and maybe you could show us the town, all the sights and things?"

"Well, I'm not much of a guide, but I'll be happy to see you and show you and Mr. Katz around."

"It's a date, Rabbi."

They met the next morning in the lobby of the hotel. Markevitch and Katz had just finished their breakfast in the cafeteria, but they thought they would like another cup of coffee, and so the three men sat around a table sipping at coffee and talking about Barnard's Crossing.

Markevitch jokingly called Joe Katz his silent partner—"on account I'm apt to do all the talking." Whereas Markevitch was big and expansive, with a wide smile seemingly cutting his melon-like head in two, Katz was a small, worried man with sad eyes and a shy smile. As Markevitch talked, Katz was silent, nodding at his partner's sallies, wincing occasionally when he felt his partner had uttered an indiscretion.

Markevitch's voice was not so much loud as never lowered. Regardless of where he was, he spoke in his normal conversational tones. In the lobby, he spoke as though he were addressing all the guests in the hotel. So all the guests heard that the Mazurs were getting a divorce. Josiah Goldfarb's boy had been arrested for drugs. The Hirshes had sold their hardware business in Lynn and were moving to Florida. Max Kaufman's boy, Al, had won first prize at the high school science fair. There was a new traffic light on Elm Street just before the temple, which should make it safer for the kids going to the religious school. Lenny Epstein had pledged a thousand dollars to the School Fund.

Finally, the rabbi managed to ask, "And how is Rabbi Deutch getting along?"

"Ah," said V. S. beaming, "we hit the jackpot with that one, Rabbi. I thought when I heard you were taking a vacation, you'd palm off some kid out of the seminary on us as a substitute. Or if not that, then some *shlemiehl* who couldn't normally get a decent job. But when you picked Rabbi Deutch, you picked a good one. And the *rebbitzin* too. She's a real high-class lady."

"I didn't pick him," said the rabbi. "He was picked by the committee. I had never met him."

"Oh, is that so? I thought it was you who picked him. I went to the reception, if you remember. And seeing you folks and the Deutches standing there so chummy and talking and all, I just assumed—well, anyway, he's a good man. I mean when he gets up there in the pulpit"—he straightened up in his chair and looked around the room in imitation of Rabbi Deutch in the pulpit— "and gives a sermon in that voice of his, sometimes the shivers go up and down your spine. Of course, I haven't had much to do with him, but you hear people talking and they're pretty impressed, even Gentiles in town, I mean. You know they asked him to serve on the Library

Committee? Now for an outsider. . . . And the *rebbitzin,* did you know Dan Stedman is her brother, the TV commentator, I mean? They took right over as soon as they came to town, and they fit right in."

"That's nice. Then he's happy in Barnard's Crossing?"

"That same question V. S. Markevitch addressed to Rabbi Deutch no later than last Friday night at the *Oneg Shabbat.* We were all standing around drinking tea and V. S. Markevitch sashays up to the rabbi and says"—his voice became businesslike—"'Rabbi Deutch, we like you here, and we all think you're doing a swell job, but do you like it here?' A lot of people say that V. S. Markevitch is always shooting off his mouth, but he says if you don't ask you don't find out."

"And what was his answer?" the rabbi asked.

"Well, now you tell me, you be the judge, if he likes it in Barnard's Crossing. He says in that high-toned way of his, 'It's a lovely, pleasant town, Mr. Markevitch, and in addition, for me, it has the added advantage of being only a half hour's ride from the great libraries of Boston and Cambridge.' He's a great scholar, you know. Now what do you think? Does he like it, or does he like it?"

The rabbi smiled. "I get your point, Mr. Markevitch."

Markevitch's voice suddenly changed to a hoarse whisper not a decibel lower than his normal speaking voice. "There's even talk around that maybe we're big enough now to have two rabbis and that maybe Rabbi Deutch might be willing to stay on. What do you think of that?" He sat back in his chair and looked quizzically at the rabbi.

"Well, I can see some problems that—"

"Sure, that's what Markevitch said when he first heard about it. Didn't he, Katz?" He leaned forward again and went on confidentially, "Rabbi Deutch is the older and more experienced man, so he couldn't be assistant to Rabbi Small. On the other hand, Rabbi Small had the job first, so he's not going to like the idea of stepping down to play second fiddle to Rabbi Deutch no matter how old and experienced he is."

Katz winced. He touched his partner. "Please, Markevitch."

Markevitch turned and stared. "Whatsamatter, Katz?" Then he turned to the rabbi again. "What I say is, why can't there be like two associate rabbis, both equal, especially where it looks like we're going to have to run two services, one upstairs and one downstairs in the vestry? And the way I see it, where our holidays all run two days, they could take turns conducting the service upstairs, which it will no doubt be the more important one. And they could toss a coin for who gets first whacks. What do you think, Rabbi?"

Rabbi Small pursed his lips. "It's an interesting speculation."

Markevitch poked his partner with his elbow. "See, Katz, you don't ask, you don't find out. Rabbi Small is interested. You think about it, Rabbi. Now, how's about seeing the town?"

"I suppose you'd like to see the Wall first?"

"Yeah, we'd like to see the Wall. We got a special reason." He smiled and winked at his partner.

They took a cab, and all through the short ride, Markevitch, who sat in the middle, kept turning from side to side so as not to miss any sight they passed. "Look at that, Katz, out there . . . it's past now. It was a—What's that, Rabbi? . . . Oh, look at that old Jew with the whiskers . . . Hey, that's an Arab, isn't it? I mean when they wear those checkered *shmattes* around their heads, then they're Arabs. Right? . . . Hey, that must be some kind of a church. . . ." He kept it up until they were deposited at Jaffa Gate, asking questions and not waiting for answers, pointing out whatever he thought unusual—people, buildings, signs.

"I thought we'd go this way, so you'd get a chance to see the Old City," the rabbi explained.

They crossed the plaza beyond the gate and approached the tunnellike street.

Katz drew back. "You mean we go through there? Is it safe?"

"Sure, Katz. Look at those two old geezers with the beards. If they can go through, I guess it's safe for us."

They entered. Markevitch commented, his words expressing not so much wonder as incredulity. "Imagine, Katz, this is a street. . . . This is by them a regular street. . . . Imagine . . . look at those women with the veils. What are they afraid of? . . . How can people live like this? . . . Look, there's a shoe store. Better not stop, Katz, or you'll maybe have to buy . . . this junk . . . who buys it? . . . How can they make a living. . . . Look, there's a guy selling halvah. . . . When was the last time you ate halvah, Katz? . . . This is what they call a butcher shop, I suppose. . . . Look, everything open . . . I guess they never heard of sanitation. . . ."

At last they came to the Wall. They surveyed the plaza in front of it, and Markevitch said, "Now this is something like. I guess you come here practically every day, huh, Rabbi?"

"Well, I've been here a few times."

"Gee, I'd think you'd be here every day, praying, I mean."

"No, Mr. Markevitch, I don't feel it's necessary. Prayers are no stronger for being made in front of the Wall."

"Can we go right up to it?" asked Katz. "Or do we have to buy a ticket, or make a contribution—that guy at the desk there—"

"He's just distributing paper yarmulkes for those who don't have head coverings. No, you can go right on up. There's no charge."

"Imagine, Katz, no charge. Not even a silver collection. Look, Rabbi"—for the first time Markevitch dropped his voice—"we were wondering if you could say a prayer for us. What we had in mind was some special kind of prayer maybe where you could ask for the success of our enterprise—"

"Especially the financing," said Katz.

"That's right, especially the financing, but I was thinking of the whole *shmeer*."

The rabbi shook his head. "With us it's every man for himself, Mr. Markevitch. We Jews have no intermediary between man and God. You can stand right up close to the Wall if you feel that will be especially efficacious, and you can say what you have in your mind and heart."

"But I don't know any Hebrew except maybe some of the prayers, you know, like the blessings for bread or wine—"

"I'm sure God will understand if you speak in English or even if you just think it."

"You don't think He'd mind where it's a matter of business? After all, it's for the good of the country."

The rabbi smiled. "People ask for all kinds of favors. Some who come here even write little notes and stick them between the stones. See?"

"Yeah." Markevitch looked around and, seeing that he was unobserved, pried loose several of the rolled-up bits of paper. He unrolled one and, as it was in Hebrew, passed it to the rabbi. "What's it say?"

The rabbi read: "I have six daughters and my wife is heavy with a seventh child. Grant, Dear God, that it should be a male so he can say the Kaddish for me and my wife after we are gone."

Markevitch unrolled another, and the rabbi read and translated: "My wife is sick. She is a burden to herself and to me. Dear God, either take her to your bosom or make her well."

Markevitch shook his head and made little clucking noises of pity. He felt constrained to justify his intrusion on another's grief. "It's not that Markevitch is nosy, rabbi. It's just he wants to get the general picture." He unrolled the third. "Oh, this one is in English. This is more like it," and he read aloud to them: "American Telephone—52, IBM—354, Chrysler—48, General Motors—81. I ask not for riches, just for enough of a rise, dear God, so I can bail out."

He folded the bits of paper carefully and reinserted them in a crevice in the wall. "It's worth a try, Katz. Give me a pencil and piece of paper."

The rabbi waited while they wrote out their petition and insinuated it in a crack between two stones. They stood in front of the Wall, muttering what scraps of Hebrew they knew. Even though he was standing at a little distance, he could not help hearing the voice of V. S. Markevitch reciting the blessing for wine, the blessing for bread, and then after a pause, the four questions that the youngest child at the Seder asks on Passover. Then for a couple of minutes Markevitch stood silent, his eyes shut tight, his brow furrowed in deep concentration. Finally, he said, "It's V. S. Markevitch that's asking, dear God," and stepped back.

People continued to arrive, and just as they turned to go, they saw a group of Americans, prosperous middle-aged people like themselves, under the leadership of one of their number whose black hat and more sober costume suggested that he might be the rabbi who was conducting their tour. "Just spread out and stand right along the Wall," he ordered. "Don't be afraid. Don't be bashful. You've got just as much right here as anyone else. Now, if you'll all turn to page sixty-one . . ."

Markevitch looked significantly at his partner and nodded in the direction of the praying Americans.

They left the Wall and took a cab to Zion Square. They strolled along Ben Yehuda Street and Jaffa Road, the business area of the new city. They were obviously disappointed in the narrow streets and the small, poorly decorated shops.

"This sure ain't no Fifth Avenue, eh, Katz?" said Markevitch.

"Fifth Avenue it ain't, or even Boylston Street or Washington Street, but look how little capital you need to start a business here."

The rabbi thought they might be tired and steered them to a nearby café. They ordered coffee and looked about them at the occupants of the other tables, several of whom were reading the newspapers and magazines.

"They come here to read?" asked Katz.

"They come to meet their friends, to read, to talk, to break the monotony of the day over a cup of coffee," the rabbi explained.

"I guess they never heard of customer turnover here," said Markevitch, putting down his cup. "Where to now, Rabbi?"

The rabbi nodded to the waitress. She came over. "Anything else, gentlemen? Then three coffees—three lira."

"I thought we might take a look at the university now," said the rabbi, reaching in his pocket.

Markevitch put a restraining hand on his arm. "No, Rabbi, when V. S. Markevitch eats, V. S. Markevitch pays. How much is it?"

"No, Mr. Markevitch," said the rabbi, and he clinked some coins into the waitress's outstretched hand. "You are guests, visitors to the country, and I am a resident."

At the university the partners expanded. This was more like it. They had been obviously disappointed in what they had seen so far. The Old City had been quaint, to be sure, and the people picturesque which was interesting in movies and picture postcards, but up close, the quaint and the picturesque were dirty and ragged and smelly. The Western Wall—well, it was just a wall. They had not felt the anticipated magic of it. And Zion Square, too, was old and shabby, not like the Old City, to be sure, but also certainly not what they had been led to expect from the slides and movies that were shown at fund-raising meetings they had attended. But the university—new, modern buildings, wide plazas, open and spacious surroundings, this was what they had expected the whole city, indeed the whole country, to be like. Over the years, they had bought Israeli bonds and made contributions. Now, at last, they could see that their money had been put to good use. They walked about, breathing deeply of the clean, fresh air as though it had been generated by the new buildings. They stopped and conscientiously read each of the bronze plaques as they came across them.

"Donated by the Isaacson Family, Montreal. . . . Through the generosity of Arthur Bornstein, Pough-keepsie. . . . Established in memory of Sadie Aptaker. . . . The Harry G. Altshuler Room. . . . Morris D. Marcus Memorial Library of Industrial Design. . . ."

They read aloud and commented. "You think that's maybe the Marcus from the Innersole Marcuses?"

"Look, Katz. Montgomery Levy from Rhodesia. Imagine, from Rhodesia."

"They got Jews there, too. Here's one from Dublin, Ireland. . . ."

Over a cool drink in their hotel room, the partners discussed the day. "To tell the truth, Katz, I was a little disappointed in our rabbi. I mean he's a rabbi, so I should think that every time he went to the Wall, he'd want to say a prayer. By his own admission, he's only been there a few times. That don't seem right, living right here in Jerusalem, and him a rabbi. And why was he so snooty about saying a prayer for us? That's his job, isn't it? To me, it seemed like he was tired of the rabbi business."

"So he's on vacation. The rabbi business is like any other business. You go on vacation, you want a rest from it."

V. S. shot him a glance. "You sure it's a vacation?"

"What then?"

Markevitch dropped his voice to a hoarse whisper that could be distinctly heard through the closed door by anyone who happened to pass by in the corridor. "Maybe he's not planning to come back. Maybe he plans to stay here. That's why he didn't want to say a prayer for us. It's like we're no longer his congregation. You remember how in the coffeehouse he insisted on paying. Now when does a rabbi ever put his hand in his pocket? But you remember what he said how we're the guests and he's the resident? You remember?"

Katz inclined his head in agreement. "You got a point there."

Markevitch drained his glass and sat back in beaming admiration of his own perspicacity. "Mark my words, Katz, he's not coming back. And I'll tell you something else, if he doesn't come back and if Rabbi Deutch stays on, V. S. Markevitch for one, wouldn't lose any sleep."

"And how did it go?" asked Miriam.

The rabbi did not answer immediately. He frowned as though trying to find the words with which to frame his reply. "You know, it's curious," he said at last, "you live here for a while—and it doesn't have to be a long time—and you start feeling like a native, at least toward tourists. You find yourself embarrassed by them, and you resent their failure to understand what they see. You resent their patronizing airs; you resent the comparisons they make with America, the ones they voice and the ones you sense they feel even when they don't say anything; you resent their attitude that they own the country because of the contributions they've made—"

"You're really talking like a native."

"I suppose I am. Maybe I'm beginning to think and feel like one."

She rose and walked over to the table to busy herself rearranging the books, the vase of flowers, the ashtrays that were on it. With her back to him, she said, "I get the impression, David, that you're hinting that you'd like to remain here."

"I think I might," he said quietly. "At least for a while. Would you mind?"

"I don't know. It would depend. What would you do—I mean about making a living? You couldn't be a rabbi here."

"I know."

She turned around and faced him. "David, are you tired of being a rabbi? Are you planning to give it up?"

He began to laugh. "It's funny: rabbi comes to the Holy Land and loses his religion. Of course I knew, even before I went to the seminary, that I couldn't be the kind of rabbi my grandfather was in the little *shtetl* in Russia where he lived or for that matter in the Orthodox community that he came to in America. He was a judge, applying his knowledge of the Talmud to settle the problems of his congregation and his community. That was impossible in America. But I thought I could be a rabbi like my father, a leader in the community who steered his congregation along the lines of basic Judaism and kept them from straying into the romantic Christianity that surrounded them. It involved certain traditional practices, set prayers to be said at certain times of the day, that were not in keeping with the modern world, but they had the merit of keeping us different from our neighbors, and so they were a cohesive force. Well, since coming here to Israel, I have begun to think that they were the religious practices of the Exile, the *galut*. I felt the spirit of the Sabbath most on our first day here when I did not go to the synagogue and again at that nonreligious kibbutz. They had worked hard all week, and on the Sabbath they put on clean clothes and feasted and rested, and it renewed their strength for the coming week. Somehow, I felt that was the way it was intended to be. It seemed to me that here, in our own land, our traditional practices had become a kind of mumbo jumbo, useful in the Exile, but meaningless here. I could see it in the wondering eyes of Itzical's little boy at the kibbutz as he watched me praying in my shawl and phylacteries. To bind a black leather strap around my arm in a certain way and around my forehead, to wrap a special fringed cloth around me in order to recite words that had been written for me hundreds of years ago—that was useful in America to remind me that I am a Jew. But here in Israel, I don't need anything to remind me.

What is my work in Barnard's Crossing but purveying religious hocus-pocus—marrying people, burying them, saying an appropriate prayer at all kinds of occasions? That's what Markevitch and Katz expected of me today." Hands in his trouser pockets, he began to pace the floor.

"But they're not typical of the congregation."

"They're a little extreme, I admit, but their attitude is not too different from that of most of the congregation."

"David, have you made up your mind? Have you definitely decided you want to leave the rabbinate?"

"No—I don't know," he said unhappily, looking moodily at the floor. "But—"

"But you'd like to know how I feel in case you should? Well, I married you before you were a rabbi, and if you had flunked out at the seminary, I wouldn't have asked for a divorce. But you still have to make a living. What would you do?"

"Oh, I could always get a job." He looked up, and his voice was buoyant again. "Or maybe we could join a kibbutz. Or I could teach. Or write for one of the newspapers. My Hebrew is good enough. Of course, we'd have to make some adjustments. We'd have to get used to a lower standard of living. Instead of the volunteer work you're doing at the hospital, you'd have to get work that you'd be paid for—"

"That wouldn't bother me. I could even do the same work I'm doing now. The others in the department *do* get paid. But it might be some little while before I could start."

"Oh?"

"Today at the hospital, I begged off for a while and went to see a doctor on my own." She hesitated. "I'm going to have a baby, David."

23

THEY met as usual in the hotel lobby, before going up to dinner at the Artist's Club, and the first thing Roy said was, "I got an exam tomorrow, so I'll have to leave early." On the other occasions, he had made similar announcements—that he was tired and planned to get to bed early; that he had an early class the next morning or a date later that evening—any excuse to leave immediately after dinner. Each time Dan had been disappointed and even a little hurt, but had been careful to give no indication of his feelings. He felt it was important that Roy feel he had complete freedom. He was determined not to play the role of the heavy-handed father. "If we're to be friends," he told himself, "he's got to want to see me the same way I want to see him."

He had tried to get Roy to talk about his studies with little or no success. "Courses, like courses in the States. You get one prof that's interesting, you're lucky. The time passes a little quicker. Most of them just cover the ground."

He had tried telling him about his own work, interviews he had taped, his methods of procedure. It drew little response.

He had tried to ask about Roy's friends and even offered to have one or two join them for dinner.

"Well, most of the kids are pretty busy."

"I don't need to make any special preparation. Give me a call."

"Yeah, I'll keep that in mind."

Deciding that perhaps Roy interpreted his interest

as interference in his affairs, prying, tonight he was determined to keep the conversation in neutral channels and take his lead from his son. They walked to the restaurant in silence, and only when they arrived did Roy finally say, "This is not a bad place, you know."

Dan agreed, saying that considering location, service, quality of the food, he found it as good as any place in Jerusalem.

After some discussion of the menu, they ate in silence for the most part. When they were served their dessert and coffee, however, Roy ventured, "I called you last night, and they said you'd gone to Tel Aviv."

Dan wondered if he resented the trip. "Yes, I went down for a couple of days. Bob Chisholm was having a little party. He's head of the AP office down there." Roy did not appear to be interested, but Dan continued if only to fill the vacuum of silence. "I took the *sherut* down and when we arrived, I called the Sheraton to see if they could let me have a room for the night. They were full, of course—they always are—but I got hold of Phil Bailen, the manager, and he said he'd fix up something. So that way I was able to stay down there for a couple of days."

"M-hm."

"It's quite a town," Dan continued. "There's no telling who you'll run into. When I got to the hotel late that night, after the party, who do I see but Alfred Northcote? He's with the BBC, and when I was stationed in London a couple of years ago, I used his digs because he was off to Spain at the time."

"Uh-huh."

"It didn't surprise me either. You know, between the time I registered at the desk and the time I got into the elevator I met three different people I knew. I had just finished registering when Colonel Girande, whom I met in Paris, oh, six or seven years ago, spotted me and came over and we chatted for a few minutes. And while we were talking, Bob Chisholm—the one that gave the party—he joined us. Then while I'm waiting for the elevator, I hear somebody calling, 'Meestaire Stedman' and I turned around and it was Olga Ripescu. The minute I saw her, I remembered her, and remembered her name, too. Some years ago I did a story on the Rumanian Ballet. Most of the story was devoted to the *première danseuse* and the choreographer and the manager, of course. But I also talked to some of the young people who had just joined the troupe, and one of them was this girl, Olga Ripescu. Well, she had come with the ballet and now she was the *première danseuse*. And she had remembered me after all that time."

"Fantastic!"

Dan didn't know how to read the remark, so pretended not to notice. "There's a party at the American Embassy next week," he went on. "I was invited. I could wangle an invitation for you if you'd care to go. There's usually a number of pretty girls on hand from various diplomatic and government offices."

"Jewish girls?"

"Most of them."

"I see," said Roy. "You'd like me to meet some Jewish girls."

"From what you've told me, it might not be a bad idea," his father observed. "Yes, I'd like you to meet some Jewish girls and Jewish boys."

"That's what I thought. So you're still trying to run my life," he said bitterly.

"Well, isn't that what fathers are for?" Dan said, trying to keep the conversation light.

"No one has a right to interfere with somebody else's life. I'm an individual, and I've got a right to live my own life the way I want to. I aim to pick my own friends and do my own thing." The young man spoke with passion.

"Look, Roy, do we have to quarrel every time we meet?"

"Just don't try to steer me, and everything will be just fine. That's all, just don't try to steer me." He got up from the table. "Uh, look, it's getting late and I've got that exam."

Back in his hotel room, Dan Stedman went over the evening in his mind. What's the matter with these young people? Anything you say, they give their own special interpretation. How do you talk to them so they'll listen and respond in a reasonable, adult way?

He was reminded of a line in a letter he had received only that morning from his sister in Barnard's Crossing. ". . . although he was here more than six years, he was never very popular and has no real backing in the congregation except for the young people, most of them still in their teens, who seem to like him— and they don't vote in temple elections."

He searched in his desk drawer for an earlier letter in which she had given him Rabbi Small's address.

24

"IT'S a book of opinion, Israeli opinion, not of government officials or big shots but of the man in the street—Jew, Arab, men, women, the young and the old." Stedman warmed to his subject. "You see, Rabbi, when you talk to an official, all you ever get is the official view that has already been announced through the government press releases. But if you get the ordinary people to talk, you get insights into the political situation that underlie the official news."

"And how do you go about it?" asked Miriam. "Do you stop people on the street?"

"Sometimes I do, Mrs. Small, but I don't tell them I want to interview them because then they would either freeze up or say what they think you want them to say. I try to be a little more subtle. Here's a man walking along the street. So I ask him how to get to someplace that is in the general direction he's heading. Usually they say they're going that way, and we walk along together. We start to talk, and if it sounds as though it's going to be interesting, I switch on my tape recorder—I control it from a device in my pocket—so they don't know they're being taped. Then when I get back to my room, I label everything so that I can collate it, edit it, and write it up at my leisure."

"Are your interviews in English or Hebrew or what?" asked the rabbi.

"I have them in Hebrew, Yiddish, English and even French. My Yiddish is excellent; my French not too bad. My conversational Hebrew is all right, too. I've been here about a dozen times. The last time was for more than a year. I'd say it was adequate. Occasionally I strike a tough one, as I did the other day. He was an intellectual, and he used words I'd never heard before. But that's another advantage of the taping method. I can play it over and over again and look up the words I don't know in the dictionary."

"But how were you able to frame your replies or the next question if you didn't understand what he said?" asked the rabbi.

"Oh, I got the gist of it all right. It's the subtle nuances that I felt I was missing. Would you like to hear some of my tapes sometime?"

"Yes, very much," said the rabbi, "although I don't think my college French would be up to following a conversation."

"I don't have too many in French, just some that I got in a restaurant where there were a lot of Sephardic Jews from North Africa. I tell you what, maybe you'd like to come along. If you're not doing anything tomorrow morning—"

"Nothing urgent."

"You, too, Mrs. Small."

"Oh, I'd like to, but I have to be at Hadassah in the morning."

When they met the next morning, Stedman said, "Perhaps it's just as well that Mrs. Small couldn't make it. It might be harder to develop a conversation if there were three of us."

"I suppose so. By the way, Miriam asked me to ask you if you'd care to take dinner with us tomorrow night. And we'd like to have your son come, too. When you mentioned on the phone you had a son in the university, we rather expected he might be with you last night."

"Well, Roy is kept pretty busy. I see him about once a week; we have dinner together. I try not to interfere in his life too much. I'm not sure he'll be able to make it tomorrow night, but I'll ask him."

"I thought tomorrow being the Sabbath he'd be likely to be free. He might enjoy a Sabbath meal, and I'd like to meet him."

"I'd like you to meet him, Rabbi." He hesitated and came to a decision. "To tell the truth, I'm at something of a loss as to how to deal with him. After I was divorced from his mother—he was ten at the time—I had visiting rights, of course, but my work was apt to keep me away from the States for long periods of time. My wife wouldn't let me make up the time lost when I was home, and I don't blame her, because it would have disrupted his life. But the net result was that I didn't see much of Roy, except a day now and then. I tried to keep in touch with him—letters, phone calls—but it wasn't the same thing. I thought that with both of us here alone, we'd get to know each other. But he's cold, distant. I can't seem to reach him. Sometimes I think he resents me. If I try to interest myself in his work, in his problems, if I try to advise him, he acts as though I'm intruding on his private affairs."

"You probably are."

"But I'm his father."

"Biologically," said the rabbi. "Your son treats you like a stranger because you are a stranger."

They stopped at the curb for the traffic light to change. Stedman waited until they had crossed before answering. "But what am I supposed to do? I see him doing all sorts of foolish things. Am I supposed to see him make mistakes and not interfere? As near as I can make out, all his friends at the university are Arabs. When I suggest that he cultivate some of the Jewish students, that his present associates might be unwise or even dangerous, he only gets annoyed with me."

"Just as you'd be annoyed with him if he presumed to criticize your friends."

"There's a difference."

"Not much, really, and none in his eyes." The rabbi shrugged.

"So what's the answer?"

"There might not be any, at least not the kind you hope for. If you think of him as a stranger, as a young man whom you've met but whom you have no claim on, after a while you might get to be friends."

Stedman spread his hands, pleading with the rabbi to understand. "But I want to help him. I want to help him shape his life, influence him, steer him in the right direction."

"Well, as a friend you might be able to." The rabbi could see that Stedman was disappointed and that his advice was not likely to be taken. They walked along in silence for a block, and then suddenly Stedman seized his arm and pointed.

"There, that could be the answer."

The rabbi looked about, but saw nothing unusual.

"That sign: Memavet Auto Brokerage Agency. When I first came, I told Roy I was planning to get a car to tour the country, and I invited him to come with me to pick one out. Come to think of it, he was pretty enthusiastic about that."

"And you think if you got a car, that would do it?"

"Rabbi, unless you know how kids feel about cars,

you don't know kids. Do you mind stopping in for a minute? This place advertises in the papers. I'll just see what the deal is and what sort of cars they have to offer."

It was a repair shop with several disemboweled cars being worked on. In one corner, near the window, was a flat-topped desk, untidy with dusty papers, with a cardboard sign set in a wooden holder: MEMAVET AUTO BROKERAGE AGENCY. An elderly mechanic with a beard approached them.

"Mr. Memavet?"

The mechanic pointed to the desk. "You want the Memavet Agency? That's it." He pointed to the desk. "Memavet is not in. He's been out sick a couple of days."

"Isn't this his place? Isn't there somebody else I can talk to?"

"No. We got nothing to do with Memavet. He just rents the desk space."

"Oh." Stedman was disappointed.

"You wanted to see him about a car, maybe? Buying or selling?"

"I'm interested in buying, but—"

"So go to see him at his house," the bearded mechanic said. "It's all right. Sometimes, even when he's well, he stays home for a few days. The same business he does here, he can do there."

"Well, I thought I'd look at his stock and—"

The mechanic laughed. "He has no stock. He doesn't work that way. You tell him what you want, and he tries to get it for you. He's a crazy old man, but I'll say this for him, he knows cars and he'll give you a good buy."

"In what way is he crazy?" the rabbi asked. "Is it because he gives good buys?"

"Your young friend is a joker," said the mechanic. He went on to explain. "He's crazy because his mind works funny. He's had troubles that he'll tell you about at the drop of a hat. But who hasn't had troubles, especially in this country? Take his name: Memavet. 'From death'—is that the name a sane man would choose?" He shrugged. "But he knows cars, and he's honest. If he sells you a car, he'll tell you exactly what condition it's in, and you can believe him."

"Well, maybe I'll call him," said Stedman. "Do you have his phone number at home?"

"He doesn't have a phone yet. He moved into a new place. There's a public phone in the lobby of the house, just outside his door, but I don't know the number. But you don't have to phone him in advance. Just go to see him. He'll be home, all right."

"Well, if he's sick—"

"He's got a cold. Believe me, he won't mind."

"Well—"

"Here," said the mechanic, "take down the address: Number One Mazel Tov Street. It's a new street that runs off Shalom Avenue. You know where Shalom Avenue is, don't you?"

"Yes, I know Shalom Avenue," said Stedman.

"So this is a new street running off the avenue. It's a block of apartments. You can see him anytime— today, tomorrow, the day after—"

"The day after is the Sabbath," said the rabbi, smiling.

"So? The Sabbath means nothing to him."

"Are you going?" asked the rabbi when they left the shop. "Is it within walking distance?"

"Every place in Jerusalem is within walking distance. I don't know. I'll have to think about it."

25

THE day started for Miriam much as usual, except that her morning sickness was a little more acute, and as a result, the common sounds of the morning which she thought she had got used to were more than normally irritating: the noise of cars and trucks shifting with a great grinding of gears—their house was on a slight hill—the *ozzereth* across the way thwacking at rugs spread over the railing of the porch with a large bamboo carpet beater—seemingly the only way of cleaning rugs in Israel—the *ozzereth* in the apartment above sloshing buckets of water on the stone floor and then sweeping it with a squeegee where it gurgled down the drain—presumably the only way to clean a floor—while her mistress was already preparing the noonday meal, the main meal of the day, by chopping something in a wooden bowl, where every stroke of the chopper was transmitted through the bowl to the table to the floor and thence to the ceiling above Miriam's head—seemingly the only way to prepare a meal.

And because this was one of the mornings when her husband had decided to go to the synagogue for the morning prayers rather than recite them at home, he was not there to complain to, and worse, was not there to help ready Jonathan for school.

And Jonathan had been cranky. Normally, he went to school with Shaouli, a child in the upstairs apartment and his bosom friend; but Shaouli had a cold and a little fever, and his mother had announced the night before that he would be staying home today. So Jonathan wanted his mother to walk to school with him. She had refused since it was only a block away and involved no street crossings, and he had finally set off alone but not without complaining, and it was a further aggravation.

And it took time, precious additional minutes she needed to make a bus to get her to the Hadassah Hospital in time to keep her appointment at the Obstetrics Clinic.

Then Gittel called from Tel Aviv.

Gittel called frequently, usually for some specific purpose—to say she had received a letter from Miriam's mother, to give her a recipe she had tried and found good, to say she would be in Jerusalem for an hour or two in connection with her work and to make elaborate arrangements for a meeting for a few minutes. But today she called merely for a nice long conversation with her niece before starting work. And Miriam, watching the minutes flit by, had in desperation explained that she had an appointment at the hospital and would have to hang up. She mentioned the hospital on the assumption that her aunt would not have accepted any other kind of appointment as sufficiently urgent to justify cutting short their conversation.

But immediately Gittel was alarmed and demanded to know what was wrong. "Who's treating you, Miriam? It may be someone I know. If it's something serious, perhaps I can arrange to have the head of the department look at you."

Since she was planning to tell her anyway when next she saw her, she told her now over the phone that this was a routine visit to the obstetrical clinic because she was going to have a baby.

"Oh, wonderful! *Mazel tov!* The best of luck! When will it be? Oh, Miriam, the baby can be born in Israel. When David has to go back to his work, you can stay on here. You can come down to Tel Aviv with Jonathan. And I can take care of Jonathan while you're having your baby. It will be a little crowded, but here in Israel we can always manage, Miriam dear. If Uri should come home on leave, he can sleep on the divan in the living room, or I can if necessary."

When Miriam finally managed to break off and hurry to the bus stop, her bus was just pulling away. Then because she was late, she had to wait all morning at the hospital. And then the doctor was annoyed with her for missing her appointment, and neither his English nor her Hebrew was up to an explanation of the events of the morning. He was cold and his manner forbidding, which made it impossible for her to ask him all the questions that bothered her.

It had continued. The bus going back was crowded, and although she got a seat, the young man standing in the aisle near her was eating away at sunflower seeds, cracking them between his front teeth and spitting out the husks on the floor near her feet. It disgusted her, and again because her Hebrew was not good enough to enable her to hold up her end of the argument that would certainly ensue, she did not ask him to stop and suffered in silence. Her relief when he finally got off turned almost immediately to acute embarrassment when a new passenger, moving up the aisle to a seat, saw the husks on the floor at her feet, assumed she was responsible, and glared his indignation at her.

When she got home, she found that her husband had eaten his lunch and gone out, leaving his dishes in the sink. And the water, although she let it run for some time, continued tepid. Then the doorbell rang, and it was Gittel.

"Oh, Gittel!" She embraced her aunt, tears of relief streaming down her cheeks, as she clung to her until she regained control. Only then did she ask how in the world she ever managed to get away.

"Any social worker in Tel Aviv who can't scare up some business in Jerusalem should be in another profession. Besides, when my sister writes me and asks me what I did when I found out that her daughter was pregnant, am I going to answer that I couldn't get away?"

She listened to her niece's recital of the events of the morning, and finding in Gittel a sympathetic listener, Miriam went on, luxuriating in self-pity, to recount whatever had troubled her since her arrival—her difficulties with the language, the new kind of housekeeping she had to adapt to, and even her uneasiness over the change in her husband's attitude toward his work.

Gittel held up a hand. "David's desire to leave the rabbinate, I can understand. It is not work for a modern man of ability. And I can only applaud his desire to settle here. I may have misjudged him. But you are about to have a baby, and we must be practical. Your mother is not here, so I must act in her place and advise you as she would. There is the problem of making a living. Your husband cannot simply walk away from his job and his profession. If he wants to leave them and come here, he must make preparation. He must plan and make arrangements. Even if he should find a job here tomorrow, you would still have to go back to the States to wind up your affairs. And much as I would like you to stay here, I'm afraid for this you would have to go. Husbands can't be trusted to pack furniture, close up a house properly, especially if the husband is a rabbi." She eased her niece back into a chair and slid a hassock under her feet. Then she placed a chair in front of her and sat down to face her. "So, let us be practical—and methodical. First we must deal with your particular problem. You are in the early stages of pregnancy. What you need is calm, tranquillity, freedom from fear and doubt. You don't need a lot of tests and X rays; you don't need a specialist who thinks of you only as a line on a chart. What you need is a nice family doctor, a general practitioner, someone who will sit down with you and answer any questions you may have and tell you what to expect from time to time."

"Oh, that would be wonderful, Gittel, but who do I go to? Do you know a doctor who—"

"In Tel Aviv I could give you the names of a dozen. Here in Jerusalem—but just a minute—my friend Sarah Adoumi, the doctor who's treating her, Dr. Ben Ami, he's been wonderful, a real old-fashioned doctor. When he comes to see her, he's never in a hurry. He sits down to a cup of tea with them afterward. Maybe it's good for him, too; he's a widower or a bachelor, in any case alone. He even got them their present apartment because she mustn't climb steps. He's that kind of doctor. Give me the phone book. . . . Ah, here he is, Dr. Benjamin Ben Ami, 147 Shalom Avenue. I'll call him."

"Maybe I ought to talk to David first," Miriam suggested doubtfully.

"What do husbands know about these things, especially a rabbi. .. . Dr. Ben Ami? I am a close personal friend of Sarah Adoumi. I would like to make an appointment with you for my niece. . . . You can see her now? Excellent, I'll bring her right over."

26

THE Jerusalem Café in the Old City is not far from the Damascus Gate. Thousands of tourists pass its open doors daily, but few venture inside. A couple, tired and anxious to escape from the hot sun, to sit and rest over a cup of coffee or a glass of orange juice, might halt momentarily and look in, but probably would decide against it and hope for another place farther on. It is obviously not intended for tourists.

The radio is tuned up to a deafening pitch, interminably playing melancholy Arab music in a minor key. In the dimly lit rear there is a pool table with several Arab youths usually playing, every stroke accompanied by noisy exclamations.

A number of plain wooden tables are scattered over the remainder of the room where some sit drinking coffee and smoking and others play at cards. To one side is the cashier's desk. He twists his head to listen better as the customer tells what he had, makes computations on little slips of paper, and then puts the money in the table drawer and offers change from little stacks of coins he keeps on the edge of the table. He is respected because he handles money and can figure rapidly and because he is also the owner. Just beyond his table, there is a sink where the dirty dishes are washed by his son, who is also the waiter.

If the tourist pair *had* entered, the waiter would have politely taken their order, served them, and then paid them no further attention. The other customers would have ignored them, too, even to the point of not looking in their direction. Just as Abdul, with an open book in front of him as he sipped his coffee, was ignored. Because he was not of them. His clothes, the book— all proclaimed him to be of a higher status and even a student. He had already been there twenty minutes and was sipping at his second cup of coffee when Mahmoud came in. He did not hail Abdul but wandered over to the pool table in the rear and watched for a few minutes, then moved on to one of the tables where a card game was in progress. He spoke to several of the card-players in friendly joking fashion. Then he took a stool and brought it over to Abdul's table and sat down beside him.

Abdul continued to read his book, but he nodded the waiter over.

"Coffee," said Mahmoud.

When the coffee had been brought and the waiter returned to his customary station by the sink, Mahmoud said, "We found out where she lives, but Leila thinks we ought to wait awhile."

Abdul shrugged his shoulders.

"It's easy like that." He snapped his fingers. "It's a new apartment, a whole new development. He's the only one in the block, and his apartment is on the street floor. The apartment house fronts on Shalom Avenue, but his entrance is way at the end, next to an embankment. And it's a new street; no houses on the other side."

"So?"

"So Leila thinks maybe it's too easy. Maybe it's some kind of a trap."

"Women!" said Abdul scornfully. "They worry all the time—about everything."

"No, Abdul, Leila is not like that. She's got a head on her. And she's as good as any man in the movement. But Leila found out that in Tel Aviv he lived on the top floor even though his wife was sick and the stairs were hard for her. Why would he take an apartment on a street floor here?"

"Because his wife is sick and climbing stairs is hard for her. You just explained it," said Abdul. "Besides, apartments are not so easy to come by in Jerusalem."

"But if he is ordered up here, wouldn't the government see to it that he got the kind of apartment he'd want?"

"The government doesn't even bother finding apartments for some of their real big shots, heads of ministries, when they move them up here. Believe me, they wouldn't go out of their way for *him*. If that's what's worrying Leila, she's an old woman. Get word to the Swiss to have the gadget ready. And to check it. Last time it went off prematurely."

"There's a place between two entrances where he parks his car," Mahmoud said. "He rides right over the sidewalk and parks between those two buildings. There's a little space. The Swiss can rig up something that we can attach to his car—"

"Was that Leila's idea?" Abdul asked contemptuously. "That's a wonderful idea! You'd wait until late at night so that the raising and lowering of the hood can be easily heard. No, the best way is the regular gadget. It's still daylight when we plant it, and if you're walking along the street, no one would think of stopping you to ask what you're doing there."

"All right, I'll tell the Swiss." He sipped at his coffee, and Abdul turned back to his book. Then, "Leila was wondering about this American you are so friendly with."

Abdul closed his book and turned to face his friend for the first time. "So Leila now feels she can decide who my friends will be? Does she approve of my friendship with you?"

"No, but Abdul—an American and a Jew."

"I have plans for the American."

"She thinks maybe he has plans for you."

"Roy?" Abdul tossed his head back and laughed. "She thinks Roy may be playing *me*?"

"She saw him in a restaurant with an older man once. They ate their whole meal in silence. But they stayed on after everybody had finished and left. They were just sitting drinking coffee and not saying a word. It looked suspicious."

"Tell Leila to stop looking for agents everywhere. That was his father."

"No, Abdul, because she went back after a few minutes. She told the waiter she thought she had left her scarf on the chair. And they were quarreling. The young one, your friend, was speaking harshly to the older man. No son would talk that way to his father."

Abdul smiled. "You don't know Americans."

27

THE rabbi met him at the King David where Stedman shook his hand effusively as though he were an old friend he had not seen in years. "I can't tell you how glad I am that you agreed to come, Rabbi. I called you on the spur of the moment. If I had thought about it, I wouldn't have because of the Sabbath."

"I gathered that you were anxious that I come. Besides, my Sabbath routine has changed since coming here. I don't always go to the synagogue."

"Oh?"

"I go when I feel like it now. It had become a matter of habit with me in America, and I didn't want it to be a matter of habit."

"It will have to be when you go back, won't it?"

"If I go back."

Stedman waited for him to go on and, when he did not, decided not to press him. "Roy's going directly to the auto dealer's house," Dan said as they set off in that direction. "And I thought this would be a good chance for you to meet him. I called and told him about our little visit to the garage and that I might drop in to see Memavet. Well, he was pretty excited. He suggested we go today, and I agreed because I didn't want to disappoint him. You know, if I had said it was the Sabbath and maybe we'd go next week, he might think I was trying to put him off. I'm sure this is the key to the problem of our association."

"You mean buying his friendship?"

"No, of course not. But while he's at the university, when do I get a chance to see him? For dinner once a

week maybe. And he usually has to get back early.
But if I had a car, he'd take a few days off every now
and then and we'd drive up to the Galilee or down to
the Negev. We'd see a lot of each other. I know people
all over the country. He'd get a chance to meet them,
Israelis, and he'd get their point of view. Back at school,
he'd have a different slant on things. He'd—"

The rabbi saw the street sign. "Here's Shalom Avenue now."

"Good. We're meeting him in front of the apartment
block. It's quite a way down. Tell me, do you know
anything about cars?"

"I can drive one. That's about all."

"Then if you don't mind, I'll just say that we had a
prearranged date, and you agreed to come along."

"All right."

Roy was already there when they arrived, studying
the sign in front of the new building. It was a large
sign and was already considerably weathered. It stated
that the Resnik Construction Corporation was going
to erect a large complex of apartment houses—central
heating, central gas supply, outlets for television and
radio antennas, adequate closet space—and that it
would cover the entire block. According to the archi-
tect's drawing painted in one corner, there would be
seven entrances on Kol Tov Street and a like number
on Mazel Tov Street, and the two rows of houses would
enclose a sizable area which would be landscaped with
trees and shrubbery, shaded walks and terraces. Little
stick figures were shown walking along the paths. The
original notice stated that the apartments would be ready
for occupancy early in 1971, but it had been painted
over, and it now read: READY FOR IMMEDIATE OCCU-
PANCY.

The rabbi looked about him, at the vacant lot they
had just passed, an acre or two of stones and rubble
with here and there a patch of grass or a low bush to
give a touch of green to the yellow clayey soil. The
few trees were low gnarled olive trees, with tortured,

twisted branches. Beyond the house was another such lot, but this a little less depressing by the accident of a Bedouin sitting on a rock eating his lunch while his little flock of goats nuzzled at the few bits of greenery.

Mazel Tov Street, like Kol Tov which paralleled it on the other side of the complex, was as yet unpaved, narrow and rutty, and slippery with the thick yellow mud of Jerusalem.

"What was it, number One? Then it must be down at the other end," said Roy. "This is number Thirteen."

Fastidiously, they picked their way along Mazel Tov Street—a street by virtue of a couple of passes by a bulldozer—hopping from one dry patch to the next until they came to the embankment at the end. They looked over it curiously at the roadway below, then walked back to the door of the house.

"There doesn't seem to be anybody living here," said Roy.

"There's a name card in the letterbox," observed his father. "This must be it."

He knocked on the door, and a gruff voice from within called out, "Come in. The door is open."

They entered to a large, bare room. They saw a few folding chairs, but nothing in the way of furniture— no tables, no rugs, no curtains, no lamps. The lone figure in the room did not rise, but motioned them to sit down.

He was a short, thin man, and almost totally bald. He was in pajamas and bathrobe. A vein throbbed perceptibly in his right temple, and periodically a tic developed in the cheekbone below which he seemed able to control by a quick grimace, a pulling away of the right corner of his mouth. Otherwise, the corners of his mouth drooped so that the lower lip seemed to push against the upper in a perpetual pout.

"You are the people who made inquiries at the shop the other day?" He spoke in a throaty, guttural Hebrew.

"That's right," said Dan. "My name is Stedman,

and this is my son. This is my friend, Small." A natural delicacy kept him from identifying him as a rabbi.

On a narrow marble shelf attached to the wall about shoulder height, a kind of mantelpiece, there was a bottle and some glasses. Memavet poured himself a glass and looked inquiringly at his visitors. "Some brandy? I'm afraid it's all I can offer you." When they shook their heads, he went on, "I've got a little cold and this helps." And indeed, his voice was very hoarse, and he ended with a spasm of coughing.

"That sounds like a pretty bad cold," said Stedman.

"Yes, my neighbor across the way, who is herself not well, recommended her doctor to me. He was on my *Kupat Cholim* list, so I called and he said he'd come— today, tomorrow, maybe the day after, whenever he gets here. In this country you have to learn to be patient. My furniture, rugs, a sofa and some chairs, I ordered them more than a month ago, before I moved in. I'll be lucky if I get them in another month. These chairs and my bed and a table in the kitchen, I brought them from my old place. But you're not interested in my troubles. You want to buy a car. Tell me what you want, how much you want to spend, and I'll get it for you." He had switched from Hebrew to Yiddish and, when he got on the subject of cars, to a heavily accented English, as if he wanted to be sure they understood every word. This was the pattern he followed for the rest of the meeting—Hebrew for general matters, Yiddish for personal matters and English when he talked business.

"You don't have any cars actually in stock?"

"No, I'm a broker. You wish to buy an apartment or a house, you go to a broker. You don't expect him to be the owner of the house. The same with stocks and bonds. Why not with cars? In this country, a man comes to stay for a year, a university professor maybe. Then there's a death in the family, and he has to rush back to England or the States, and he has no idea when he will return. The best thing for him to do is to sell his car. If he takes it to a secondhand dealer, he will get a fraction of its value. If he advertises in the papers, he may have to wait who knows how long. But if he comes to me, I can probably sell it for him in a day or two and at a better price than the secondhand dealer will offer him, although perhaps not as good as what he could get if he sold it himself. How do I do it? People know of me. One tells another. So people come to me—those who want to buy and those who want to sell, and it's just a matter of matching them up, the buyers and the sellers."

"Are there many like you in the used car business?" asked Roy.

"I don't know of any others, young man, and if I did, you wouldn't expect me to give you their names, now would you? And it's not always used cars. You'd be surprised how many times a dealer in new cars finds it necessary to sell off one or more of his cars at a sizable discount—quietly, discreetly. And at how much of a discount will depend on what his situation is. And I am apt to have information about that, too."

"You got a line on a new car now?" asked Roy eagerly.

"Not right now. How soon do you want a car? How much do you want to spend? What make are you interested in?"

They talked cars for a while, largely Roy and Memavet, with Dan Stedman occasionally interjecting a remark. They discussed the relative merits of Fiats and Peugeots, of Renaults and Volkswagens; power and fuel economy; cost and resale value. Finally Memavet said, "I think I know what you want, and I've got a line on just the car for you. Be here tonight at seven o'clock, and I'll have something for you."

"How can you be sure?" asked Dan.

"When you've been in this business as long as I have, my friend, you get to know your customers," said Memavet.

"Did you originally have a car agency?" asked the

rabbi, curious about this strange man and his gruff manner. "Or did you start out as a broker?"

Memavet grimaced. "I came to this country without any money, and with no friends or relatives to help out. I came with just the clothes on my back, and they were practically rags. I knew cars, or rather gas engines. So if I had been healthy, I would have become an auto mechanic. But since I was a sick man, just risen from the dead you might say—"

"What do you mean, risen from the dead? Then your name—"

"That's right. Memavet means 'from death.' The government here is eager to have you change your name to a Hebrew one. You pay a lira and fill out a form and that's it. So why should I continue to carry a name given to my grandfather or great-grandfather by some Cossack, when for a lira I could change it to something meaningful. I rose from the dead, so I called myself Memavet." He laughed, a throaty gurgle of a laugh, pleased at the effect on his visitors.

"You mean you were so sick?" the rabbi persisted.

"No, I mean that the Russians—may the sun stop shining on them—left me for dead. That the spark had not actually gone out is a minor detail that they overlooked. It's a national characteristic with the Russians —may all their children be girls—to overlook minor details. Their machinery frequently doesn't run because they cannot be concerned with minor details like oil or even small parts that drop off. As they say, it's only a little part and it's such a big machine. Officially, I was dead."

"This was during the war?" Stedman asked, picking up the lead.

"World War Two. Because I was in the wrong place at the wrong time, I found myself in a concentration camp. The rest of the camp was made up of Poles mostly and a few Russians. I was the only Jew." His voice suddenly became dry and didactic like a professor lecturing a class. He spoke in Yiddish. "The

Germans are efficient. When they are engaged in a sadistic cruelty, they do it efficiently. But the Russian is inefficient. Much of the time, his cruelty comes from his negligence and inefficiency. He tends to forget minor details like food or the clothing and shelter needed to face a Russian winter.

"I was an educated man, and there weren't many there. I was a mechanic, an engineer. Nevertheless, I was put to rough work, unskilled work out of doors. In the first month I lost fifty pounds. The only thing that sustained me was the knowledge that we were due for a visit from the district medical officer. He checked on the health of the prisoners, and it was on his decision that we were assigned to various details, inside or outside, or worst of all, the Forestry Detail. And he was a Jew."

Memavet tilted his head back and closed his eyes. "I can see him now: Dr. Rasnikov of Pinsk, scientist and good party member, the new breed of Jew in the Socialist paradise. You wouldn't believe what it cost me for the chance to see him, but I managed it, just long enough to tell him I was a Jew and that if I were continued at the outside work, I would be dead in a month. I was sick and running a fever, and the only shoes I had were a couple of pieces of cloth I had torn from my coat and wrapped around my feet. He didn't answer me, only stared. And I withdrew. It was enough. I didn't expect him to answer. But he would remember my face. He could not answer because it was dangerous for him, too.

"The next day we were lined up, and he walked along the line, putting a hand to a forehead of one, ordering another to open his mouth wide, taking the pulse of a third. That was the medical examination. An aide had a list and called off the names and then noted down his recommendation beside each name. He came to me, looked me over, and then said to the aide, 'Forestry Detail.'

"This Forestry Detail was engaged in clearing a road

through the forest by chopping down trees, clearing out brush, piling up logs. Because you were working in a forest where it was theoretically possible to escape, the discipline was brutal. Small groups worked in marked-off areas. If you stepped outside the line, you were shot. You were led out on the double before dawn, and you worked until after the sun set and then marched back to camp. Anyone who couldn't keep up was beaten, and then if he still could not keep up, he was shot. Every day fewer came back than went out.

"I managed for three days, and then on the fourth when we were being marched back to camp, I slipped and fell. It had begun to snow, and they were racing us back against the storm when I fell. The guard kicked me and ordered me to get up. I tried. How I tried! I got to my knees only to collapse again. Another guard shouted back to the one who was standing over me to hurry up. Again he ordered me to get up, and when I could not, he pointed his rifle at me. Again the other guard shouted, and my man pulled the trigger of his rifle with as little concern as if I had been a rabbit scurrying across an open field."

"He shot you?"

"He shot me, and I don't suppose he wasted another glance at me. If the shot were not fatal, I would freeze to death—if the wolves didn't get me first. He would report the matter back at camp, and the next day they would send out a burial detail to bring me in. It's a curious thing, but do you know the last thought that ran through my mind before I lost consciousness? It was, now will Dr. Rasnikov think I was fit for the Forestry Detail?"

"But you obviously did not die," said Stedman.

"It was a superficial wound, and maybe the cold congealed the blood. Anyway, I was found by an old peasant woman who was out gathering firewood. She kept me hidden and fed me until I was able to travel. It took me more than a year to get here, and believe me, many a time I regretted that the shot had not been fatal."

"Then here, here it must be a paradise for you," Stedman said with emotion.

Memavet's face relaxed in a horrible grimace of a smile. "After you've been dead, my friend, you just live from day to day." His voice suddenly became brisk and businesslike, and he shifted to English. "Come here tonight at seven, and I'll probably have a car for you. Don't fail. A good buy doesn't wait."

Outside Roy asked, "What was that long rigmarole in Yiddish? Was he telling you the story of his life?"

"No, the story of his death," said the rabbi.

"Oh, yeah?" He saw that the rabbi was smiling and assumed it was an example of rabbinic humor. "Well. . . ." He was at a loss how to respond. He turned to his father. "Look, I got to split now. Do I meet you at the same place tonight?"

"Oh, I have no intention of coming back tonight," said Stedman.

"But, Dad—"

"If I return tonight," the elder Stedman went on, "he'll see that we're interested and I'll pay through the nose."

"But—"

"He has my name, and he knows where to reach me. If he gets something, you can be sure he'll call."

Seeing that Roy was obviously disappointed, the rabbi stepped into the breach.

"Your father is coming to Sabbath dinner Friday evening," he said. "Mrs. Small and I would be pleased if you would also come, Roy."

"Well, thanks. Sure, I guess I could make it," he said.

As they strolled along after Roy had left, the rabbi remarked, "That was quite a story that Memavet told us."

"It was," said Dan, "and I have it all on tape."

"You taped it? Then this expedition was not to buy a car?"

"Oh, I came for a car all right, but I thought it might make sense to have a record of our conversation. If there's any hanky panky about the deal—if he's peddling hot cars, for example—then the tape would show that my hands are clean."

The rabbi nodded. They walked in silence for a while, and then the rabbi said reflectively, "It's quite a story, but the man's name suggests that it's probably true."

"Oh, I'm sure it's true, at least he thinks it is. But it's not as unusual as you seem to think, Rabbi. Here in Israel, everyone has a story. Either they fled from the Nazis, or they fought the Arabs. Practically everyone is alive as a result of a minor miracle. Miracles are part of the climate here."

28

DR. Ben Ami, a big, stocky bear of a man, parked his Volkswagen against the embankment, extricated himself from behind the wheel together with his bulky doctor's bag in one fluid motion born of long practice, and then realized that the Adoumi apartment was dark. He stopped to consider for a moment and then walked up the street a few paces to check the area between 2 and 4 Kol Tov Street where Avner Adoumi usually parked his car. It was not there. He was quite sure that his patient, Sarah Adoumi, had not left the house. She had probably dozed off before dark, and her husband had not yet returned.

He could ring the bell, and that would awaken her. After all, he was expected, and perhaps she was not asleep but merely resting. On the other hand, he felt a certain reluctance about examining her when her husband was not present. It was almost seven, and Avner would no doubt be along in a few minutes. Perhaps it would be best to wait.

Then he remembered his other patient, a certain Memavet whom he had never treated before, only the next street over at 1 Mazel Tov Street. Probably a minor upper respiratory infection from what he had said over the telephone. Aspirin, rest, perhaps a cough syrup to relieve the throat irritation. He could be out of there in ten or fifteen minutes, and by that time Adoumi would be home. And he rather liked the idea of ending up his day at the Adoumis. He could take his time, have a glass of tea and some friendly talk before going on home.

Rather than get into his car and turn around in the narrow, muddy street, he set off down the alley between the embankment and the houses. It was dark and he swept his flashlight ahead of him to light his way.

Halfway down he stood quite still and thought hard. Then he retraced his steps. There was a public phone in the lobby of the apartment house, and he rang Adoumi's office number.

"Avner? . . . Ben Ami. . . . I'm here at your house, in the lobby I mean. . . . No, I haven't seen Sarah yet. The house is dark, so I guess she dozed off. . . . No, I thought I'd wait until you got home. But there's something important I have to tell you. . . . No, I'd rather not over the phone. How soon will you be home? . . . Half an hour? That's all right. . . . No, it's quite all right, I have another patient in the next block. I'll see him first."

At the corner of Shalom Avenue and Mazel Tov Street, Roy Stedman paused and looked at his watch. It was almost seven o'clock.

It was a cloudy, misty night, and now it began to rain. He turned up his coat collar and trudged down the street. He came to Memavet's house. There was no car there, new or used; there was no car anywhere on the street. His watch still showed a few minutes before seven, so he waited.

By quarter past, there was still no car, and he was quite certain that none would come.

He crossed the street and was about to ring the bell when a man came out of the apartment and carefully closed the door behind him. He looked at Roy in surprise.

Roy saw the black bag. "Oh, you must be the doctor. I've got to see Mr. Memavet."

"That's right. I am his doctor. Mr. Memavet is not well. He's in bed and I don't want him disturbed. Besides, I've just put him to bed and given him a shot. He'd have to get out of bed to open the door."

"Oh, yeah, well in that case, I guess I can come back tomorrow morning."

"Yes."

"Well, I guess I might as well go. Er—good night."

"Good night."

Roy started up the street. He looked back and saw the doctor standing there, watching him. Halfway up the street he looked back again, and this time the doctor was gone. Roy stopped and then turned and retraced his steps.

29

THE explosion was not loud. Save for the gaping hole in the wall of the Memavet apartment and a few broken windows property damage was not great. But unlike the explosion in which Professor Carmi had lost his life a couple of months earlier, because it was early in the evening, a large crowd had gathered, drawn by the noise of the fire engines, if not by the sound of the explosion itself, and the police were hard put to cordon off the area.

Again, the reaction to the death of the old man was quite different from that to the death of the professor. After Carmi's death, there had been speculation in the press about why he in particular had been selected. And after a few days, it had come out that he was engaged in important agricultural research which might have resulted in a remarkable increase in the yield of certain types of ground crops. The papers had been vague about the precise nature of his research, and while one paper had announced authoritatively that he was engaged in investigating a new miracle fertilizer, another announced equally authoritatively that his work involved using brackish water to open up for cultivation thousands of acres that were now considered useless. In any case, it was generally accepted that he was an important scientist whose death was a major blow to Israel.

But Memavet was not anyone important and was not engaged in anything that could either help or hurt Israel. And this was all the more infuriating because it meant that the bombing was a senseless and meaningless taking of life.

There were other reactions stemming from the irony of the situation as revealed by the statement of the doctor who had visited him just shortly before the explosion. Dr. Ben Ami's statement to the police was widely quoted in the press:

"He was a new patient who had chosen me from the *Kupat Cholim* list because I lived nearby, I suppose. I had a full schedule of patients for the day even though it was the Sabbath. Sickness keeps no Sabbath, you know. But I was able to squeeze him in since I had another patient in the next street and I was early for my appointment. It was just luck that I was able to see him at all. I got there a little before seven. I rang

the bell, and he called to me to come in, that the door
was open. He had a bad cold and had been coughing
a great deal. He had not slept, for several nights, he said.
I gave him something to relieve the irritation in the
throat and a hypodermic to let him get some much-
needed sleep. I saw to it that he went to bed, and then
I turned off the light, locked the door and left, planning to look in on him again in the morning. But evidently he did not fall asleep immediately. He must have
got up a little later to get a glass of brandy from the
bottle on the living-room shelf. Had he stayed in bed,
he would have been alive today, I'm sure, since the
main force of the explosion occurred in the living room
and his bedroom window was not even broken."

"Imagine, he calls the doctor, gets treated right then
and there, and the doctor even sees to it that he goes
to bed. Believe me, my doctor wouldn't take the trouble.
He looks at you and writes a prescription, and he's
gone. You want to talk to him, to ask him some questions? He's too busy. Five minutes—that's his limit.
And where you're going to get a prescription filled on
the Sabbath, or any night after seven, that's no concern
of his. So after all that, the poor devil gets up to pour
a drink for himself—and bang!"

"How do they know he got up to get a drink?"

"That was in the papers. I saw it in *Hamaariv*. He
still had the bottle in his hand when they found him.
The way they figured it, the force of the explosion
knocked him against this marble shelf he had in the
living room. So he must have been standing near it.
Smashed his skull."

A shaking of heads and a moment of silent reflection
on the tragedy of the human condition.

On the other hand, in certain cafés in East Jerusalem
where young Arabs were wont to gather for coffee and
cards and heated political discussions and where the
report of any Israeli mishap, however trivial, was
received with considerable joy, a joke was gleefully
circulated that the name of the victim of the explosion

should have been Lamavet rather than Memavet—
that is, "to death" rather than "from death."

Of course, the terrorists immediately claimed full
credit. All the various groups did, in fact. Al Fatah,
based in Jordan, issued a statement: "Our brave commandos have demonstrated that they can penetrate the
very center of the Jewish stronghold and that no Jew
living in Palestine is safe from our vengeance. There
will be no letup until the United Nations resolution is
implemented and the Palestinian is given justice."

Intellectuals for Arab Independence, based in Leb-
anon, pointed out that the Israeli government was up
to its old tricks of trying to enlist world sympathy by
pretending that the victim of the bombing was a harmless civilian. It was well known that Memavet was connected with the Jewish Agency and had been on a secret
mission to Zurich only a few days before.

The Palestinian Committee, based in Syria, explained
that 1 Mazel Tov Street was a secret Israeli Army installation, an electronic nerve center which their brave
commandos had destroyed and that Memavet's death
had been purely accidental.

Cairo's *Al-Ahram* asserted that the Israeli government was concealing the true facts of the incident. It
quoted the head of the Palestine Liberation League
who said that a secret strategy meeting was being held
at 1 Mazel Tov Street at the time, that it had been
attended by a number of high Israeli officials and that
the death toll might reach fifty.

The Anglo-Arab Friendship League in its newsletter
suggested that there was ample evidence that the bombing had been done by Israelis for the purpose of en-
listing world sympathy as they had attempted to do
by planting bombs in commercial airliners and blaming
the Arabs for it.

The rabbi heard the news on the late radio newscast.
The first shock of realizing that the man killed was
someone he had been with, spoken to, only that very

morning was immediately translated into the feeling that he should take some action. He called Stedman.

"Yes, I heard the news earlier around the lobby here. Shocking!"

"I think we should go to the police," said the rabbi.

"To the police? Why should we go to the police? What can we tell them that will be of any earthly use, Rabbi?"

"We could tell him what he told us. You could play that tape for them. About his enemy—"

"Forgive me, Rabbi, but you just aren't thinking straight. If it had been whatsisname—Rasnikov—who had been killed, then our story of Memavet's enmity might be of some use to them. But it was Memavet that was killed."

"Still, I think they should know."

"Believe me, they know. Or if they don't they'll know soon enough. They'll just inquire at that shop where he had his desk and—"

"How do you know he told the story there?"

"Come now," said Stedman, "you heard what the mechanic said. He said he was a crazy old man who'd tell you his troubles—how did he put it? Oh, yes— at the drop of a hat. You don't suppose we were the first to hear that story, then, three perfect strangers? If he told it to us, you can be sure he's told it to anyone who would listen."

The rabbi was uncertain. "But still, I think—I mean it would do no harm if—"

"Rabbi," Stedman said with assurance, "I've done a lot of traveling in foreign countries, and there's one thing I've learned: You don't get involved with police if you can avoid it. I know in Israel you think it's different, but take my word for it: Police are the same the world over. Now there's nothing we can tell them except that we saw him on the morning of the day he was killed. There may have been any number of visitors after us. That doctor saw him just a little before it happened."

"Still, I'd like to talk to you about it. Perhaps we could get together sometime tomorrow—"

"I'm sorry, Rabbi, but I'm off to Haifa first thing in the morning. I'll be away a few days. We'll get together when I get back."

The rabbi hung up, but he was troubled. Everything Stedman had said was true, but he still felt that they ought to go to the police. And yet, he could not go alone. It might raise questions of why Stedman had not similarly reported, and that might make for the very involvement his friend was trying to avoid.

30

"HEY, how come the tan, V. S.? You been in Florida, or did you buy one of those sun lamps?"

"Florida? No, Katz and I were in Israel."

"Israel? No kidding. Hey, guys, V. S. was in Israel. When did you get back?"

"Day before yesterday. We just went over for ten days—on business."

It was the Sunday morning Brotherhood Breakfast, and the members were still drifting in, still standing around greeting one another, as the members of the committee set up the round tables, laid the tablecloths and silverware—quite unlike Sisterhood affairs where everything was made ready the day before.

They crowded around Markevitch. "How was it there, V. S.?"

"How was the weather?"

"Any Arabs take a shot at you, V. S.?"

"You starting a branch in Israel, V. S.? You becoming one of these international financial wizards?"

"Tell me, are the people worried? Are they scared?"

"Scared?" boomed V. S. Markevitch. "Let me tell you something: You can go out walking, any city there, anytime day or night. We'd go out for a walk after midnight, me and Katz, and on dark streets, and nobody thought anything of it."

"Did you get to see all the sights? Where'd you go?"

"Oh, most of the time we were in the hands of the Ministry of Industrial Development guys. They showed us around, and they introduced us to some of the big shots in the government. It was quite a trip."

"Did you get to Jerusalem? Did you see the rabbi?"

"Yeah," said V. S., "we saw him. We were with him pretty much all one day. He showed us around."

"Did he show you King David's Tomb?"

"How about the Chagall windows? That was the first thing I saw when I went."

"You went to the Hadassah Hospital, didn't you?"

"I hope you visited Meah Shearim."

"The most impressive place we saw when we went over was the Yad Vashem. You got a chance to see that?"

Markevitch, grinning from ear to ear, turned from one questioner to the other. Finally, he held up both hands as if in surrender. "To tell the truth, guys, we didn't get a chance to see any of those places. Like I said, the rabbi was showing us around. He figured we'd want to see the Wall, which we did. And he showed us through the Old City, which we could have done without. I mean, as far as I'm concerned it's just a bunch of smelly little alleys. And then we went over to take a look at the university, and that took up pretty much the whole day. To tell the truth"—he lowered his voice to a loud whisper—"I got the impression that the rabbi didn't know half the places you guys mentioned."

"Yeah? By now I would've thought he'd know every little nook and cranny."

Markevitch shrugged. "That's what we figured. To

tell the truth, that was one of the reasons we called him. We figured he'd know what there was to see."

"I guess maybe he just hasn't had time to go sightseeing. I suppose he's at the university library all day long—"

"You kidding?" Markevitch was scornful. "When he took us out there, he admitted he'd only been there a couple of times before."

"So what's he do there?"

"As near as we could make out, he just loafs, maybe takes a walk, stops in at a café for coffee—like that."

"I know he's no ball of fire, but I figure in Jerusalem and all—say, did he mention when he was coming home?"

Markevitch shook his head slowly. "Not a word. And that's kind of funny when you come to think of it. I mean, you'd think that saying good-bye, he'd say something like 'See you in Barnard's Crossing.' But not a word. Just good-bye."

"What are you getting at, V. S.?"

"Well, you know that idea I talked about at our last meeting, you know, about us having two associate rabbis. Well, I kind of sounded him out on it."

"You didn't, V. S.!"

"Sure, I did. You know my motto: If you don't ask, you don't get to know. Why shouldn't I? Maybe I'm not a board of director, but I'm a member in good standing. My dues are paid up."

"All right, so you asked. What happened?"

"Nothing!" said Markevitch triumphantly. "He wasn't happy, and he wasn't sore. He just wasn't interested one way or the other. Just kind of polite."

"Maybe he was playing it cozy."

Markevitch gave the other a prod with his elbow and winked knowingly. "Maybe he was, and maybe he just wasn't interested one way or the other. To tell the truth, we were kind of a little annoyed with our rabbi. I mean if he's our rabbi, we got a right to expect him to rabbi for us. You go to Washington, and you tell your Congressman you're there, and he'll be interested in your problems. He'll try to help you, or at least he'll make you think he's going to help you. The least he'll do is have someone from his office show you around. Right? Well, we figured we could count on the rabbi the same way. Take like for instance we went to the Wall. Right? So you expect you're with your rabbi right there, he'll say a prayer for you at the Wall. That's the holiest place we got, and if you got a chance to have a prayer said there, well that's something you wouldn't want to pass up. Right? So when we asked him, he says he'd rather not, and we should do it on our own. Well, of course we did, me and Katz, but you know it isn't the same thing. We had to say it in English for one thing—"

From the head table came the sharp rap of the gavel, and the chairman called out, "Will you take your seats please? Will everybody please be seated?"

There was a scurrying to take places, while those still engaged in conversation automatically lowered their voices.

"That sure is funny. What do you figure it means, V. S.?"

Markevitch dropped his voice to a whisper that could not be heard much beyond the six or eight tables in the immediate vicinity. "Let me put it this way: Markevitch is not one to shoot off his mouth, but Markevitch has a sawbuck which he'll bet against anybody's V-note that our rabbi when he took off for Israel took off for good."

31

WHILE the police, in the person of Chaim Ish-Kosher, and the Shin Bet, as represented by Avner Adoumi, were "cooperating," the fact that they were meeting in Adoumi's small dusty office on the top floor of Police Headquarters that had been temporarily assigned to Intelligence rather than in Ish-Kosher's much more comfortable and spacious office on the first floor at the opposite end of the building suggested that the cooperation might be a little one-sided.

The personal styles of the two men were different. Ish-Kosher, in blue uniform with a white shirt and black tie, his tunic pressed and buttoned, exuded an air of brisk, businesslike efficiency; but he also smiled easily, an executive type of smile, a quick flashing of even white teeth to denote interest and understanding. Avner Adoumi, on the other hand, a big, burly, bullet-headed man with close-cropped hair now gray with few traces of its former blondish red, was tieless and in shirt sleeves. His collar open at the throat, like the yarmulke worn by Ish-Kosher, was something of symbol in the involved politics of Israel. He was brusque, authoritarian, and rarely smiled, and when he did, it was almost against his will.

"And how is Mrs. Adoumi?" asked Ish-Kosher politely.

"She's at Hadassah for a couple of days' observation."

"Oh, I'm sorry to hear that."

"It's nothing. Just some tests."

"The shock of the explosion?"

"The doctor says not. She'll probably be home tomorrow. And then later she may have to go in again for a few days." His eyes flicked at Ish-Kosher's yarmulke. "I understand that you people have arranged things so that I couldn't visit her on the Sabbath if she's still there."

A quick, easy smile. "My people? Oh, you mean the religious. Well, it isn't that you can't visit her. It's that you have to ride to Hadassah, by bus or by car, and that of course would be a desecration of the Sabbath."

Adoumi held up a stuffy forefinger of warning. "One day the rest of us aren't going to stand for it, Chaim."

"Then it won't be a Jewish state anymore."

"Oh, it will be a Jewish state all right, but it will be for all the Jews and not just for your little handful. Now, to business. Did you get anything on Memavet?"

"No, but I'm sure it was him they were after. The kind of business he was in—"

"Shady? Stolen cars? He was dealing with the Arabs?"

"Not as far as we know. But in that business, automobiles, there are always people who are dissatisfied. A customer thinks he's been sold a lemon, or a seller thinks he could have got more on his own. Or he might feel that Memavet was holding something back. He was a broker, after all, and only entitled to a commission, not a profit."

"But everybody you questioned said he had a good reputation, that he was honest."

"Yes, but—"

"All right, I won't argue with you. Follow it up if you like, but I can tell you now, you're wandering down a blind alley. The university professor—"

"We found an Arab connection there," said Ish-Kosher quickly.

"Sure, but it was the wrong kind for our purposes. He was going to help them. He was their friend."

"But that's just it," said Ish-Kosher excitedly. "You see—"

"I know, I know. The terrorists don't want their people helped. All this theory"—a wave of a broad, freckled hand—"it's just theory. The terrorists don't work that way. They don't think that way. Arabs don't think that way. One Arab kills another, so the victim's family will try to get revenge by killing the killer. That's understandable. That's normal. It isn't our way. It isn't the way of civilized people, but it's understandable. But if they can't get the killer, they'll get their revenge by killing some member of his family, a brother or an uncle or his father. That's already different, you see. Ever since the Six-Day War when our army defeated theirs, they want revenge. That's normal. But they can't get it by defeating our army, so killing any of us is for them a reasonable substitute. Which of us? It doesn't make any difference to them. It could be an old man like Memavet, or it could be women or even children."

"But—"

Adoumi stopped him again with a raised hand. "Naturally, the more of us they can kill, the better. And that's why they've bombed places like markets, public places where there are likely to be a lot of people gathered and where a lot can be hurt. But we're on the watch, and the danger of being caught is great. So they play it safe for a while. They pick safe targets. If we don't catch them, they get their courage back and try the public places again. Why did they bomb Memavet? I'll tell you: because he was an easy target. Here's an old man living alone in a new block of flats, the only resident on the street, and it's a dark street. They can go down the street, unseen—"

"But they were seen. The doctor saw—"

"The doctor saw a young man who said he had business with Memavet. And that's quite possible. Now, that young man might have seen something. He might be worth questioning."

"Then why did you cut out that part of the doctor's statement when we released it to the reporters?"

"Because, Chaim, I thought it would be better if he came forward on his own. That would prove he was not connected with this in any way. He didn't come forward, so it suggests that he might not be entirely innocent."

"Or just that he doesn't want to get involved," said Ish-Kosher.

"This was a terrorist bombing. Anyone would want to help." Adoumi shook his head gloomily. "I gambled in withholding that portion of the statement from the press." Then he brightened. "But if he hasn't come forward, the chances are that even if we had mentioned he had been seen, he probably would hold back. It was raining, and he had his coat collar turned up. He'd know that the doctor wouldn't be able to recognize him. I'd sure like to get a line on him, though."

Ish-Kosher smiled broadly. "Well, perhaps I can help you. How would you like to have his name?" From the briefcase on his lap, he drew a slip of paper and passed it across the desk to Adoumi. It read: "I came back at seven as I said I would. Stedman."

"Where'd you get this?"

"One of *my* men thought to look in the mailbox. It was there."

"But there's no date. This could have been left a couple of days earlier. The doctor didn't mention his writing a note. In fact, he said he watched him go up the street."

"But he could have come back after the doctor left."

"Possible." Adoumi studied the note. "Stedman, Stedman—where have I heard that name?"

"There's a fairly well-known American journalist named Stedman. He's in the country now, staying at the King David."

"No, no." He began rummaging through the folders on his desk, flipping one after another open to glance at the contents. "Ah, here it is—Stedman. That,

Chaim," he said impressively, "is the name of an American student at the university who has been seen frequently in the company of an Arab student named Abdul El Khaldi. Now, Abdul is someone we've been interested in for some time."

"You have something on him?" asked Ish-Kosher eagerly.

"Something in the sense that would interest you police people? No. Nothing suspicious about his behavior. He has been most circumspect."

"Well, then—"

"That in itself might be suspicious, Chaim."

"You mean that the Arabs who act up you are interested in, and those who don't you are also interested in?"

Adoumi laughed shortly. "Chaim, that's not far from the truth either. We are suspicious of all of them. But when I say that we're interested in Abdul, I mean that we try to keep an eye on him because while he's done nothing that we know of, there have been rumors. Arabs who for one reason or another want to be on the good side of us pass us little tips every now and then. And his name has come up more than once. So we keep him under observation. Not a twenty-four-hour-a-day surveillance, of course; we don't have the manpower. But we keep an eye on him, and the last report I have mentions a student named Stedman who is frequently in his company. So that stirs my interest in Stedman. And when I see that someone named Stedman has some connection with Memavet, maybe went to see him the very night he was killed—"

"Are you going to pick him up?"

"No, Chaim. I think for the time being I'll stay out of this. Your people will pick him up, and you will question him. Now this is what I'd like you to do. . . ."

32

ISH-KOSHER glanced through the passport and then pressed a button on his desk. To the clerk who entered in response to his ring, he handed the book and said, "Check it through." Then he turned to Roy once again.

"Now, Mr. Stedman, I'm curious why you didn't come forward. As a guest in our country, I should think that having some knowledge of a crime, you would be only too eager to cooperate with the police."

"But I didn't know of any crime. I mean I heard about the bombing, but it took place after I'd left. And I didn't see anything."

Ish-Kosher fingered his yarmulke and smiled. "You are not an ignorant man, Mr. Stedman. You are a student at our university. Surely, you must realize that negative evidence is also important. The fact that you saw nothing between, say, five minutes of seven and fifteen or twenty past means the bomb must have been set earlier—or later. Didn't it occur to you that this might be helpful to the police?"

"Well, I thought of it," said Roy, "but since this doctor was there, he was able to see anything I could see."

"Not quite," Ish-Kosher corrected him. "He was in the house while you were outside. But then when you came back to leave the note, he was gone."

"Well, I guess I didn't figure it out that fine. I just thought he was there and went to the police because he made a statement, so why should I?" Roy had been frightened when the police had first come for him and again when he had been brought into the office of the inspector. But he was at ease now. An inspector with a yarmulke—it was reassuring.

"This appointment with Memavet, you made it when?"

He had thought not to mention the earlier meeting, if only not to involve his father and the rabbi; but the inspector was so matter-of-fact that it seemed pointless to conceal it. "I didn't make the appointment. Memavet did. You see, we were there in the morning, well, it was practically noon."

"We?"

"Yes. My father called and said he was planning to see Memavet about buying a car, and since he thought I might know more about cars and besides, I'd be using it, suggested we should go the next day, Saturday—"

"The Sabbath."

"Yeah, I guess that's right but my father said Memavet wouldn't mind and I didn't have much other free time. Well, anyway, we met up at the corner of Shalom and Mazel Tov—"

"You and your father?"

"That's right. And he had a friend with him, a Rabbi Small from America—"

"Rabbi Small?" Ish-Kosher's voice gave no hint of his surprise.

"Yeah, Rabbi Small. David Small, I think."

"And he was along as another expert on cars?"

Roy glanced at Ish-Kosher. Was he being sarcastic? But the inspector's face was impassive. "He had arranged to take a walk with my father, and so he just came along."

"I see."

"Well, we saw Memavet and we talked about cars. He offered us a drink, and he talked about himself a lot, about his early life, I guess. It was in Yiddish—that part, so I didn't get any of it, just a word here and there from my German, you know. Then he says if we'll come back at seven, he'd probably have a car for us."

"But you returned alone."

"Yeah, well, my father said he wouldn't come back because he didn't want Memavet to think he was over-eager. That was after we left the place, you understand. I mean, he didn't say it to Memavet, but to me."

"Then why did you come back?"

"Well, I thought I could take a look at the car if there was one."

"But there wasn't."

"That's right. But I thought the fact we'd showed up for the appointment or at least I had, and there wasn't a car for us, would put us in a better bargaining position. After all, since he hadn't kept his part of the bargain, he might shade the price a little."

"I see."

"But then this doctor said he was asleep and couldn't be disturbed, and like what was I doing bothering a sick man—so I left. But then I thought why couldn't I write him a note and leave it in his letterbox. So I came back."

"M-hm. Your father does not live with you—"

"No, he's at the King David. But he's not there now. He's gone up to Haifa for a few days."

"His address there?"

"I don't know it. I called him at the hotel and they said he had gone to Haifa. I didn't ask for the address. Maybe they know it at the hotel though."

"All right, Mr. Stedman. That seems clear enough." He rose to indicate that their meeting was over.

"Is that all?"

"I may want to see you again, but that is all for the present." He smiled in dismissal.

"Yeah, but my passport. You still got my passport."

"Oh, of course." Ish-Kosher picked up the phone. "The passport, Mr. Stedman's passport. Will you bring it in, please. . . . What? . . . Well, look on his desk . . . oh, I see. . . . Well, I suppose it will have to do." He replaced the instrument and turned to Roy. "The man who was working on it, he's not at his desk. He probably has it with him. We'll send it to you through the mail."

When Roy had gone, he lifted the receiver again. "Avner? Ish-Kosher. Young Stedman was just here. . . . No, nothing special, except that he had been to see Memavet earlier with his father, and his father was accompanied by a friend. And who is this friend, Avner? It is Rabbi David Small. . . . Don't you remember? He lives at Five Victory Street. . . . No, he was the one tenant who was out when we checked on the Carmi bombing."

33

IN spite of the yarmulke, Inspector Ish-Kosher was not a religious man, but he was strongly traditional; he had a distinct image of what a rabbi should look like, and Rabbi Small did not fit it. A rabbi should have a beard and wear appropriately dark and somber clothes, preferably black. Rabbi Small was beardless and wore light-gray summer trousers and a seersucker jacket. At the very least, a rabbi should not go uncovered; Rabbi Small was hatless. Ish-Kosher could not help feeling a little antagonistic as he motioned the rabbi to a seat.

The inspector thumbed through a folder on his desk and then looked up and said pleasantly, "A little while ago we made an inquiry at your apartment house to see if anyone there was expecting a visitor on a certain night. You were not at home, but your neighbor, Mrs. Rosen, said you had just arrived that day, late that evening, in fact. She said you were a rabbi from America. And yet, the little card in your letterbox says only David Small. Are you a rabbi?"

"Yes, I am a rabbi."

"Then why doesn't the card say Rabbi David Small?"

"Because here I am not a rabbi."

"And yet a doctor coming from America would probably keep his title on his letterbox," said the inspector.

"The two cases are not the same. The doctor probably could practice in an emergency, in an accident for example."

"This shows great delicacy on your part, Rabbi. Just what kind of rabbi are you?"

"I am a Conservative rabbi. I am the rabbi of a Conservative temple in America."

"The training is different for a Conservative rabbi than for one of ours?"

"No, not really," Rabbi Small said. "The emphasis is a little different, but the work itself does differ. Many of your rabbis here perform largely legalistic functions. Our work is rarely legal. Most of the time it is concerned with the emotional and spiritual health of the congregation we serve."

"I see." The inspector smiled suddenly. "Just to clear up and complete our records, *were* you expecting someone the night you arrived?"

"No, no one that I can think of."

Ish-Kosher made a note in the folder, closed it, and leaned back in his chair. Again he smiled pleasantly. "You are here on a sabbatical from your congregation?"

"No. I wouldn't call it a sabbatical. I took a leave of absence for a few months."

"Ah, on vacation. And what do you do, Rabbi? Do you go sight-seeing? Are you perhaps studying at the university?"

"No, I'm not doing much of anything; just taking a vacation, resting."

"From your arduous labors with your congregation?"

He was smiling, but there was also a tinge of sarcasm in his voice.

"Something like that," said Rabbi Small good-naturedly.

"It appears that you are not only taking a vacation from your congregation and your work, Rabbi, but even from the religion you profess."

"What do you mean?" said the rabbi in surprise. "If you refer to my not going to the synagogue every Sabbath—"

"I am referring to your going on the Sabbath to see someone about buying a car, specifically one Benjamin Memavet, whose apartment was bombed and who died as a result."

"How do you know I went to buy a car?"

"Please, Rabbi," said Ish-Kosher reproachfully, "I ask the questions."

"I had an appointment with my friend, Dan Stedman, and he had made another with his son. He was anxious for me to meet him, so I agreed to come along."

"But he was going to buy a car, to conduct business —and on the Sabbath. Again I ask, what kind of rabbi are you?"

The antagonism was now unmistakable. Rabbi Small smiled faintly. "As a rabbi, like all rabbis, I give these matters more thought than does the average layman like yourself," he began patiently. "Adherence to the traditional religious practices like covering the head or even observing the Sabbath according to the strict rabbinical code, these we do partly out of habit, partly because people expect it of us and perhaps to set an example to others in maintaining rabbinic tradition and rabbinic authority. I don't think anyone who has given the matter any thought actually thinks that God requires it of man or is pleased by it. According to Isaiah, 'I am full of burnt offerings . . . it is an abomination unto Me, saith the Lord. Your new moons and your appointed seasons, my soul hateth.'

That's putting it rather strongly, but it suggests how the God of Isaiah at least might view conformity and religious conventions in general."

"The God of Isaiah!" Ish-Kosher was outraged. "Tell me, Rabbi, do you believe in God?"

"I suppose as a police officer you'd like a yes or no answer."

"I—"

"It's a difficult question," the rabbi went on easily, "since it involves three variables—"

"Variables?"

"Of course. You ask if I believe in God. Do you mean at this moment in time, or the I of yesterday, or the I of three years ago? And what do you mean by 'believe'? That's another variable. Do you mean in the same way that I believe that two and two make four? Or the way that I believe that light travels a certain number of miles per second, which I myself have never seen demonstrated but which has been demonstrated by people whose competence and integrity I have been taught to trust? Or do you mean in the sense that I believe that there was a man named Washington who won independence for the American colonies from Britain, or in the sense that I believe there was a man named Moses who did the same thing for the Jews from Egypt. If you think about it, you'll see that there are many more forms of belief, and all of them a little different from each other. And finally, the third variable —God. Do you mean a humanlike figure? Or an ineffable essence? One who is aware of us individually and responsive to our pleas for help? Or one who is so far above us that He can have no interest in us? Or any one of the other conceptions that men have had over the ages? But speaking more generally, I suppose I have the feeling of belief and certainty some times and lack it at others, just as you do, or the Chief Rabbi, or the Pope for that matter."

Ish-Kosher stared at his visitor. Then he regrouped

his forces, as it were, and said stiffly, "I did not bring you here for theological discussions—"

"I have been wondering why you did ask me to come."

"Memavet made an appointment with your friend Stedman for later Saturday evening. I want to know if he kept it."

"I didn't see Mr. Stedman later, but I remember his telling his son he had no intention of keeping the appointment. He did not want to appear overeager. Is that all?"

"That is all. Good day to you."

"My passport. You have it on your desk."

"Oh, yes. Here it is." Ish-Kosher handed the booklet to the rabbi and remained standing for some little while after the rabbi had left, his fingers drumming a light tattoo on the desktop.

34

THE rabbi had not overlooked the fact that somehow the police had learned of his presence at Memavet's. They must have been told either by Dan or Roy. If, as seemed unlikely, Memavet had made some notation of his later meeting and the police had found it, the name referred to would certainly be Stedman. There was no reason for Memavet to have noted his name as well, since he was obviously not interested in buying a car. It was unthinkable—well, almost unthinkable—that the information had come from Dan, since he had pooh-poohed his suggestion that they report to the police. But if he had changed his mind and gone after all, would he not have called him first? And if he had not, then it could only have been an oversight or because for some reason he wanted to get him involved. And what reason could he have for that? His brother-in-law was perhaps interested in the job at Barnard's Crossing and he was acting out of a sense of mistaken family loyalty?

He dismissed the idea as melodramatic, completely absurd. And yet what did he know of Dan Stedman? They had had some pleasant talks, to be sure, but he had never confided in him. Except that he had been a TV journalist, he knew nothing of his past. And this sudden decision to go to Haifa, could that have some significance? It was certainly strange. The normal thing would have been to want to discuss the tragedy that had followed their visit. He tried to put the thought out of his mind, and yet. . . .

His mind turned to Roy and he realized the son was a more likely source of information to the police. If Memavet had made a note, he probably would have listed only the name, Stedman, and a routine police check would have come up with Roy's name. And then in routine questioning they would have learned that Roy had accompanied his father and his father's friend, David Small. Roy would have no reason to conceal the information. But then why hadn't Roy called to alert him that the police might be making inquiries? The answer was simple—the thoughtlessness and inconsiderateness of the young—and from what he had heard from Dan, quite characteristic.

He called Roy as soon as he got home. There was no answer. He called again later, and the next day, with no better luck. And then the rabbi put the matter out of his mind. Roy was coming to dinner Friday night, and he would see him then. And even if Roy had to beg off for some reason, common courtesy would require him to call.

By Friday as the rabbi waited for his guests to arrive, he decided not to bring up the subject. It was the Sabbath, a day of peace and rest. Of course, if either of the Stedmans were to bring up the matter, he could not refuse to discuss it. But he would not bring it up himself.

Both Stedmans came separately but at almost the same time. He had no sooner opened the door to welcome one than the other arrived. And because it was late, they went immediately to the table, then stood while the rabbi recited the kiddush, the prayer for wine that began the Sabbath observance.

The dinner was the customary Sabbath meal of chicken soup, gefilte fish and chicken. To Roy who had been eating in restaurants and the university cafeteria, it was a treat. He raved over each course to Miriam, and agreed when she urged him to have another helping. "I don't often get this kind of food," he said by way of explanation, "at least not this kind of cooking."

Gradually, mellowed by the food and wine, he dropped his original reserve and relaxed. The atmosphere at the table and in the house, perhaps because of the presence of little Jonathan or because Rabbi Small and his wife were relatively young, was pleasantly informal, very different from the occasional Sabbath meal he had had at his Uncle Hugo's. There, in spite of Aunt Betty's attempts at lightheartedness, the solemn emphasis on the holiness of the day tended to dampen its joyousness.

As they sipped their tea afterward, the conversation focused on him and his life at the university. Completely at ease now, Roy told them of his difficulties there. "My Hebrew is not so hot, and that doesn't help matters, I suppose. But mostly it's the Israeli students. They're so cliquey. And the American is shut out. My closest friends are Arabs." He said it defiantly, but his father refused to pick up the challenge.

Instead he said with jovial heartiness, "Why, I think that's fine, Roy. I want you to see all sides." Curiously, Roy did not feel grateful. He looked at the rabbi, who had remained silent.

"I guess the rabbi doesn't agree," he said.

Rabbi Small shook his head slowly. "No, I don't think I do. If there was dissension between me and my neighbors, the Rosens, and a guest of mine, newly arrived, took their side and showed a preference for them, I think I'd have a right to feel resentful."

"Well, let me tell you, Rabbi, there are plenty of Israeli students who are friendly with the Arabs."

"I am glad to hear it."

"But I thought you just said?"

The rabbi nodded. "The quarrel is between them, and it is a good thing if one or the other or both parties to the dispute make overtures, just as it would be if Mrs. Small were to make overtures and try to become friendly with Mrs. Rosen. But the case for the guest is different."

"That's the old way of thinking—my side, your side. It's what's made for all these wars and things." Roy sat forward. "My generation, we don't think that way. We don't care whose side we were born on. It's which side that's right that's important. Look at our attitude, I mean the attitude of Americans of my generation, toward Vietnam. Your generation tells us they are the enemy, but we refuse to go along. Your generation's thinking has given us wars, pollution, hunger, disease. My generation is changing all that."

"He's got a point there, Rabbi," said Dan. "I guess we have made a mess of things, and they're the ones that are trying to clean it up."

"No." The rabbi shook his head vigorously. "It's not our generation that caused whatever is wrong with the world. It's all the generations of mankind. The same generations of mankind that are responsible for all the good things, too. It's a world we live in, not a Garden of Eden. And it is the older generation that is doing the cleaning up, too, simply because the new one has not as yet acquired the necessary skills. It will be a dozen years at least before your generation, Roy, gets a chance to try its hand. And if it is your generation that transcends national boundaries, why do you call the Israeli students at the university cliquey? They're your generation. For that matter, why don't the Arabs of your generation try to make peace in this little part of the world instead of trying to terrorize the civilian population? Most of the terrorists are of your generation, you know. If there were peace, they could begin to make inroads into poverty and disease in their own countries—"

"Why don't the Israelis do it in their country?"

"Don't they?" asked the rabbi.

"How about the Sephardim who live in slums and don't have a chance for a decent life?"

"The Israeli government is trying to help them," Dan Stedman pointed out.

"Well, they could do a lot more," Roy said, returning to the rabbi.

"Every country could do a lot more for its unfortunates than it is doing," he said mildly. "Name one that is doing all it can."

"But this is supposed to be a nation of idealists," Roy protested.

"Is it? I certainly hope not," said the rabbi.

"You do?" Roy was startled. "That's a funny thing for a rabbi to say. Don't you want the country to be idealistic?"

"No, I don't. The whole thrust of our religion is toward a practical ethics rather than an absolute idealism. That's how Judaism differs from Christianity, as a matter of fact. We don't ask of our people that they be superhuman, only human. As Hillel said, 'If I am not for myself, who will be for me?' Traditionally, we have always felt that *parnossah*, the making of a living, was necessary for a good life. We have no tradition of an idealistic asceticism, or superhuman dedication as in monasticism or self-imposed poverty."

"What's wrong with idealism?" asked Roy.

"It's the worship of an idea, and the idea comes to count for more than people. Sometimes people are

cruel because—well, because they're people. But it's
self-limiting. If someone's normal, his act of cruelty
is apt to be followed by a bad attack of conscience.
But if he's an idealist, then any kind of wickedness
can be justified in its name. The Germans killed mil-
lions in pursuit of the idea of racial purity. In Russia
thousands were slaughtered for the quite human weak-
ness of hoarding a bit of food against the winter. I
might add that right now some of your fellow students
in America are perpetrating all kinds of wickedness in
the name of peace or social equality or academic responsibility or any other ideal that someone happens
to think up."

They argued late into the night. Sometimes the
argument went in circles, as arguments frequently do,
and sometimes it slid off into areas wholly unrelated
to the immediate subject of discussion. But for the
most part the adversaries were Roy and the rabbi, with
Dan occasionally chiming in to give moral support to
his son. The subject of the bombing of Memavet's
apartment did not come up until the guests were getting ready to leave. Some mention was made of Haifa,
and Roy asked his father if he had had a successful
trip there.

"I'd say it was successful, Roy. I'm hoping you'll
think it was, too. I happened to notice that the *Athenia*
had docked and was loading. I used to be quite friendly
with the skipper, so I went down to see him. He was
just as friendly as ever, and it ended up with an invitation to sail with him—a ten-day trip to Greece, Sicily,
and back to Haifa—for both of us, if you can make it.
What do you think of that, Roy?"

"Gee, that's great, Dad. When would we go?"

"We'd leave Haifa Sunday—"

Roy snapped his fingers. "Uh-uh, I just thought of
something."

"What's the matter? You got an exam?"

"No, as a matter of fact, we get a break from school
about then. But I'll need a passport, won't I?"

"Of course. What's the matter, did you lose it?"

"*I* didn't lose it." And he went on to tell what happened. "*They* lost it—one of those Keystone Kops evidently misplaced it," he added indignantly. "And if they sent it out today, I won't get it tomorrow because it's the Sabbath and they don't deliver on the Sabbath. And even if it comes Sunday, I won't get it until noon because that's when my mail is delivered."

"I don't think you'll get it Sunday either," said his father slowly.

"Why not?"

"Because—well, because although the police here may be a bunch of bunglers, even Keystone Kops as you call them, but on passports they never make mistakes—except on purpose."

"What are you getting at?" Roy was uneasy.

"You were questioned Monday? Tuesday?"

"Tuesday."

"All right," said Dan, "and today is Friday. That's four days, and you still haven't received it. I think they've pulled your passport. And in a country like this, surrounded by countries at war, you might just as well be in jail. You can't go anywhere, not even to a hotel in another city. And any time they want to, they can pick you up. Why didn't you go down and see them when it didn't come in the mail?"

"I did. I was there this morning. Nobody knew anything about it. And when I tried to see this inspector, the one I told you about, the one with the yarmulke, they said he was out and wasn't expected back."

"That's what I was afraid of," his father muttered.

"But surely," said the rabbi, "if you go to the American consul here—"

"No, I don't think that's too good an idea. Maybe Sunday I'll take a run down to Tel Aviv and see the people at the embassy."

"But then it will be too late for the trip," Roy protested.

"There'll be other chances. Maybe his next trip out."

When the Stedmans left, Dan purposely steered the conversation away from the subject of police and passports. "How did you enjoy the evening?" he asked his son.

"I had a nice time. I liked the rabbi."

"You were fighting with him all night."

"That doesn't make any difference," Roy said. "He wasn't yes-yessing me like some of the profs do at home who are always trying to get on with the kids. You know the drill: 'Now that's a good question' or 'That's a very interesting point Stedman has brought up.' And he didn't talk down to me either. We argued like equals."

They came to where they had to separate. "Er, Roy, about that passport, don't worry about it. Maybe I'll run down to Tel Aviv tomorrow."

"But it's the Sabbath. You'd have to cab down. It will cost about fifty lira."

"Yeah, but I can take either the *sherut* or the bus back, and that's only three and a half."

As Roy trudged home, stopping whenever he heard a car to jerk out a thumb for a ride, he went over the whole business in his mind. If the police inspector thought he was really involved in the murder, why had he been so pleasant to him? Why hadn't he questioned him more intensively? On the other hand, if the interrogation had been all it appeared, why did they have to check his passport so thoroughly? Maybe his father was right and they had actually pulled his passport; then why couldn't they simply go to the American consulate in Jerusalem and have them get it back for him? Why did his father think it necessary to go to the embassy in Tel Aviv? And on the Sabbath? It couldn't be just to expedite matters so they could make the boat trip, because the embassy wouldn't be able to do much before Sunday and by then it would be too late. But then why did his father tell him not to worry? If there was really nothing to worry about, why was he going down to Tel Aviv on the Sabbath?

And if there was, why didn't he just tell him? Did he think he was a kid who couldn't be told the truth?

Then Roy really started to worry.

35

"THERE'S nothing official about this, Rabbi," said Marty Drexler. "We want to make that plain at the beginning. Don't we, Bert?"

Bert Raymond nodded. "That's right. Marty had this idea, and he spoke to me about it, and I said we ought to come over to see you first before we started doing anything—you know, talking it up among the fellows, laying the groundwork."

Rabbi Deutch looked from one of his two visitors to the other. His fingers drummed on the arm of his chair. "It's something I'd have to think about," he said at last in his deep baritone voice. It was the voice he used in the pulpit, several notches below the tones he used to tell his wife how he wanted his eggs cooked for breakfast. "I served my congregation in Darlington faithfully for thirty years. There were many who wanted me to continue, but I felt that I needed a much deserved rest. There was work of a scholarly nature that I wanted to do. Traditionally, a rabbi is primarily a scholar, gentlemen. Frankly, one of my reasons for coming to Barnard's Crossing was its close proximity to the great libraries of Boston and Cambridge. And even in the short time I've been here, I've made use of them. However, I have also enjoyed my work with the congregation, and I must admit it has not seriously interfered with the works of research and scholarship in which I am engaged. How it would work out over

the long haul is another matter. I'd have to give it
careful thought."

"Well, sure, we know that. It's not that we want
your answer right away," said Marty eagerly.

"It's not only a question of my own personal incli-
nations," Rabbi Deutch went on as though he had not
been interrupted. "There is also an ethical and moral
question. I came here originally as a substitute for
Rabbi Small—"

"But he's not the one who picked you," said Marty.
Although he felt a good deal of constraint in Rabbi
Deutch's presence, unlike his reaction to Rabbi Small,
he could not keep restrained for long. "I mean it isn't
as though he asked you to come and take his place. It
was the board that did. I mean you're not his choice,
so it isn't as though you owe him anything."

"Well—"

"Marty is right, you know," said Raymond judicially.
"I can see where you would feel bound to him if he
had asked you to come and take his place. Even if he
had recommended you to the board without consulting
you first—that is, if he had submitted your name to
the board as a possible candidate—but he had nothing
to do with it. When he told us that he wanted a long
vacation—and mind you, he didn't ask us, he just told
us—we discussed what we ought to do. There was even
some talk on the board of not engaging anyone, you
know, just arranging for someone from the seminary
to come down now and then."

"I see." Rabbi Deutch tilted his head back and looked
at the ceiling as he pondered the matter. Finally, he
lowered his head and said, "Still, the rabbinate is not
a business. I can't take advantage of a colleague's absence to take over his pulpit as a businessman would
take a customer away from a rival." He rose and began
striding the room, their eyes following him like spectators at a tennis match. "I have been very happy here.
I admit that. And I am happy to hear that my efforts
have not been in vain. I am happy to hear from you

that I am well thought of in the congregation. That makes me very happy indeed. Now suppose that as a result of my greater experience, some of you, even a majority of you, even the entire congregation"—he stopped in front of them and spread his arms as if physically to include the massed congregation—"felt that I was more attuned to your needs, and I put it that way advisedly, gentlemen, because I don't for a minute want to suggest the possibility that Rabbi Small might not be as effective in his own way as you gentlemen seem to think I am in mine, well, even then, it becomes a question of whether it is right, or at least proper, for me to take over this pulpit on a permanent basis when Rabbi Small left it expecting to come back after his vacation or leave of absence."

"But that's just the point," said Marty. "This wasn't just an ordinary vacation. I ought to know because I'm the guy that arranged it. And I came down ready to talk contract. And because he'd been here almost seven years and hadn't taken off in all that time, we were ready to give him a sabbatical. But for a sabbatical, you know, you've got to have a contract. I mean, you can't give a guy a year's salary or half a year's salary so he can go to Israel and then afterward have him say, 'So sorry, boys, I'm taking a job with this other congregation.' And he wouldn't even discuss it." Marty could not keep the indignation out of his voice. "Absolutely refused to talk about it. So, okay, he doesn't want to talk contract, but what are your intentions, Rabbi? How long do you want? You want to go to Israel? You want to get it out of your system? Fine, I can understand that. I guess a rabbi has to go to Israel at least once to say he's been. You want to take off three weeks or a month even, I guess we could manage all right. But no, he wants an extended leave, three months, maybe more. Now you understand, I'm the treasurer of the temple. I'm the moneyman, and I'm responsible to the whole congregation how I spend the temple's money. It's not my money. It's theirs, the congregation's, so while I'm handling somebody else's money I got to be careful. I mean, suppose somebody in the congregation says to me what right have I got to give away the temple's money when I don't even know is the rabbi coming back or not. So I have to figure what the congregation can be legitimately asked to stand for. And I come up with a formula. I say, 'Okay, Rabbi, let's figure on a vacation basis. You been here six years and little more. All right, practically anybody got a right to two weeks' vacation a year. So that's six times two weeks is twelve weeks or three months. I figure anybody that asks, I could justify a three-month paid vacation.' And what do you suppose the rabbi says to that? He says he'd given the matter some thought, and he's decided that he shouldn't be paid while he's on leave. And to me that means he was practically resigning," said Drexler triumphantly.

"That's the way I see it," Bert Raymond chimed in.

A faraway look came over Rabbi Deutch's face, and when he spoke, his eyes were focused beyond them as if he were addressing an unseen audience. "The responsibility of the spiritual guidance of a congregation can constitute a great drain on one's nervous energies, gentlemen. I can remember when I was a young man in my first pulpit, on more than one occasion the thought came to me that for my own peace of mind I should throw the whole business up and go into some other line of endeavor. You may have approached him when he was tired, exhausted, drained. If he meant to resign, would he not have said so?"

"Well, we thought of that," said Bert Raymond, "and that's why we didn't approach you before. But just recently one of the members, V. S. Markevitch, I think you know him—"

"Yes, I know him."

"Well, V. S. may not be the biggest brain in the world, but he's no fool either. He's a successful businessman, which means he's had experience dealing with people. He saw Rabbi Small in Israel, and he reported that he got the feeling that Rabbi Small wasn't planning to come back. Maybe he was even thinking of leaving the rabbinate."

"Still, you can't tell about these things at second hand—"

"So we're not, Rabbi," said Marty Drexler. "If we were sure Rabbi Small was not coming back, we'd have voted on it in the board and then come to you with a definite offer. All we're asking is would you care to stay on here if the opportunity arose? I mean, if you thought you were going to be through here in a couple of weeks and were flirting with another congregation—"

"No, I haven't considered—"

"So, why not stay on here?"

"As I said, I'd have to think about it. I'd have to talk it over with Mrs. Deutch and see how she feels about it."

"Of course," said Raymond quickly. "By all means, talk it over with Mrs. Deutch. Then a little later we can talk again. Right now, all we're doing is what you might call hedging our bets."

36

IN his talks with Roy, whenever the subject turned to politics, Abdul always couched his criticism of the government or of Israeli Jewish society in a teasing, half-humorous way so that it was hard to tell if he was serious or not.

"Today I went to the bank to cash a check. I stood in a long line, and when I got to the counter, the clerk told me I was in the wrong line. So I stood in another line. When I finally reached the counter, the clerk examined the check and the signature. He looked at the front of the check and then at the back, and then I had to identify myself. Then he looked through a long list to make sure that the one who had given me the check was a depositor and then to match signatures and then to see if there was enough money in his account to cover the check. Then he gave me something to sign and sent me to another clerk. Again I waited in line, and there, too, I had to sign, and only then did I get my money. This is Israeli system. And the check was for twenty lira."

"Less than six dollars American."

"That's right," said Abdul. "I could have earned more in the time it took me to cash the check."

"And is it more efficient in Arab banks," Roy asked.

"No, but with us efficiency is no virtue. *You* have work split between many people because it is efficient. With us, a job that can be done by one is split between two or three because we feel that they also have to make a living. And the cost is no greater because we do not pay them much, but everyone gets a little. And delay does not bother us because we expect it and are not in a hurry. Usually, it means that some official expects a bribe. We don't resent it because the poor man gets only a small salary and has a large family to feed and maybe a daughter for whom he has to have a dowry."

"And what if the man can't afford the bribe?"

"So perhaps he has a patron who helps him, or he waits and suffers a little. Is it different in America if a man can't afford a lawyer?"

Roy laughed. And then because he was uneasy and troubled and wanted to allay his fears, he decided to tell Abdul what had happened. Abdul would put the whole matter in proper perspective; he would cite similar cases he had known of police stupidity. "Well, maybe you're right. But let me tell you what happened to me." And he told the story from the beginning.

"Memavet?" Abdul interrupted. "You went to see

Memavet at his apartment? But that was the place
that—"

"Yeah, yeah, I know, but listen." When he told
what his father had said about returning later that evening, Abdul smiled approvingly.

"He is a smart man, your father. The big trick in
bargaining is not to appear interested. Always remember the seller has interest enough for both."

"Yeah, well—" He went on to tell of his own return
to Mazel Tov Street later in the evening. But now
Abdul was not smiling.

"This was not very smart of you, Roy," he said reprovingly. "If your father found out, he would be angry.
And what did you hope to gain in any case? You could
not buy the car on your own."

"But my idea was just to look at it. I wasn't planning to go in to see Memavet. I just figured that after
we left, he must've called somebody he knew that had
a car and told him to bring it around at seven. So it
would be parked in front of his house, and I could take
a look at it and maybe tip off my old man."

"But there was no car there."

"That's right. So then I got to thinking, here we
made an appointment and he was going to have a car
to show us. So he hasn't got a car. So I'd just go in
to show him we kept our part of the bargain and he
didn't keep his. Then he'd be obligated, see?"

Abdul shook his head pityingly. "Why would he be
obligated? And what good would it do? You think he'd
ask less when he did get a car? Believe me, more likely
he'd ask more because he'd know you were anxious
to buy."

"Yeah, well, I figured it the other way. Anyway, I
didn't get to see him because he was in bed sick, so I
left a note in the letterbox saying I had been there."

Abdul showed concern. "This note, it is probably
still there. It must be recovered. There are workmen
there now, Arab workmen, perhaps I can arrange—"

"It's been recovered."

"Ah, that's better. For a minute I was worried."

"By the police. They called me in to question me about it."

Abdul's face was impassive. "Go on."

"Well, this guy I spoke to, he was pretty decent. I told him what happened and he asked me a few questions and that was all. But he'd given some clerk my passport to check, and when the interview was over and I asked for it, they couldn't find it. I guess the guy, the clerk I mean, had left the office, maybe to go to lunch, and he had it with him. This inspector guy said they'd mail it out to me, but I haven't got it yet. My old man is worried about it, but you know how older people are—always worrying."

Abdul rose and paced the floor as Roy watched him. Finally, he stopped and faced his young friend. "Your father is a smart man, Roy. He is worried with reason."

It was not the reaction he had expected. "Look here, suppose they think they got something on me, they could just tell me straight out they were pulling my passport, couldn't they? Why would they have to go pussyfooting around and make believe they mislaid it?"

"Pussyfooting? Ah, yes, I think I understand." Abdul thought for a moment as though planning how best to say it. "You see, Roy, if they take your passport, that is an official act. So you engage a lawyer or you go to the American consulate, or the lawyer goes for you, and they demand that the passport be returned or that you be officially charged so that the case can be tried in court. But they do not have enough evidence to present the case in court; they are engaged in building it up."

"What do you mean building it up?"

"Even where the person charged is clearly guilty," Abdul explained, "it is necessary to build up the case. The police cannot go before a judge and say that this man we believe is guilty of such and such a crime and we would like the court to sentence him for so many years. They have to present proof, stey by step. It takes time. And that is a case where the accused is actually guilty. But where he is not guilty, it takes even more time."

Roy was aghast. "You mean they are trying to frame me?"

"What means frame?"

"That they know I'm innocent but are trying to convict me just the same."

Abdul shrugged his shoulders and smiled.

"But why? I mean why me?"

"Because you were there. The police naturally like to prove they are efficient. How do they do it? They arrest people and have them tried and convicted. It is not done in America?"

"Yeah, I guess it's done everywhere. But look here, they know who did it. It was done by your people."

Abdul was suddenly cold, and his eyes narrowed. "What do you mean my people?"

"It was done by the terrorists. They admitted it."

Abdul relaxed and smiled again. "The trouble is that they all admitted it, all the commando groups. I'm afraid they are apt to do that anytime something happens here in Israel. It is only natural they should want to take the credit. But for just that reason, the Israeli government would like to prove that it was done by someone else, you, for instance. It is not good for the people here, the citizens, to feel that the commandos can penetrate to the heart of the Jewish section. It makes them nervous. They do not sleep well at night. And it means also that the security is not so good as they would like people to believe. So if they can prove that it was done by an individual, it would mean that it was not done by the commandos."

Roy clasped and unclasped his hands. "But what can I do?"

"Ah, now you see the difference between the way your people run things and the way mine do. If this were an Arab country, then we would seek out the official responsible and we would offer him a bribe. Or, if this might not be possible, we would make contact with some clerk in the office who would perhaps mislay the file. You understand? It would not be difficult—"

"Be realistic," Roy implored. "What do you think I ought to do?"

"In your position, I would leave the country—no, that is not possible since they have taken away your passport. So it would be good if you could go away somewhere to hide. Go to another city for a while. Go visit someone in Haifa or Tel Aviv."

"What good would that do? The police could pick me up—"

"Not if they couldn't find you. Don't you have some friend you could visit, some friend you could trust? In the meantime, your father can go to the American embassy in Tel Aviv and see what arrangements he could make. He's an important man, you told me."

"He's down there now."

"Ah, then I am sure he will be able to make arrangements of some sort," said Abdul soothingly. "I am sure you really have nothing to worry about in that case."

"Yeah, maybe you're right." But the thought that came to him was that Abdul was just soft-soaping him because he knew the situation was grim.

37

THERE was a rectangle on the table of organization of the American embassy staff which bore the name of Michael Donahue, but it was not clear just what his duties and responsibilities were. He had no immediate supervisor but was connected with the upper echelons by a dotted line which indicated some sort of staff function. Mike Donahue was not so high on the chart as to be automatically invited to embassy parties, nor was he so low as to cause notice and comment if he occasionally attended. He was certainly not one of the pretty boys, the urbane youngish men, good-looking, well dressed, with a special talent for being agreeable to the wives and daughters of members of the diplomatic corps in Tel Aviv. On the contrary, he was a thickset middle-aged man, balding, with a round face and a nose that looked as though it might have been flattened in the boxing ring. He usually dressed in wrinkled seersucker suits and a shapeless panama. He was thought by most of the staff to have something to do with publicity since he had a wide acquaintance among journalists, and yet he did not come directly under the Public Relations Unit. The more knowing suspected that he was either CIA or its liaison with the ambassador.

It was to his old friend Mike Donahue that Dan Stedman made application when he went to Tel Aviv. "So they took Roy's passport and gave him some cock-and-bull story about its having been misplaced and they'd send it to him by mail."

"And he fell for it?"

"He's just a kid, Mike. This man at the police, the inspector who interrogated him, had been pleasant all through it—no tough stuff—why wouldn't he believe him?"

"But all this time—"

"Well, you know how it is. You don't get it the next day, so you figure the mail service is not so good. Then the next day you get a little anxious, but you figure you'll wait one more day. Then the next day he did go down to inquire, and no one there seemed to know what he was talking about, and this inspector he had dealt with was not around. If this business of the little trip I'd planned hadn't come up, chances are he might have waited another few days or a week before telling me about it."

"The police don't lose passports," said Donahue flatly.

"That's what I thought. The whole business didn't seem kosher."

"Obviously not. And I don't think it's the sort of thing the police would do, not to an American citizen, especially a student at the university, and especially one whose father was in the media. No, it's definitely Shin Bet. The police are acting for them."

"So what do I do?" asked Stedman. "Do I play it straight and go down there and raise hell or go to the American consulate in Jerusalem and have them make a formal demand, or maybe ask them to issue a replacement?"

Donahue shook his head. "I wouldn't do that. Because if it is the Shin Bet and they don't want your boy to leave the country for a while, they'll see to it that he doesn't leave even if they have to put him in a hospital to keep him here."

Dan was indignant. "C'mon, Mike, this is a democracy with a code of laws—"

"You c'mon. You've been around long enough to know better. What country democratic or otherwise can control the individual actions of its Intelligence? If the Shin Bet wanted your boy around for a few days, even if word came down from Golda herself, do you suppose that would stop a convenient automobile accident? They'd reason that it was for the security of the state and that she didn't know what was involved. The agent wouldn't change direction until he got word from his chief."

"So what do you do about a thing like this?"

"Well, that depends on what the thing is."

"What's that supposed to mean?"

"I'll spell it out for you, Dan. There was a terrorist bombing in Jerusalem and your kid was there—in a quiet, deserted street where no one would normally go for a stroll in the evening, mind you. Or put it another way: He's in a place where he would normally

have had no business to be unless he had business. And
he was not just taking a walk there because it was
raining. All right, that's one item. The second item is
that his close friends at school are Arabs—"

"I didn't say they were his close friends."

"No, but you said he was friendly with them because
he hadn't been able to make friends with the Israeli
or American students. So I could amend that and suggest that whether they were close or not, they were his
only friends. Does that make it any better? All right.
So it's perfectly possible that one of his good friends,
or one of his only friends, asks him to do a little favor
for him. 'Leave this box on the windowsill of my friend
in One Mazel Tov Street, will you, Roy?'—That's his
name? Roy? Or maybe: 'I've got to drop off something
at the home of a friend of mine, Roy. How about walking down with me?' And then when they get there,
'Would you mind waiting on the street for a minute,
Roy, and cough or whistle or something if someone
comes along?'"

"My son wouldn't—"

"Yeah, I know, your son wouldn't do that kind of
thing. Let me tell you, anybody's son could, especially
these days. I'm just suggesting possibilities, you understand. Well, if it were something like that, I'm not sure
that much could be done. That is, if he's guilty or has
any connection with this, I don't know if anything could
be done except wait while they built a case and it came
up in court. Then about all you could do would be to
hire the best lawyer you could get. But if he is completely innocent, and they really have nothing on him
except the coincidence of his having been there, maybe
we can do something."

"Like what?"

"Well, we could pass the word along until it reaches
the right party. Favors have been asked and favors
have been done and you slip this one in as a favor in
exchange."

"I see," said Stedman. "And what do I do in the meantime?"

"Not a damn thing. You just wait. Were you going back to Jerusalem tonight?"

"Why, yes, I was planning to take the *sherut* and—"

"Why not stick around for a day or two? Maybe I'll have some news for you."

Stedman nodded.

"Oh, and, Dan, a suggestion: If and when we get this cleared up, it might not be a bad idea if your son went back to the States as soon as he gets his passport."

Stedman looked over in surprise. "But why?"

"You can't always tell about these things," Donahue said. "Sometimes there's more than one person involved, and not everybody gets the message at the same time. Besides, your son's evidently got off on the wrong foot. He came here to find something and so far obviously hasn't succeeded. There's no reason to believe that if he stays on for the rest of the year, he'll do any better."

"I hate to take him out of school, right in the middle of the year," Dan said. He thought a moment. "Maybe you're right."

"And, Dan—"

"Yes?"

"Look out for yourself. Be careful."

"What do you mean?"

Donahue hesitated. "Well, all Intelligence services are suspicious, not to say downright paranoid. They might get to thinking that a youngster like your kid might be acting on instructions from his dad."

38

ADOUMI would never actually send for Ish-Kosher; instead, from his dusty little office on the third floor he would phone the inspector.

"Chaim? Avner. Are you busy?"

And even though he was doing nothing more important than reading the newspaper, Ish-Kosher would say, "Well, right now, Avner, I'm kind of tied up. But in five or ten minutes. . . ."

"I'd like to see you for a few minutes. Shall I come down?"

"Perhaps I'd better come up to your place. We're less likely to be disturbed. I'll be along as soon as I can." Then he would twiddle his thumbs until he had judged sufficient time had elapsed, and only then, gathering up his briefcase, would he march down the corridor, not hurrying because that would not be in keeping with his status as inspector, but walking purposefully, then up a flight of stairs to a crossover to the next building, and again a long corridor and another flight of stairs. Then he would stop to draw several deep breaths to compose himself after his exertion, after which he would casually saunter down the short corridor to Adoumi's office.

He sat down, his briefcase on the floor between his legs. "Mrs. Adoumi is better, I trust."

Adoumi rotated a palm. "Like this, like that. Dr. Ben Ami wants her to go into Hadassah again for observation and some more tests. He's going away for a month or more and wants to get her in before he leaves."

"For a month? A vacation? These doctors do very well for themselves."

"He's supposed to be going to a medical convention in Geneva. Then on to another in Valparaiso. You know how these things work: They sign in, and so that means they've officially attended. And they can deduct it from their income tax. He'll be going around the world because from Valparaiso it's just as easy to go west as it is to go east. You and I are lucky if we can take a week off to go to Eilat. But Ben Ami is a good fellow and I don't begrudge him." He swept aside a folder to clear the top of the desk as if to invite Ish-Kosher to produce any papers he had. "Well, do you have anything?"

Ish-Kosher drew a folder from his briefcase. "Just some routine stuff on the boy's father. He was a foreign correspondent for one of the American TV networks up until recently. In fact, you may remember, he was their Middle East correspondent and stationed here before and during the Six-Day War. His Hebrew is pretty good. Right now, he's living at the King David and doesn't seem to be doing much of anything. The story is that he's writing a book on opinion in Israel. He gets into a conversation with someone and makes a tape recording. He uses a concealed recorder and a lapel mike. According to the chambermaid, he's got a number of tapes in his room, all neatly labeled."

"She's one of yours?"

"M-hm."

"Then arrange to have copies made of the tapes."

"All right. Oh, here's something interesting: one of the tapes is labeled 'Memavet.' "

Adoumi shrugged his shoulders. "If the son's story about buying a car is right, and I guess it is because the rabbi fellow confirmed it, then it's probably just a recording of the meeting." He looked off into space and murmured, "He goes around recording conversations, eh? When you think about it a bit, it's a good cover.

He can talk to anyone and claim he's recording it for possible use in his book."

"You think he's an agent? CIA?"

"All those American correspondents are," Adoumi said matter-of-factly. "If they're not actually paid by the CIA, at least they swap information with them. Anything else on him?"

Ish-Kosher shook his head. "Except that he's gone to Tel Aviv for a couple of days. He called the hotel from there to ask if he'd got any calls and said he'd be at the Sheraton for a couple of days."

"At the Sheraton? That's interesting."

"What's interesting about it?"

"Just that that's where he went when he came to Israel. Instead of going direct to Jerusalem, he drove into Tel Aviv and registered at the Sheraton."

"You were having him watched?"

Adoumi's jaw dropped to make a slow, sly smile. "It was not him we were watching. There is a Rumanian dancer, the *première danseuse* of the Rumanian ballet troupe that played in Tel Aviv, Olga Ripescu. She is a Russian agent. It was she we were watching. Almost immediately after Stedman registered, she spotted him, and they were together for a while. What do you think of that?"

"They could have known each other for some time. After all, these foreign correspondents get around."

"True, but it's interesting. Now did you get anything on this rabbi fellow?"

"Just what I told you after I questioned him," Ish-Kosher said. "He seems harmless enough. He doesn't do much of anything, just walks around the city, sometimes with Stedman, goes to the synagogue some mornings—"

"And just happens to live at number Five Victory Street, which was the house to which someone asked the civilian guard to direct him, the night a bomb went off in the next street," Adoumi said dryly.

"That could be just coincidence. It proves nothing."

"Ah, Chaim, you are a policeman. You think always in terms of proof, of what can be presented by the government lawyers in a court of law, a chain of evidence leading to a definite conclusion. But in Intelligence, where we are concerned with the safety of the state, we can't afford the luxury of absolute proof. We look for a pattern, or some oddity, or better still, a pattern of oddities." He tapped a stubby forefinger on the desktop.

"What do you call an oddity in this case?"

"Chaim, Chaim, it's full of oddities. Take any one of the people we are concerned with. Every one of them shows anything but normal behavior. Start with Stedman. He arrives in Israel, and instead of going directly to Jerusalem, where his son is, he goes to Tel Aviv for a couple of days first."

"But he has friends there—"

"It can be explained, of course, but it's still a little odd where he hasn't seen his son for some time. He could always run down to Tel Aviv afterward. It's even odd that he was not met at the plane by his son. But on top of that, one of the first persons he meets in Tel Aviv is Ripescu, a known agent. Now that's odd. But it doesn't end there. He comes to Jerusalem, and he is engaged in an odd occupation, which could serve as a cover. It enables him to talk to anyone in seeming innocence. No meeting in special places, no whispered remarks in passing, but all open and aboveboard. If we confronted him and asked him why he was talking to someone we happened to be watching, he merely points out it's his normal method of gathering material."

"But look here, if some intelligence were passed to him, it would be right there on tape as proof against him."

"Come, Chaim, I wouldn't expect him to be that simple. If it were dangerous information, he would simply wipe the tape. Conceivably, if he were confronted on the street by one of our men, he could wipe the tape right then and there with one hand in his pocket while our man was holding him by the arm. Believe me, it has excellent possibilities—this writing a book based on street conversations. Has it occurred to you, Chaim, that he might have been the one who approached the civilian guard to ask for number Five Victory Street, in which case we would have still another oddity."

"It's possible. That we might be able to check out. We could get hold of the civilian guard and bring him down to the King David." Ish-Kosher seemed pleased at the prospect of a definite assignment.

"It might be worth trying," said Adoumi. "But let's go on. We next run across him in connection with Memavet. And the very evening of the day he goes to see him, Memavet's apartment is bombed. Now, that's damn odd."

"It's certainly an interesting coincidence, especially if he was the one who spoke to the civilian guard, because that would connect him with both bombings."

Adoumi went right on. "And now, the most interesting oddity: He is the father of Roy Stedman, who was not only present at the right time for the Memavet bombing, but who is friends with Abdul El Khaldi, who is someone in whom we have been interested for a long time."

"Have you ever brought him in for questioning?"

Adoumi shook his head. "No, he's an intellectual. We treat these Arab intellectuals with kid gloves, especially if they are students at the university. That's government policy, and insofar as it's feasible, we respect it. Now let's go on. I've already mentioned that it is odd that Roy didn't go to meet his father's plane. And it's odd that a Jewish boy should be so friendly with the Arabs. But take the two together, father and son, and there you come up with another oddity. We pull the boy's passport, and instead of doing the normal thing, making representations to the consulate, they do nothing—just sit and wait for it to come in by mail. Let's assume that the boy doesn't know any better, but his father certainly does. And then you have the rabbi—"

"You are suspicious of him, too?" asked the inspector.

"He lives one street away from where the first bombing occurred, and it occurred the very night he arrived in the city. Coincidence? All right. But someone who could have placed that bomb inquired about the location of the house where our rabbi lives. Coincidence? Perhaps. Finally, he becomes friends with the Stedmans and goes with them to buy a car from a man who is subsequently killed in a bomb explosion, that very night. And this on the Sabbath; a rabbi to go to a business conference on the Sabbath? Coincidence? Well maybe, but to me, it looks like a pattern."

"Still—"

"It's a chain, Chaim. Don't you see it?" He held up a large hand and ticked off the links on stubby fingers. "Ripescu, a known agent, the older Stedman, the younger Stedman, Abdul, an Arab we suspect. And Rabbi Small somewhere in the middle as one of the connecting links."

"It's interesting," Ish-Kosher admitted, "and odd, and there seems to be a pattern of sorts, but there's nothing there that I can take action on." He seemed disappointed.

Again Adoumi displayed his slow, sly smile. "You couldn't, but I could."

"You mean you'd go ahead and—"

Adoumi shook his head regretfully. "Not yet. I don't really have enough. But if Stedman were the man who was wandering around looking for Victory Street, that would help a little. There's also the note that young Stedman left in Memavet's mailbox."

"What about it?"

"You remember how it read: 'I came back as I promised.' That could mean just what he said it meant. But there's a chance that it might mean something else."

"Like what?"

"Well," said Adoumi, "suppose he'd had dealings with Memavet before, and there had been some trouble and he had said, 'Look, I'm not forgetting this. I'll be back!' "

"But before you were sure that Memavet was killed by accident, by the terrorists and that they probably had nothing against him personally."

"True, but in the light of what we know now, it could be that Memavet was killed because someone wanted him killed. It might be worthwhile checking through his business records a little more carefully, going back as far as you can, questioning the people at the shop, perhaps."

"I'll see what I can do," said Ish-Kosher purposefully.

"That would give us a motive, you see."

"I understand. And that would do it for you?"

"That plus a lot of checking among my own people," said Adoumi. "In this crazy business you never can tell what you're liable to run up against. These people could all be agents and yet in some crazy way working for us. I'd have to check it out."

"I see." Ish-Kosher nodded sympathetically.

The two sat in silence for a while, and Ish-Kosher wondered if their meeting was at an end. Then he remembered that Adoumi had said he wanted to see him about something. "Did you just want to talk it out, Avner?" he asked. "Or did you have something special to tell me?"

"There was something. I have received word that the Americans would consider it a favor if we did not interfere with the Stedmans, father and son, leaving the country. That's what Stedman went to Tel Aviv for, to arrange to have this favor asked."

Ish-Kosher was surprised. "You mean he went to protest to the embassy?"

"Oh, not protest. That's too strong a word. He spoke to someone who passed the word to one of our people—"

"Let me understand this, Avner," the inspector said carefully. "You mean if we come up with proof that Roy Stedman murdered Memavet, the Americans would want us to drop the case against him?"

"Oh, no. If we had proof that he had broken one of our laws, they would not think of trying to beg him off. It's just that if all we have is a pattern that might lead to proof eventually, but right now is nothing but a pattern—you understand."

"So what are you going to do?" asked Ish-Kosher.

"Your people might come up with something, but it would probably take some time. And we can't just go on keeping these people on ice. Right now, the situation is essentially static. Maybe if they started acting up. . . ."

"And if they don't? Do I just send Stedman's passport back with a note saying I'm sorry if I caused him any inconvenience?"

"I was thinking maybe we could nudge them a little."

"What do you mean?"

"Well," said Adoumi, "suppose we put a little pressure on one end of the chain. It might cause reactions all along its length. We can't at the Ripescu end because she's gone. But how about the Abdul end. One of their group is a girl named Leila M'zsoumi. Now suppose a couple of your men were to pick her up. . . ."

39

AS Rabbi Hugo Deutch, still in pajamas and bathrobe, went to the stove to pour himself a second cup of coffee, his wife, still in nightgown and housecoat, said anxiously, "Hadn't you better get dressed, dear? You don't want to be late for the board meeting."

"I'm not going. It was suggested that I stay away today. I gather that they're going to discuss the question of my staying on here. So I decided to take a holiday and pass up the minyan as well."

"Then why don't we take our coffee out on the porch? It looks lovely and warm out. Smell that air!" She opened the porch door and stood on the threshold, coffee cup in hand.

"It's an offshore breeze. We're getting the smell of the ocean."

"Spring in New England, Hugo—I never enjoyed it so much before."

"Well, Darlington is a factory town and spring breezes there were apt to be full of smoke and that sulfur smell—remember?"

"Mm. Oh, I'm glad, Hugo, that we're going to stay. I was afraid you were going to be stuffy about it."

"Just a minute, Betty." He brought his cup and sat down on a porch chair beside her. "I haven't changed my position. I just said I'd be willing to stay on if Rabbi Small decided not to return."

"But you said—"

"The meeting today? That's to decide if they want me—if Rabbi Small doesn't come back."

"You mean that Drexler told you that they want Small, and you are just their second choice?"

He sipped his coffee. "No, my impression is that if we were both equal candidates, I would be their first choice. But it's really his job."

"Is that their opinion, Hugo, or is it yours?"

"That's my opinion," he said stubbornly. "I'm not taking a man's job away from him."

She bit her lip to keep back the angry words that welled up within her. She knew how her husband reacted to opposition when he was having one of his stubborn streaks. Then her face cleared, and she smiled. "It's an easy job for you, Hugo, isn't it?"

"It's a real vacation. I've thought about it—why it's so much nicer here than it was in Darlington. I think it's a matter of money as much as anything. The rabbi depends on the congregation, on the board really, for his salary, and so subconsciously they can't get over the feeling that he's a salaried employee. Since they're the ones that are paying, that gives them the whip hand, and it's only human nature when you've got a whip in your hand to flick it occasionally. But they know I'm on a pension and don't need their salary. So that puts me on a somewhat different plane."

"Oh, I don't think it's only that. I think they're a nicer class of people than the congregation we had in Darlington."

He shook his head. "No, I won't go along with you there. These people may be a little better off financially, but it's new money that they've made in the last ten or twelve years. And a lot of the lovely homes we've visited are mortgaged to the hilt. As a matter of fact, there's a kind of meanness that I detect every now and then, that I didn't notice in Darlington. Take this matter of Rabbi Small's not drawing a salary while he's in Israel."

"Yes, but you said it was a matter of his own choice."

Rabbi Deutch nodded. "That's what *they* said. But you know how these things work. They back a man into a corner, and he practically has no alternative. The decent thing would have been not to mention it at all, but to just go on sending him his checks."

"And this bothers you? Is this why you won't come right out and accept the job?"

"Oh, for myself it doesn't bother me at all. I was just thinking of poor Small. As far as I'm concerned, it's probably a little wicked of me, but I rather enjoy the situation. You see, here I have the upper hand, I don't need them. We have enough for our needs, and I have no long-term career here that I have to safe-guard. If I remain here, it will be for three years? Five? Seven at the most. You notice in the time I've been here, I haven't had any rows, no crises of the sort that seemed to come up every other week at Darlington.

They know that when I take a position, I'm going to stick to it." He smiled complacently.

"But you don't take a position quite so often here," she pointed out.

"I guess that's true, too. Since I think of the job as essentially temporary, I don't have the same feeling of urgency on most things as I did in Darlington. There, when some minor matter came up, I sometimes had to make an issue of it, not because it was important in itself, but because I was afraid of what it might lead to. Here I don't bother. If it should develop into a major crisis, I feel strong enough to handle it then. Do you remember Mr. Slonimsky in Darlington?"

Mrs. Deutch laughed. "Abe Cohen was in the hospital a whole week, Rabbi, and you didn't go to see him," she mimicked.

"He also kept tabs on the number of times I missed the minyan." The rabbi chuckled.

Now that he was in a good humor, she tried again, cautiously. "Did you ever think that it has been a welcome change for me, too, Hugo?"

"How do you mean, my dear?"

"As the *rebbitzin,* I had to be careful and circumspect. My behavior might affect your job. I had to trim my friendships to the politics in the synagogue. Arlene Rudman would call me practically every morning and chat at me for as much as an hour at a time, and I listened and never cut her off, because her husband was the big moneyman in the congregation and one of your strongest backers."

"But you continued to talk to her on the phone after I retired," he said.

"Only because when you form a habit, it's hard to break." She looked off into the distance. "Whenever they came to visit us, I always had the feeling that she was making an inspection of the premises."

"Really! I thought you liked her."

"I never really liked her, Hugo. I just got used to her. And when you retired, things didn't change for me. The attitudes of the women of the congregation to me and my attitude toward them had been developing for thirty years. You can't change that overnight. I never had any real friends; friendships that you cultivate on the basis of the importance of their husbands to the congregation don't mean much."

"But when I retired—"

"That made it worse. I was no longer the official *rebbitzin* and didn't have to be consulted. And I had no children or grandchildren to visit and busy myself with. Except for Roy, we never had any young people in the house. And we only saw him when Laura would pack him off to us when she wanted a little rest herself. And I always felt that he was in your way and was disturbing you. I think he felt it, too, poor boy." She seemed on the verge of tears.

"Believe me, Betty, I'm fond of the boy. As for Darlington, I had no idea—but—but we don't have to go back to Darlington when I get through here," he soothed. "We can live anywhere now and meet new people and make new friends. We can take an apartment in Boston or Cambridge, where I can work at the library—"

"It's no good, Hugo. Scholarship just isn't your cup of tea. If you had a real interest in it, you would have done something about it long ago. Grubbing away at dusty books just isn't your forte. You have to deal with people. You're good at that. I know you'd make a bluff at it and trot off to the library every morning with a briefcase full of notebooks and pencils, but the first bit of bad weather, you'd stay at home, and that would break the routine, and you'd hang around the house more and more after that until finally you gave up all pretense and just followed me around from room to room as I did my housework—two old people with nothing to say to each other, getting in each other's way."

He did not answer immediately, and there was a long

silence between them. Finally, he said, "What do you
want me to do?"

"Take the job if they offer it. Leave the question of
the ethics of the situation for them to answer. That's
where it belongs."

40

IT had been midmorning when Ish-Kosher had
had his conference with Adoumi, and by noon one of
his sergeants was driving down to Tel Aviv with
Shmuel, the civilian guard, on the passenger seat beside
him.

Shmuel was far less assured than he had been when
Ish-Kosher had questioned him. "You understand, it
was late at night and dark. And since then, I've seen
so many people. How can I be sure that it was this
man and not someone else who spoke to me that night?"

"You know how these things are," the sergeant said.
"Maybe you can't describe a man, but if you've seen
him once, there's usually something familiar about
him—"

"And if not?"

The sergeant was patient. "I explained that. You go
up to him and greet him. If he greets you back and
the chances are he will—almost anybody will whether
they know you or not—then you say, 'Did you find
the house on Victory Street all right?' If he's the man,
he'll say, 'Oh, yes, no trouble,' or something like that.
Then he may ask what you're doing in Tel Aviv, and
you tell him you had to come down on business or you
are meeting a friend—anything."

"And if he says, 'I don't know what you're talking about'?"

"Then you've had a nice ride to Tel Aviv and back, a little vacation."

And early in the afternoon, another of Ish-Kosher's sergeants was questioning the elderly bearded mechanic at the auto repair shop where Memavet had had his desk.

The mechanic looked despairingly at the clock on the wall and then to the interior of the shop, where he had been working on a car whose owner was expecting it soon.

"I've been through this half a dozen times with you people," he said. "I had nothing to do with his business, and I know nothing about it."

"I know, I know," the sergeant said soothingly. "But if the man occupied a desk right here, he must have talked to you about his customers occasionally. He couldn't have been so busy that he'd just sit at his desk all day long. There must have been plenty of times when he had nothing to do and he'd wander over."

"Sure, but—"

"And he'd talk to you, wouldn't he?"

"Of course. Dumb he wasn't."

"So what does a businessman talk about? About some deal he missed out on; about a shrewd deal he pulled off; about some customer he had trouble with. Some of his customers he must have had trouble with. They couldn't all have been perfectly satisfied."

"Naturally, if you're in business—"

"So, all I want you to do is to think back and try to remember."

The old man seized on the suggestion. "All right, I'll think back and try to remember. You come in next week sometime and I'll tell you what I remembered."

"No, no," said the sergeant. "Right now. Look, when you're working, you can still see the front of the office here where the desk is. Right?"

"When I'm working, I work. I pay attention to what I'm doing—"

"Sure, but you look up every now and then. You have to stop to get another tool. You can't help seeing who is sitting by the desk."

"All right," said the mechanic. "So I see somebody sitting beside the desk."

"And if there were an argument, you'd listen. You couldn't help it. It's human nature. Don't tell me you never heard Memavet arguing with a customer."

"Who's telling? Sure, I heard."

"Now did you ever hear a customer who got so angry that he slammed out of the door—"

"Look, young man, in business customers are always slamming out of the door, but later they usually come back. If you were in business, you'd know."

"Sure," said the sergeant affably, "and I bet that many a time Memavet came back here afterward and told you about it, and you both laughed maybe, and you reassured him and said, 'Don't worry, he'll come back.' "

"Why not? Two people working in the same place, they encourage each other, if they're not in competition in the same line of business."

"That's right," said the sergeant. "Now, did anyone ever get so angry that he said he was going to get even? I have in mind a young man, a foreigner, an American. . . ."

Early in the evening, Roy and Abdul were sauntering along the street after dinner together. When they reached Roy's apartment house, a figure detached itself from the shadows. It was Mahmoud.

Roy said hello, and Mahmoud flashed a smile in greeting. Then in rapid Arabic he spoke to Abdul. "I thought you'd be coming here," he said. "I've been looking for you. They've picked up Leila."

"That's serious, Mahmoud. You think she will talk?"

Mahmoud shrugged. "If it were the other way and

we got a girl of theirs who knew something, I'd make her talk."

"I suppose you're right. What are you going to do?"

"I have a place in the Old City. I suggest you go north."

"Yes, it would probably be advisable. I'll need the car."

"I can have it here in half an hour."

"Good. We'll leave then."

"We? You mean the American?"

"That's right. I'll try to take him with me. It could be insurance."

As they mounted the stairs, Roy asked, "What was that all about?"

Abdul waited for Roy to open the door and snap on the light. Then he said, "My uncle is marrying off a daughter. There is a big feast lasting several days to which we are invited, Mahmoud and I."

"Are you going?"

"Mahmoud cannot get away from his job. He will let me have his car, though, but it is a long drive. My uncle's place is in the Galilee. I am not anxious to drive two or three hours at night alone."

"Well, you could leave tomorrow morning—"

Abdul shook his head. "You don't understand. The family will be gathering, and unless I get there tonight, the most desirable rooms and beds will be all gone. No, if I am to go at all, it must be tonight."

"Gee, that's—look, did Mahmoud say anything about me? Seems to me I caught the word 'American.' "

"Oh, that was something else. Yes, he mentioned you." He sobered. "While he was waiting here, the police came and rang your bell."

"They did? Gosh, maybe it was to return my passport."

Abdul shook his head. "There were two of them. They don't need two to deliver your passport. He heard one say they could come back in the morning."

"Well, what do you think I ought to do?"

Abdul considered. "I think if you were out of the way for a few days while your father is working out things in Tel Aviv, it would—" He slapped his hand against his side. "I have an idea, come with me."

"You mean to the wedding?" Roy asked.

"Why not? There will be feasting and dancing, and there'll be girls," he said with a broad smile, "lots of girls."

"But I haven't been invited."

Abdul laughed. "But I am inviting you. I will present you to my uncle as my friend, and you will be his most honored guest. You'll have a chance to see Arab hospitality."

"You mean it? You'll take me with you?"

"Of course. You are my friend." He was struck by a thought. "Your father he is in Tel Aviv, you say. Why don't you call the King David and leave a message for him that you are going to visit friends for a few days, so he won't worry if he doesn't find you when he gets back?"

41

MONDAY, Gittel came up to Jerusalem. "There is a conference," she explained. "Normally, I do not go to these conferences, you understand. A waste of time. It just provides audiences for people who have nothing better to do than write papers. But this time I came because it gives me a chance to visit with you and also to see my friend Sarah, who goes into Hadassah tomorrow for observation and tests."

"What's the matter with her, Gittel?" asked Miriam.

"If they knew, would Dr. Ben Ami send her in for tests? Of course, I know what's wrong with her—"

"You do?" the rabbi asked. Normally, he and Gittel had little to say to each other. She usually talked woman's talk with Miriam, and he remained silent or even wandered off to another room. But he was startled by the seeming contradiction in her remark.

"Of course," she sniffed, contemptuous at his male, not to say, his rabbinic, lack of understanding. "She's nervous, poor girl. She's all tensed up all the time."

"What's she nervous about?" asked Miriam.

"If you were married to a man holding her husband's position, you'd be nervous, too."

"Why, what's he do?"

"He's an important official with the government," she said primly.

"Everybody in the government here seems to be an important official," the rabbi teased.

"You mean she's afraid he'll make some mistake on an important matter?" asked Miriam.

"I mean when he leaves the house in the morning, she doesn't know when he'll come back or even *if* he'll come back."

"His work is dangerous?" asked the rabbi.

She detected incredulity in his voice. "You think not, Rabbi?" The title was pure irony; normally, she called him David. "No doubt you heard about the bombing that took place a little while ago where an old man, an automobile dealer, was killed. Well, that happened practically next door to her."

The rabbi smiled. "The night we came there was a bombing in the next street and someone was killed then, too. Are you suggesting—"

"But he was an important person, a professor at the university."

"So?"

"So he was a natural target for the terrorists," said Gittel. "But this automobile dealer, he was a nobody. I am sure it was Avner they were really after. *Him* they would want to kill. It's just that they made a mistake."

"That's a little far-fetched, Gittel," said the rabbi. "I can see where they might want to blow up a new apartment building and kill a harmless old man in the process. But I find it hard to believe that they would plant a bomb to kill a specific person and then make a mistake and leave it at the wrong address."

"That's how much you know about Arabs, especially the terrorists," sniffed Gittel. "Don't tell me they were after this automobile dealer."

"All right, I won't," said the rabbi good-naturedly.

She looked at him suspiciously and turned to Miriam.

"Sarah was lying there in bed, in a deep sleep, mind you, when the bomb went off. Do you mean to tell me that wouldn't affect a woman who hasn't been in good health for the last ten years at least?"

"You mean that's why she's going to the hospital?" asked Miriam. "That's what the doctor said?"

"The doctor! Not that I have anything against Dr. Ben Ami. But he is only a man. He is a man of sympathy and understanding. You know that, Miriam. But he can know only what a man can know. The mind of a woman, it takes a woman to know. I told Avner to his face, 'If you want your wife to get well,' I told him, 'you'll get another job.' And he couldn't think of anything to answer."

The phone rang, and Miriam went to it. It was Dan Stedman calling to invite them to have dinner with him at the King David that evening.

"Oh, we'd like to, but my Aunt Gittel is up from Tel Aviv and—"

"Bring her along."

"Just a minute." She cupped the receiver. "It's Dan Stedman, a friend of ours. He wants us to come to the King David for dinner tonight."

"So go. I can stay home and take care of Jonathan."

"No, he asked me to bring you along."

"Well, I don't know. I—"

"He's a nice fellow—and unmarried," said the rabbi.

Gittel gave him a look of annoyance and indignation. "What do you say, Gittel? Please come."

"All right, what can I lose?"

Miriam spoke into the instrument. "It's all right. We can all make it. Is it some special occasion?"

"Not really, but I'll be returning to the States soon and—"

"Oh, really? Something unexpected came up?"

"I'll tell you all about it when I see you."

42

THE assistant dean of foreign students placed the fingertips of one hand very carefully against the fingertips of the other and nodded slowly as Stedman talked. Not for one minute did he believe what the other was saying, that his son was homesick and wanted to return to America. He had had experience with the parents of American students who came to see him because they were withdrawing their sons or daughters from the university. Usually, it was because the youngster had got involved and wanted to marry someone whom they considered completely unsuitable. The last time, it had been an ardent lifelong Zionist, indignant because his daughter had decided to remain in the country and join a kibbutz.

"Who can tell what is educative, Mr. Stedman," he said soothingly. "Students come here from all over the world, but mostly from America to study at our university. Is it because we have better teachers? Not any better than America or the other advanced countries have. So what benefit do they derive by coming to school here? Not what they get in the classrooms, but what is available outside the classrooms, the life here, the people."

As soon as he had been assured by Mike Donahue that matters had been arranged, Dan Stedman had returned to Jerusalem to arrange for Roy's return to the States, only to find a note from him saying he had gone off for a few days to visit with friends and that he would call when he got back. Anxious to expedite matters, Dan had gone to the university to see what arrangements had to be made.

"I understand," said Dan, "but I was primarily interested in what could be done about credits and that sort of thing."

The dean smiled and spread his hands. "Obviously, we cannot give credit for courses in which your son has not taken the examinations, but we are very flexible in the matter of examinations. The student can take them at various times of the year. We have to have this kind of arrangement of course, because so many are called up for military duty throughout the year, faculty as well as students."

"But he can take nothing back with him to apply toward his degree at Rutgers?"

The dean shook his head slowly.

"Then he's wasted a year, because the educative value outside the classroom, getting to know the people and the life here, I don't think he got that either. He had almost no friends—"

"I'm sorry to hear that, Mr. Stedman. You sound disappointed, and I suppose that reflects your son's feelings. It is not easy for a student from an American college. I think our courses are a little harder, or at least they demand more work, but it's not that. Even the difficulty with the language is not the principle cause of the disappointment for some of our American students. It's that the tone is so different from what they're used to.

"We want them to come here, partly because they bring dollars of which we are in desperate need. But also, we hope that some of them will like what they find here and remain on or come back to settle. Because we need people as well as dollars. But we cannot change the university whose primary purpose is to serve our own students, merely to please the foreign student. Our students are older than yours by an average of three years—the time they spent in the Army. And at that time of life, three years is a considerable difference. But there is also the difference resulting from the maturing experience of the Army. For them college is not a relaxation, a vacation before going on with the serious work of making a living. It is the serious work. Most of them have jobs, and as soon as classes are over, they hurry off to them. We have no fraternities here, Mr. Stedman." He got up from his chair and came around to the front of the desk as if to remove a barrier between them.

"And yet, in a sense, everyone here belongs to a fraternity, but it is the fraternity of his Army squad. And this kind of fraternity is even more exclusive to the outsider than the most exclusive clubs in your colleges because their lives depend on it. They have no time and little inclination for friendships outside their circle. And it's no different with the women students. They are all of marriageable age, and it is more intelligent for them to date Israelis where there is a good chance of friendship resulting in marriage than some outsider who wants companionship while he is here and who will then leave the country at the end of his study. So all this makes it hard for the American student who comes here."

"It makes it damn close to impossible," said Dan.

"Not altogether, Mr. Stedman. There are some who come here properly motivated. They come from strong religious or Zionist backgrounds, and just being here is enough for them, at least at first. They persevere. They acquire a good command of the language. And they win out and integrate with the life of the country. And many of them elect to stay on."

"Well, Roy's background is neither strongly religious nor strongly Zionist," said Stedman. "My own sympathies are strongly with Israel, but I belong to no Zionist clubs or organizations."

The dean nodded. "Which brings us back to where we started. How do we know what is educative? Perhaps the experience your son had in living for several months among serious, dedicated young people, even if he couldn't participate, will have a greater influence on his future than if he had found here a duplicate of what he had back in America. Right now, he might feel only disappointment, but there may be also a feeling of grudging admiration. And when he is a little older and amusement and entertainment are not so important in his life, he may think back to this as an example worth following."

Stedman nodded. He even managed a smile. "It sounds convincing when you say it, Doctor. I wonder how it will sound when I tell it to the boy's mother."

43

EVERY time Abdul shifted gears the car growled in protest and Roy dozing on the seat beside him stirred uneasily, shifted his position, and dozed off again. When they had first started out, he had pointed out that there must be something wrong with the transmission or the clutch.

"It's been this way for a couple of years," said Abdul. "Nothing to worry about."

The shock absorbers were not in good condition either, and whenever the road was the least bit rough, they were bounced around unmercifully. But as Abdul remarked cheerfully, "It's better than walking."

"Would you like me to drive for a while?" asked Roy.

"No—maybe when I get tired. Why don't you take a nap? When we get to my uncle's house, we may be staying up late."

"Oh, I'm all right. You know there's a knock in the engine?"

"A knock? Oh, you mean that little tick you hear? It's nothing, believe me. Mahmoud is very good with automobiles, and he keeps this one tuned like a watch. Well, maybe not like a watch, but like a good serviceable alarm clock. It is perhaps not so quiet as the cars you are used to, nor is the ride so smooth; but it always starts, and it always goes."

"Yeah, well. . . . It's pretty good on gas. I'll say that for it. We've been driving for over an hour and the needle on the tank gauge hasn't moved."

Abdul chuckled. "The gauge doesn't work. The needle never moves."

"Then how do you know when you need gas?"

"Mahmoud knows. Every now and then he fills it. Never once has he run out. He assured me we had enough gas to get to my uncle's house."

"Just where is your uncle's place, Abdul?"

"North, up in the Galilee. Not far from the border," he added lightly.

"I mean, is it in some town or—"

"Up there, in that area, there are only a few small villages. I'm sure no place you've ever heard of."

"He lives in the village?"

"He has a house in the village, several houses, but he lives on his farm which is away from the village. It is to his farm that we are going."

"You know the road all right?"

"Oh!" Abdul shrugged his shoulders expressively.

"And you're sure I'll be welcome? I mean, he doesn't know I'm coming."

"You don't understand about Arab hospitality, Roy.

I am his nephew. That means more with us than it does with you. It means I am of his family—like a son. And you are my friend. His house is like mine, and if I invite you, it is just the same as if he invited you. Do you understand?"

"I think so." He lay back in his seat and stared up through the windshield at the bright stars in the inky sky. "And he will not mention that I am there? I mean—"

"I know what you mean, Roy. To whom would he mention it? To the police? Even if he thought they might be interested in you and that you were hiding from them, you would be perfectly safe. You are a guest, and a guest is sacred."

"Yeah, well that's nice to know. Maybe by the time we get back, my father will have straightened matters out at the embassy—"

"I am sure, it will all be straightened out." He glanced at his companion and saw that his eyes were shut. "Roy?" he said softly. The only answer he got was a drowsy murmur. Abdul smiled and focused his eyes on the road. Once or twice he glanced over, but Roy slept on.

He woke up suddenly as the car came to a bone-jolting stop. He was flung against the door and then back against the seat. "Wha-what's the matter? Are we there already?"

"We are in a ditch," said Abdul. "And we are out of gas."

"But—"

"It is no matter, Roy. We are practically there. As a matter of fact, we are on the edge of my uncle's estate —but the far edge. We will go the rest of the way on foot. It's just as well, because from here the road— road?—a couple of ruts in the ground—goes way off and then loops around. We will take a shortcut through the woods—"

"But the car—what do we do about the car?" Roy grumbled as he climbed out.

"I will have my uncle haul it in with a team of mules. It will be all right where it is for the present. Follow me." He plunged into a thicket of bamboo.

"You know the direction?"

"Oh, sure, but keep your voice down, Roy. Some of my uncle's people might be out and think we are trespassers."

"Yeah, well, maybe you could call to them," he said as he trudged along behind the shadowy figure of his friend. He was still not fully awake, and he found himself stumbling over the rocky and uneven ground.

Suddenly, from the side there came a shout of "Halt!"

Roy froze in his tracks, but Abdul began to run. "This way, Roy. Run. Run."

A shot rang out, and he saw his friend stagger and fall.

44

"I'D know you anywhere," said Dan when he was introduced to Gittel. "You look just like your niece."

"*Tcha!* The idea of comparing a fresh, handsome girl like Miriam to an old woman like me."

"On the contrary, I'm sure David is very happy to know what his wife will look like when she grows older."

He ushered them into the Grill and was gallantly solicitous about seating the older woman where he judged she would be most comfortable. "Sit here, Gittel, there's a little draft from the air conditioner on that side." While they waited for the waiter to take their orders, he directed most of his conversation to her. He pointed out people he knew among the diners. "That man that just came in, he's a tire manufacturer who's here to build a big new factory. I was talking to him the other day in the lobby." He waved as the man saw him and nodded. "That woman, the one near the post. She was president of Hadassah two, no, three years ago." He caught her eye and smiled. "Oh, you know who that is coming in now, don't you? That's the Finance Minister. I interviewed him last year. I wonder if he'll remember me."

Seemingly he did, for when he saw them, he stared for a moment and then came striding toward them.

"Gittel! It's been ages since I saw you. What are you doing in Jerusalem?"

"Hello, Boaz. How is Leah? And the girls? I'm here attending a convention." She introduced him to the others.

"And Uri, he's still in the Army?"

"Still in the Army."

"How do you know him, Gittel?" asked Miriam when he left.

"Boaz?" She shrugged as if to indicate that she was not impressed by his importance. "We were in the same unit in the Haganah." Nevertheless, she was obviously pleased that the opportunity had arisen and that the Finance Minister had remembered her and been so effusive in his greeting.

"I was going to introduce you," said Stedman with a chuckle, "and he didn't even remember me."

"Boaz? He has a lot on his mind these days."

"I suppose. Was it your son he asked after? He's in the Army? He is a professional and planning to make a career of it?"

"Who knows about young people? They can change their minds from one week to the next. The last time I saw him, weeks ago, he was saying that he thought he might leave. He's got himself tied up with a girl, and I suppose she has been making plans for him."

"When are we going to meet him?" asked Miriam.

"A first cousin and we've been here almost three months—"

"Well, he doesn't get off every week. And I suspect that there have been some leaves he has had that I didn't know about. He is seeing this girl. She lives here in Jerusalem, and he wrote me that although he is getting this next week off, he will not be coming to Tel Aviv, but will come here instead. What do you think of that? His own mother he passes up to see a girl."

"But if he's coming here," said Miriam, "why don't you write him to drop in on us, if only for an hour or two? Tell him to bring the girl along. And you could come up from Tel Aviv for the Sabbath. Tell him to come for dinner—with the girl. And Dan, can you come?"

"I don't think so, Miriam. There's a good chance Roy and I will be gone by then, and if not, we'll be getting ready to leave."

"Oh, yes," she said, "you were going to tell us all about it."

"There isn't much to tell. My friend at the embassy arranged it for Roy, and I thought under the circumstances it would be a good idea if I went along with him. I've got all the material I need, and the rest of the work—the editing and the writing—I can do back in the States just as well."

The menus were distributed, and the waiter, a young man prematurely bald, was helpful to the point of being avuncular. "The pâté, I guarantee you've never tasted liver like this, madam." They took his advice, and it *was* good. "Trust me, choose the steak." And when Dan chose fish instead, the waiter shrugged his shoulders as if to say that there were always people who had no faith.

When he was not fetching for them, he hovered over them, filling their wineglasses, offering Dan a light when he put a cigarette in his mouth, picking up Gittel's napkin when it slid off her lap. The talk flowed pleasantly, Gittel telling how it was in the old days and

Dan chiming in with his memories of his earlier visits
to the country.

Just after the waiter had served the coffee, the headwaiter approached their table. "Mr. Stedman? There's
a phone call for you. This way."

"That could be Roy. Excuse me."

"He's a very nice man," said Gittel at his retreating
figure.

He was not gone long, and when he rejoined them,
they could see that he was upset.

"Was it Roy?" asked Miriam.

"No, it wasn't. Look, you'll have to excuse me.
I have to leave for Tel Aviv immediately, but please
don't go. Please stay and finish your dinner." He
looked from one to the other. He saw their bewilder-
ment and their concern.

"They caught Roy trying to cross the border," he
blurted out and hurried out of the room.

45

"YOUR pajamas fit you better than your suit,"
said Dan Stedman sourly. And indeed they did because
unlike his seersucker, the pajamas were unwrinkled.

Donahue smiled. "Yeah, they're some new kind of
drip dry. You hang them on a clothes hanger after
washing and they come out like you just took them out
of the package from the store. My daughter gave them
to me last time I was in the States. Drink?"

Stedman shook his head. He was silent, sitting
hunched forward in his chair, his hands folded, his
forearms resting on his thighs, staring down at the floor.
"Sorry I got you out of bed," he said awkwardly.

"I wasn't asleep, just reading. Why didn't you tell me you were coming down when I spoke to you?"

"I wasn't planning to. I didn't think I could. I was giving this dinner party in the Grill. Nice people—I didn't see how I could run out on them. Nice evening, good dinner, interesting conversation—when I came back to the table, that's what got me, the conversation. How was I going to go on talking pleasantly with Roy . . . there? So I excused myself and got a cab. I didn't think to call ahead."

"It's all right. But you know I can't do anything. The case is different now."

Stedman looked up. "Why is it different?" He knew, of course, but he wanted to talk about it.

"C'mon, Dan. Before, they had nothing on him. He was friendly with an Arab. So what? Lots of American students, and Israelis too, are. He was in the vicinity of the bombing—at the site even—but he had a plausible excuse. No overt action, no official action, had been taken by the police."

"They pulled his passport, didn't they?"

"No, they didn't. You know they did, and I know they did, and they know they did, but officially they had just mislaid it and hadn't got around to sending it back to him."

"Sure."

"But now they caught him trying to cross the border," Donahue hurried on. "That's a crime at any time in any country. But in a country at war, it can be a serious crime. And if it means crossing into enemy territory, it can be damn serious."

"But he didn't know he was crossing the border," cried Stedman.

"I told you he said he didn't know," Donahue corrected. "His story was that this Abdul had invited him to visit an uncle—some big shindig that would last a few days. So they drove north, presumably to Abdul's uncle's place. And when they were almost there, they abandoned the car to take a shortcut. And

Roy isn't too clear as to just why they abandoned the car—it either conked out or Abdul ran it into a ditch. The whole story is a little weak, Dan—you got to admit. I mean, this kid of yours has the normal amount of smarts. He has to have to be in the university at all. But at this point, leaving the car and taking a shortcut through the woods—dammit, driving all that time, he must've known that they were damn close to the border."

"Why would he have to know? Chances are he's never been up that way before. And if the other was driving, he could have dozed off."

"All right, but he found out damn quick when suddenly there were Israeli soldiers all over the place." He cocked his head to one side and considered. "That's a little unusual, their being in force right at that point."

"You think it was a trap?"

"Could be. It wouldn't surprise me. Anyway, your boy showed some sense for the first time: He stopped and put his hands up. The Arab tried to make a run for it, and they shot him."

"They killed him?"

"No, just through the leg. I guess they wanted him for questioning."

"And of course he'll implicate Roy," said Stedman bitterly.

"Not necessarily. Why should he? It wouldn't make it any easier for him. And if he did, they'd probably discount it. The whole affair is a little funny. It has a Shin Bet flavor. I get the impression that they're not really concerned about the border crossing. That's a matter for the border guard, I should think, which comes under the Police Ministry, but they don't seem to be handling it. The case seems to be directed from Jerusalem. That would suggest to me that they're really interested in the possible connection with the bombings they've had up there. And if they tied your boy in with the bombings, it would be a murder charge. I'm sorry,

Dan, but there's no sense in trying to minimize the situation."

"No, no sense at all," said Stedman dully.

"The thing to do would be to get a lawyer."

"That's the last thing to do. You know what it would mean to Roy even if a lawyer managed to get him off? An Arab—he's a hero among his own people, and even the Israelis have some understanding of his reasons. But an American and a Jew! Even if he got off scot-free, what kind of life would he have? I can't have him stand trial. There must be something you can do."

"Be reasonable, Dan. Now a lawyer—"

Stedman nodded quietly. "If worse comes to worst, of course I'll get a lawyer. But first—well, that's why I'm coming to you."

Donahue got up and poured himself a drink. "There's no way I could make a deal if it's murder. The ambassador himself couldn't. You can't go to the government of a sovereign state and say that this man killed one of your nationals but I want you to let him off."

"No, I suppose not."

"Well, then—"

"Look, can you find out who's in charge in Jerusalem?"

"I guess I could," Donahue said. "What good would that do?"

"I don't know. I could try to see him, maybe convince him. What else can I do?"

"I'll see what I can do."

Stedman rose and headed for the door.

"Dan."

Stedman stopped.

"Are you sure he didn't do it?"

Stedman hesitated. "I don't know. I don't want to think of it." He turned to go and then stopped. "I suppose I don't really know my son."

46

ALTHOUGH the monthly *Haolam* ran articles on science and politics, and regular sections on literature, the arts and fashion trends, it was essentially a picture magazine. It used photographs not only to illustrate its articles, and because they were newsworthy, but also because they were simply dramatic or arresting or bizarre camera shots. So although the excitement engendered by the explosion on Mazel Tov Street had died down, the front cover of *Haolam* featured a picture of Memavet lying dead on his living-room floor.

They ran it not to revive interest in the affair; in fact, there was no comment other than a small note of identification and explanation in a box on the masthead page. They ran it because the angle from which the photograph had been taken made a strikingly dramatic shot. The photo showed Memavet lying on his left side, his knees drawn up in the fetal position. The outstretched right arm, flung across the body, clutched a brandy bottle like an Indian club. The eyes were open and staring and from the right temple ran a trickle of blood. What made the picture so unusual was that it had been focused along the line of the bottle, and the whole figure had been fantastically foreshortened as a result. At the bottom of the picture, dead center, was the iridescent arc of the heel of the bottle. Lying along the swelling shoulder of the bottle and pointing directly at the viewer was the tip of the forefinger. And above that, the knuckles of the hand curving around the neck of the bottle, and—the foreshortening having all but eliminated the arm—in the very center of the picture, the upturned face of the dead man, eyes open and staring.

"Yeah, it's quite a picture," Adoumi admitted. "But there's something about it that bothers me."

"I know," Ish-Kosher agreed. "Me too. No matter how you hold it—away from you or one side or the other—the finger seems to be pointing right at you and his eyes seem to be looking right at you, too. I asked the boys at the photo lab about it and they said it was because the camera was focused right on the tip of his finger. That's what gives that effect."

"I wonder who took it."

"They don't say," said Ish-Kosher. "It could have been almost anybody—maybe even a tourist. They have their cameras with them all the time. Before we could get the place cordoned off after the explosion, there must have been fifty or a hundred people there on Mazel Tov Street, and half of them had cameras and were snapping away. A fellow gets an unusual shot like this and he might send it to *Haolam*. They'd pay pretty good for something like this, I'd say. Or it could even have been a press photographer for one of the dailies."

"I understand all that, but why did they decide to run it now? Do you suppose they've heard something?"

Ish-Kosher shook his head decisively. "Impossible. The arrest was made only a few days ago, and the copy for this issue of *Haolam* must have gone to the printer at least a couple of weeks ago."

"You mean they couldn't change the cover at the last minute?"

"It's possible, I suppose," Ish-Kosher said cautiously. "I don't know enough about the printing business or the magazine business, but what would they gain?"

"Maybe they figure we're about to break the case, and it will give them a journalistic scoop. I don't like to think that there might be a leak in our outfit, Chaim."

"Believe me, Avner, the only ones in my organization that know about this case, I can trust absolutely. You have nothing to fear from that quarter. I'm sure it's just a coincidence."

"It'd better be."

Stedman saw the picture in the magazine rack in the hotel lobby. He bought a copy of the magazine and took it up to his room. He, too, wondered why it should appear at just this time. Was it part of a subtle campaign to revive interest in the matter? Was it intended to arouse public indignation? Would articles on the subject of the explosion begin appearing in the daily press? He thought of going down to the editorial offices of the magazine and making inquiries. Then it occurred to him that his very inquiry might arouse curiosity and start an investigation where none was planned. But if it should be part of a campaign, and he did nothing to scotch it, then. . . .

He decided that he needed someone to talk to; that he was going around in circles; that he needed a normal, healthy mind to look at the situation calmly and objectively.

47

GITTEL drove up Friday early enough to help Miriam prepare dinner.

"Really, Gittel, it was kind of you, but I can manage all right by myself."

"Look, Miriam, with me you don't have to stand on ceremony. I don't want to interfere. With my experience with hundreds and hundreds of families where there was a daughter-in-law and a mother-in-law living in the same apartment, no one had to tell me that there is no kitchen big enough for two women. My idea was to just sit quietly and keep you company." But she made suggestions. "An onion in the soup, Miriam. Always cook an onion in the soup. Uri says it makes the soup taste like homemade." To Miriam's objection that David did not like onions, she answered, "But an onion—that's the whole beauty of the soup. And we don't leave it in. We just cook with it. It gives to the soup a perfume." And later, at the dinner table, when the rabbi praised the soup, she managed to catch Miriam's eye and nod an I-told-you-so at her.

"No, Miriam, the fish you don't grind it. You chop it. In America I know women grind the fish like they grind the liver because it's easier that way. I understand that in America they even have a grinder that works by electricity, so all you do is drop it in and press a button. But when you grind, it comes out like a paste and cooks hard." She rummaged around in the cabinets and found the chopper and a large wooden bowl which she set on her lap, and in spite of her initial protestations, she was soon chopping away rhythmically "to show how you're supposed to do it." While she chopped, she talked—of the owner of their apartment, whom she had visited only last week and who was getting along nicely with her sister; of the new supervisor in her department, whom she was not sure she was going to like; of Sarah Adoumi, whom she had stopped off to visit for a few minutes at Hadassah before coming and about whose treatment she had grave doubts—unconsciously accelerating the rhythm of her chopping when she mentioned anything that annoyed her.

But most of all, she talked of her son, Uri, and then she chopped at a furious pace to express a kind of bewildered disappointment in him. "He is tall like his father, and handsome. That is not just my opinion as a mother. You will see for yourself when he comes. And popular. The girls are all crazy over him. He could have his pick. And he gets involved with a girl from a poor family, Tunisians or Moroccans or something like that, one or the other. *They* claim there is a difference, but I could never see it. And she's dark as an Arab, too. And suddenly, he becomes religious because her family is very observant. That kind always are. She even has an exemption from serving in the Army because she's religious. Uri claims she wanted to go, but her father wouldn't let her. Maybe. If it's true, then she shows more respect for her parents than he does for his. He even prays every morning, with phylacteries. How could it happen? He was raised in an enlightened home."

"My David prays every morning."

"Even now? I thought you said—"

"He is thinking of changing his profession, not his religion," said Miriam.

"Well, a rabbi has to; it's his business. And now he's got into the habit, I suppose." It was plain that she did not regard her nephew's example as conclusive proof of the validity of the practice. "And now he talks of going into a religious kibbutz when he gets out of the Army. You know what that means? He'll have a child every year and he'll be a farmer all his life."

"Don't you approve of kibbutz life, Gittel?"

"Of course. It is one of our great sociological contributions. In the old days it was necessary to the development of the country. But things are different now." When Miriam did not seem to understand, she said, "I mean, now that the country is established, it is no longer necessary. He could be a doctor or an engineer or a scientist. He has a fine mind." And when Miriam still did not seem to understand, she said impatiently, "Is it so strange that a mother should want for her son, not an easier life, but a chance to realize his fullest potential?"

It seemed to bother Gittel, so Miriam did not pursue the subject but retreated to neutral ground. "Do you think he'll bring his girl?"

"I spoke to him on the phone yesterday. He said not. Her father objected; he did not think it proper. That will give you some idea of the kind of upbringing she's had. They are, after all, Orientals."

"Aren't you anxious to see her?"

"This pleasure I can wait on."

In the early evening the rabbi went to the synagogue, and when he came home after the service, the candles were already lit and the table set with the two braided Sabbath loaves and the wine decanter and glasses beside the rabbi's plate at the head of the table. The women were puttering in the kitchen with last-minute preparations for the meal, and the rabbi paced up and down the living-room floor humming a Chassidic melody as they waited for Uri.

"Will he be in uniform?" Jonathan asked Gittel.

"What else?"

"And will he have his gun with him?"

"He is an officer and so does not carry a gun."

"Oh." Jonathan was so obviously disappointed that she hastily added, "He carries a revolver strapped to his waist. He will probably be wearing it."

The minutes stretched out to a quarter of an hour and then half an hour, and Miriam noted that her husband glanced at his watch occasionally as he paced the floor. She was on the point of asking Gittel if perhaps they ought not begin, when they heard the outer door open and close. Then their doorbell rang, and Jonathan ran to open it, and there stood Uri.

He was all his mother had said he was. He was tall and bronzed and carried himself with assurance. With Jonathan he made an instant hit—the uniform, the boots, the beret, and, above all, the gun in a holster on his hip. With the rabbi he shook hands when he was introduced, but Miriam he kissed heartily on the lips. "A pretty girl you kiss like a pretty girl," he explained. "You do not mind, David?" With his mother he acted as though he had last seen her only an hour ago. Out of deference to Miriam, he spoke in English, a heavily accented English where the words seemed to be formed deep in the throat.

"So did you have a good time at the conference last week?" he greeted his mother.

"To a conference you don't go for good times," she said reprovingly.

They had not kissed or embraced; only the proprietary way in which she had picked some lint off his jacket and then smoothed a wrinkle on the shoulder indicated their relationship.

"What then? You go to learn something?" Then teasingly, "What can they teach you?" To Miriam he explained, "She sees all her old cronies—from Jerusalem, from Haifa, even from Tel Aviv. Some of them live right in the city with her, and she doesn't get to see them except at these conferences."

Gittel's manner with him was matter-of-fact, and the pride she had displayed when talking of him to Miriam she now carefully concealed. Her tone, when she spoke to him, was mildly ironic, but when she referred to his girl, it became a studied and bitter sarcasm. On his part, his answers were tolerant and good-natured; but sometimes he was stung to momentary anger, and he made a biting response, usually in Hebrew, as though his native language gave him greater scope for emotional expression or perhaps to avoid offending his hostess.

"Her father didn't let her come because he thought maybe it wasn't kosher here?" Gittel asked.

"Look, I told you that over the phone because I didn't want to argue with you. But it was *my* idea for her not to come tonight."

"Oh, you didn't want her to meet me? You are maybe ashamed of your mother?"

"Don't worry. You'll meet her. And Miriam and David will meet her, I hope. But not together, at least not the first time. Because you'd say something and then we'd fight. And I don't want to spoil the Sabbath for David and Miriam. She wanted to come, but I persuaded her not to."

"Shall we go to the table?" the rabbi suggested mildly.

They stood behind their chairs while he intoned the kiddush for which Uri had replaced his beret with a black silk yarmulke. Gittel said nothing, but the twist of her lip showed her disapproval. When they sat down to eat, she said, "That bit of silk is holier than your Army beret? It covers more maybe?"

He smiled good-naturedly. "To get out of uniform, even just a little bit, makes you feel that you're really on leave."

"This is a reasoning I'm sure your girl understands better than I do. You saw her today, I suppose."

"Yeah, I saw Esther," he said defiantly in Hebrew. "We disengoffed in the park for a while, and then I hitched a ride here. What of it?"

The rabbi pricked up his ears. "Disengoffed? What is it, to disengoff?"

Uri laughed. "That's Hebrew they don't teach you in the yeshiva, David. It's Army slang. In Tel Aviv there's this big, wide street, full of cafés, the Disengoff. The boys go there and just stroll with their girls. So to disengoff is just to walk along with your girl."

"With a mother, you understand, David, you don't disengoff," said Gittel. Then to her son, "I'm surprised her father didn't insist you go to *shul* with him, to the Wall probably."

"He asked me, and if I weren't coming here, I would have gone. He doesn't go to the Wall. He goes to a little *shul* in the Quarter, and I like to go there."

"He has preferences in *shuls,* my son. He's getting to be a regular rabbi. Every day he puts on phylacteries and prays—"

"So what? You want to remember something, you put a string around your finger. So what's wrong if I tie a strap around my arm and another around my head—"

"To remind you of what?" his mother demanded.

He shrugged his shoulders. "I don't know. Maybe that when I am alone on patrol, I may not be alone. There's a chance of catching a sniper's bullet or stepping on a mine. It's not pleasant to think that it is just a matter of luck, that if you hadn't taken one extra step, it wouldn't have happened. It's better to think that there is a great design of which I am a part, yes, and even of which my being shot is a part. Look, all this business here, the candles, the wine, the challahs, the whole idea of the Sabbath—it's beautiful. Can something be beautiful and have no meaning? You yourself light the candles at home."

"The Sabbath is not really religion," said his mother stoutly. "It's a major sociological contribution that we have made."

"Aren't all religious practices sociological contributions?" said the rabbi mildly.

Gittel canted her head to one side and considered. "Your husband has a curious way of looking at things, Miriam," she said. Then to the rabbi: "You may be right, but even a major sociological innovation can in time become a mere superstition. Take my son—"

"Oh, come on, Gittel," Uri protested, "there must be other subjects of conversation besides me. Did you get to see Sarah?"

"I saw her, and I saw Avner, too. He was there at the hospital when I came in. And I told him to his face, 'Avner Adoumi,' I said, 'if you want your wife—'"

"Yes, I know," Uri interrupted. "He should give up his job."

"You still didn't explain why it's so dangerous," said the rabbi.

"The exact nature of his work, I don't know," Gittel said, "only that he's a high government official—"

"Come on, Gittel, you know very well he's in the Shin Bet," said her son.

"I know nothing of the sort. Neither he nor Sarah ever told me, and I wouldn't think of asking. And I should think you, in the Army, would know better than to mention it."

"Why? You think David and Miriam are going to spread it around? Maybe I ought to go out and see her while I'm in the city."

"When? Tomorrow? You can't. Your friends, the religious, won't let you because you would have to ride. No visitors at Hadassah on the Sabbath. Even Avner can't go see his own wife. By them it's a terrible crime. So they impose rules on the rest of us. They're not even true Israelis; they don't even talk the language—"

"And the bunch of Anglo-Saxons and Yekkies that run Hadassah and your hospital, too, you call them real Israelis? As for the language, they don't even want to learn it. Some of them have been here thirty years or more and still can't read a Hebrew newspaper or understand a Hebrew news broadcast."

"So there is a 'real Israeli' question here?" said the rabbi pleasantly. "I suppose that's a sign that the state is fully established. During the formation and founding of a state there's usually no time for such arguments."

"You don't understand, David," said Uri earnestly. "You haven't been here long enough. It's a matter of principle—"

"No, Uri, it's a matter of logic," said the rabbi firmly. "Anyone who is a citizen of Israel is automatically a real Israeli. Some are perhaps more typical than others. I suppose that a Pekinese is a less typical dog than a foxhound, but he is still a real dog. What else could he be? Your test of language would exclude a lot of people who came here and died to establish the country. Your own father, I understand, did not speak Hebrew."

"My husband was a Yiddishist," said Gittel stiffly. "He did not speak the language out of principle."

"So the religious groups, some of them at least, don't speak it out of principle either," said the rabbi. "They consider it a holy language and hence not to be used for mundane things."

"No one really objects to their not speaking Hebrew or to their strange dress and outlandish costumes for that matter," said Gittel. "What we object to is that they are less than fifteen percent of the population and they try to impose their customs on the rest of us."

"Would you deny to a political group the right to use their intelligence to increase their influence and propagate their ideas?" the rabbi demanded. "And remember, with them, it's a matter of not just political principles. They may be mistaken, but they think they're carrying out divine commandments."

"Fanatics!" said Gittel. "That's what they are."

The rabbi tilted his head to one side and smiled. "Even fanatics have their uses. They form one end of the normal curve that comprises all of us. If they were a little nearer the center, then those on the other end would have been just that much farther away. If a couple of hundred years ago we had all been 'enlightened,' would we be a people today?"

Gittel pushed her plate aside, planted her elbows on the table, and leaned forward, the light of battle in her eyes. "David, you are a rabbi, but you don't know what you're talking about. It's not your fault," she added magnanimously, "you haven't lived here long enough to know what's going on. It's not only in the restrictions they impose on the rest of us on the Sabbath, but there are whole areas in which they have complete control. They control marriage; they control who is a Jew. They practically control our hotels and restaurants. And all on the basis of ancient regulations that have no bearing in a modern society. Because a man's name happens to be Cohen, they refuse him permission to marry a divorced woman on the grounds that he is of the family of Cohanim or priests, and according to Leviticus or Deuteronomy or someplace, the priest must not marry a divorcée. A woman suffers all kinds of cruelty and abuse from her husband, and she cannot get a divorce because only the husband may grant a divorce."

"The husband can be ordered by the rabbinical court to grant a divorce," said Uri, "and they can even put him in jail if he refuses."

"And what if he is already in jail?" his mother demanded. "And how about the children of Jewish fathers and non-Jewish mothers who have been declared by the courts to be non-Jews—"

"But if she converted—"

"But they decide if it's a proper conversion," she ended triumphantly.

The rabbi leaned back in his chair. "And what law, anywhere, has ever affected everyone exactly the same? There are always exceptional cases which are unfair to the individual. But society tolerates them because a perfect law is impossible and life without law is unthinkable. If there are too many such exceptional cases —that is, if the cases stop being exceptional and become the rule—then either changes are made in the law, or it is bent a little, reinterpreted, to accommodate to the new situation. And that's what's happened here in the matter of mixed marriages. But if there were not a group of zealots dedicated to the preservation of the strict interpretation of the law on this matter of who is a Jew and who isn't, say, how long do you suppose Israel would remain a Jewish state? How soon before it became completely cosmopolitan? And then what justification would there be for having it a separate state?"

Jonathan yawned prodigiously, instantly drawing all attention to him.

"The poor child," said Gittel, "our talk has tired him."

"It's past his bedtime," said Miriam. "Come, Jonathan, kiss Daddy and Aunt Gittel and Uri and say good night."

Jonathan dutifully made the rounds, ending in front of Uri. "Are you going away tonight?" he asked wistfully.

"Uri will sleep here tonight," said Miriam, "and if

you go to sleep right away, you can be up bright and early and go to *shul* with him."

Much later, when the adults finally decided to retire for the night, Gittel announced that she would sleep on the sofa so that Uri could have the bed in Jonathan's room. He protested, but Gittel insisted that she preferred the sofa. To Miriam, she explained, "I'd like him to have a comfortable bed for one night at least. Besides, Jonathan will like seeing him in the room with him when he wakes up."

As she helped Miriam make up the sofa, she said, "Your friend, this Stedman, has he gone back to America yet?"

"No, I'm sure he hasn't. I'm sure he'd call us to say good-bye before he left."

"His son, he's in real trouble?"

"I don't know," said Miriam. "We've been worrying about it. We haven't heard a word from Dan since that night at the King David. He's probably in Tel Aviv seeing what he can do at the embassy."

"Too bad, he is a nice man."

"Maybe he'll drop by tomorrow for kiddush. He usually does."

"So maybe I'll see him. Maybe I can help. I know lots of people."

48

IT was no accident that Marty Drexler and Bert Raymond stopped in at the Deutch house Saturday morning; they knew the rabbi would be at the temple, and it was the *rebbitzin* they wanted to see.

She came to the door in response to their ring. "Oh,

Mr. Raymond—and Mr. Drexler. The rabbi is in the temple."

"Oh. Yes, I guess he would be, wouldn't he?" Raymond sounded disappointed, but he did not turn away.

There was an awkward pause, and then to fill it, Mrs. Deutch said, "Won't you come in? Was it something urgent?" She stood aside for them. "I'm just having a second cup of coffee. Would you care to join me?"

"That would be very nice, Mrs. Deutch," said Marty.

She motioned them to the table and brought cups for them. They sat and chatted as they sipped their coffee. They both refused a second cup. Marty held up his hands to emphasize his refusal and said, "It's good coffee, but one's enough for me. What we wanted to see the rabbi about is if he'd come to any decision on a matter we talked to him last week. Did he tell you about it?"

"Yes, he mentioned it," she said cautiously.

"I guess you're concerned as much as he is. How do you feel about staying on here, Mrs. Deutch?" asked Raymond.

"The decision rests with Hugo." She removed the cups. "I'm sure you understand that, Mr. Raymond."

"Sure," said Marty. "I make the decisions in my house, but my wife tells me what to decide. I got an idea it's the same in most households. Now I got an idea that the rabbi listens and sets store by what you got to say."

"Well, of course—"

"I mean, that if you don't like the idea, if you think the rabbi is too old to undertake a new job or you got it in your head to retire to Florida, then we're barking up the wrong tree, and the sooner we know it, the quicker we can start making some alternate plans."

"As far as I'm concerned, I like it here. And I know Hugo does. Whether he's too old is up to you and your board to decide. I know he doesn't think so. And I

don't think so. As for retiring to Florida, I'm sure it's
the farthest thing from his mind."

"Well, if we've got you in our corner—"

"But I can tell you that what concerns him most,"
she went on, "is whether there is really a job here."

"I know what you mean," said Raymond earnestly,
"and of course, I explained to Rabbi Deutch that we
were approaching him because we had reason to believe
that there is a job here."

"Look, Mrs. Deutch," said Marty Drexler impulsively. "Let me lay it on the line. When Rabbi Small
took a leave of absence, and I mean took it, because
Lord knows it wasn't offered, as far as I was concerned,
the job was available right then and there. If it had
been in my office, I would have had a replacement before the guy had cleared his whiskey bottle out of the
desk drawer. And I don't think I'm tough; I'm just
fair. I don't mind giving the other guy what's coming
to him so long as I get what's coming to me. But a
lot of guys on the board, they took the view that it
was different with rabbis. So all right we agree to hire
somebody temporary, namely, your good husband, while
Small takes off for three months or so. But in all that
time, we haven't heard a word from him. Not one word.
Not so much as a line saying, 'Be seeing you soon.'
Let alone any letter asking for what's happening here.
So now a lot more guys have come around to my way
of thinking—that there is a job here, and that we can
take a hint that's like a knock on the head with a
hammer as good as the next guy."

"Have you written him?"

"No, we haven't, and if somebody suggested it in
the board, I'd get up on my hind legs and holler loud
and clear, because I don't think it's dignified for us to
write him and beg him to tell us what his plans are."

"And on top of that, Mrs. Deutch," Raymond added,
"a couple of our members were in Israel and spent a
day with Rabbi Small, and they got the impression—I

want to be fair—that he wasn't coming back, and might even leave the rabbinate altogether."

"Well, I'll admit that we thought it strange that Rabbi Small hadn't written to us," said Mrs. Deutch.

"That's good enough for me!" exclaimed Marty. "As far as I'm concerned, Rabbi Small is definitely out of the picture."

"Now, Marty . . ." Raymond temporized.

"Look, Bert, that's not just my attitude. I've sounded out the guys on the board, and a clear majority of them say that if they have to pick between Rabbi Small and Rabbi Deutch, they're going to pick Rabbi Deutch, even if it means a fight. He's our kind of man. He's what the temple needs. And I'll tell you something, Mrs. Deutch. Bert here feels the same way, but he's a lawyer, so he can't say anything without putting in a lot of wherefores and whereases. But I'll lay it on the line to you, Mrs. Deutch, the job is open, and your husband can have it if he wants it; but he can't sit back and let it drop on him. He's got to reach for it."

"I'm afraid I don't understand."

"Sure you do. He's got to show he wants it. There never was a job or a deal that was all clear sailing. There's always some little bind. That's life. You got to expect that. And in this case, I don't see it as any big problem. But Rabbi Deutch got to show that he wants the job. Otherwise, when Rabbi Small comes back, there are going to be people who will say that even though they prefer to have Rabbi Deutch, still and all, Rabbi Small is a young man with a family and all that kind of thing. And the first thing you know, we've got a fight on our hands, and things kind of sour, and some of the mud hits your husband."

Mrs. Deutch nodded. "Yes, I think I see your point."

"So is it a deal, Mrs. Deutch?"

"Well, as I said, the decision is up to Hugo, but I'll undertake to talk to him."

"That's all we ask," said Marty. He rose, as did

his colleague. "If I happened to run in to Rabbi Deutch, I wasn't planning to mention that I'd been here."

"Yes, I think that's good strategy," she said. "I won't mention your visit."

"That way he'll think it all comes from you."

She smiled. "Yes, I think that might be better."

When they were back in the car, Bert asked, "Do you think she can bring it off?"

"It's in the bag," Marty chuckled. "I'm no philosopher or psychologist or anything, but in my business I've had a lot of experience sizing up couples—you know, they come in together for a loan—and I can usually tell who wears the pants. Believe me, in that household, she does."

49

URI had left to go to his girl's house; Jonathan had already changed from his "good" clothes he wore to the synagogue into his regular shorts and jersey and was playing in the yard with Shaouli; and the Smalls and Gittel were dawdling over wine and cake and nuts at the kiddush table when Dan Stedman arrived. He had the copy of *Haolam* with him and thrust it into the rabbi's hand.

"You see, the propaganda machinery has already been set in motion. There will be more in the days to come, and when the trial comes, the verdict will already have been decided in the press." He looked haggard, and there were dark circles under his eyes.

The rabbi glanced at the cover picture and then flipped through the magazine. "This is a monthly," he said, "and must have gone to press some time ago. Besides, it's a picture magazine like our own *Life*.

They're apt to print any picture that's interesting. Did you notice that one on page thirty-two? That aerial photograph must have been taken right after the Six-Day War. Now this one of Memavet is interesting just as a piece of photography."

"I suppose so," Stedman agreed wearily. "I've been so involved that I'm probably not thinking straight. I imagine I've become paranoid on the subject. And there was no one I could discuss it with—"

"What happened?" asked Miriam.

"I—" He paused, uncertain, and looked from one woman to the other.

"If you don't want to talk in front of me," Gittel offered, "I can go into the kitchen."

"No, it's all right. In a few days at the most everyone will know." He giggled hysterically. "You might as well get my side of the story first." As he began to talk, his voice grew calmer, and soon he was speaking matter-of-factly and objectively as though he was recounting to a rewrite man. He kept interrupting the flow of his narrative with editorial comments—"I can see where the police might come to this conclusion" or "It was terribly stupid of Roy." The eyes of both women were fixed on him while the rabbi stared at the magazine cover on the table in front of him. Dan finished with, "I can't believe that Roy did this terrible thing," and then weakened it somewhat by adding, "I'm sure they don't have the evidence that would be needed in a regular trial."

Gittel's feelings as she listened were ambivalent: On the one hand, the government seemed to think that the young man was tied up with the terrorists and had actually perpetrated an outrage in which a man had lost his life, and on the other hand, she was sorry for this very nice man opposite her, so it was hard to imagine a son of his being guilty of a criminal act.

"Why don't you get a lawyer?" she asked. "At least, he'd be able to arrange for you to see your son."

Stedman shook his head and gave his reasons just

as he had explained them to Donahue. "Besides, according to my friend at the embassy, this is a Shin Bet affair and it's not being handled according to the regular routine."

"So what are you planning to do?"

"He managed to get the name of the man in charge, a certain Adoumi, and I've been trying to see him, but he's been dodging me."

"Avner Adoumi?" asked Gittel.

"That's right. You know him?"

"I know him well."

"If you could perhaps arrange an appointment," he pleaded.

Her face grew stern. "This is a terrible crime against the state of which your son is suspected, Mr. Stedman. The Shin Bet, I'm sure, does not act capriciously. But Avner Adoumi is a public servant, and you have a right to see him. He must not be permitted to dodge his responsibilities. I will take you to see him—right now, if you like. He's likely to be home."

Dan couldn't contain his gratitude. "But I can't ask you to put yourself out. If you'll just give me his address—"

"And what would you do if he slammed the door in your face? Believe me, Avner is quite capable of it. No, I'll take you there and I'll see to it that he at least listens to you."

"Do you mind if I come, too?" asked the rabbi.

"Not at all," said Stedman, now in high spirits. "The bigger our gang, the better. He'll see that he can't bottle this thing up."

The Renault started without trouble. Gittel drove, of course, and Stedman sat beside her while the rabbi sat in back. They were curiously silent during the short trip, each engrossed in his own thoughts. Gittel drove up to the house on Kol Tov Street and, with the two men trailing, marched up to the door and rang the bell.

Adoumi came to the door. "What are you doing here, Gittel?" he asked. "Who are these men?"

"This is my friend Daniel Stedman, and this is my nephew, David Small."

He smiled. "Oh, the rabbi from America, the one who doesn't keep the Sabbath. What do you want?"

"We want to talk to you," said Stedman. "*I* want to."

Adoumi hesitated for a moment and then shrugged. "Well, come in then," and stood aside for them to enter. He made a vague, apologetic gesture at the newspapers on the floor and the general disarray of the room. "My wife is in the hospital."

"So you have to make a regular pigpen here for your wife to clean up the first day she gets back?" stormed Gittel. "You're afraid she won't have enough work to keep her occupied?"

"I was planning to clean up the place before she got back," he said meekly.

"I'll clean up. You talk to Mr. Stedman." She began to pick up the newspapers. Adoumi motioned the two men to chairs.

They watched her for a moment, and then Stedman said, "My son, Roy—"

Adoumi cut him off sharply. "Your son tried to cross the border into enemy territory. That is a military matter when a country is at war and a matter for the military courts. I have nothing to do with it."

But Stedman was not to be intimidated. "My information is that the matter rests largely with you. And my informant is reliable," he said evenly. Before Adoumi could reply, he added, "This attempted flight across the border—did you arrange it?"

"What do you mean?" But Adoumi was not angry; he was grinning.

"I mean that it was too apt. The police questioned him about the bombing and then conveniently neglected to return his passport. If they had any real evidence to tie him in with it, they would have arrested him right then and there. But since they didn't, I do not rule out the possibility of your inducing him to do something foolish like running away."

"The innocent do not run away," said Adoumi.

"Unless they are frightened into it," said Stedman. "This Arab friend of his, was he one of your people? Was he by any chance an *agent provocateur*?"

"We do not shoot our own agents," Adoumi said. "You have been seeing too many spy movies, my friend."

"Anything a Hollywood director can dream up, an Intelligence man can also think of," said Stedman. "He could even have pretended to be shot."

"Oh, he was shot all right, believe me. But he's alive and can be questioned."

"And *has* been questioned, I think," said the rabbi.

Both men turned to him, and Gittel paused in her work.

"What do you mean?"

"If he were critically injured," the rabbi began diffidently, "I think you would have interrogated him immediately to make sure you got what you wanted from him before he died. And if he were not critically injured, I don't think you would wait until he were fully recovered. So I think you have questioned him, and obviously he has said nothing to implicate Roy, or you would not have referred earlier to his crime of crossing the border; you would have had something more serious to charge him with."

Gittel did not continue with her tidying up. She gave her nephew an approving nod and slid into a chair. Adoumi, too, looked at him with respect.

"That's a rabbinic pilpul," he said. "I didn't think you American rabbis went in for that kind of thing. I do not say you are wrong." He considered a moment. "No," he corrected, "but the interrogation of the Arab is still going on—"

"Sure," Stedman chimed in bitterly, "and before you finish with him, he will have guessed what you want him to say."

"We don't work that way here," said Adoumi angrily.

"Every police force works that way, or for that matter, anyone asking a series of questions, like a teacher, if only subconsciously," said the rabbi quietly. "I don't know what induced Roy to leave Jerusalem. It may be that his Arab friend persuaded him, and he in turn could have been frightened by your people. Or he could have had some reason of his own. But if it was a crime for Roy to leave the country, it surely is not a serious crime. You do not retain people here by force as in the Iron Curtain countries. You merely require them to fill out certain forms and follow certain procedures if they want to leave. So, from that angle, all you have against him is that he did not follow official procedure. Normally, that would involve what? A judicial reprimand? A small fine? A few days in jail? So it must be something else that you are holding him for. And that can only be the bombing of the apartment on the next street. Now if it can be proved that he could not have had any connection with that—"

"And how can you prove that?" Adoumi challenged him.

The rabbi tossed the copy of *Haolam* on the table in front of Adoumi. "That picture proves it. Have you seen it?"

Adoumi glanced at the magazine. "I have seen it," he said. "You say there's something here that proves your man could not have done it?" He picked up the magazine, and no one spoke as he studied the picture. He left the room and returned a moment later with a magnifying glass to look at it more closely. Both Gittel and Stedman had twisted in their seats and leaned over to look at the magazine that he left lying on the table, but as soon as he returned, they straightened up again. He went over every square inch of the photograph with the glass, his head moving up and down while they waited in silence. Finally, he put down both the glass and the magazine and looked his question at the rabbi.

"The doctor saw him to bed before he left," the rabbi began. "He assumed, and I suppose you people agreed, that he must have got out of bed to get a drink from the bottle on the mantelpiece."

"So?"

"So the way he's holding the bottle, he could not have poured a drink," said the rabbi.

Adoumi glanced at the picture again.

"If he tilted the bottle, it would go down his arm," the rabbi offered.

"So perhaps he was going to take the bottle back to bed with him, maybe to leave on the floor and to sip from every now and then." Adoumi was not impressed.

Stedman and Gittel looked at the rabbi, who shook his head slowly and said, "No, he wasn't going to do that either. The bottle was kept on the shelf. These apartments are the same, yours and his, and the shelf is like this one"—he broke off to walk over to it and measured himself against it—"about shoulder high for him. In the picture he's holding the bottle with the thumb down like an Indian club—"

"Indian club? Oh, yes, I know."

"Well, he couldn't take it down from the shelf that way, not without twisting his arm and shoulder in a most unnatural way. Even for you, who are much taller, it would be unnatural."

Adoumi got up and walked over to the shelf and went through the motion. "All right," he admitted. "So why—"

"Why did he hold it that way? To use as a weapon, of course. It's the only reason for holding the bottle like a club, because he was going to use it as a club. And that means that there was someone in the room that he was either going to attack or from whom he was going to defend himself," he added.

"But—"

"And it couldn't have been Roy, because when he got there, the doctor was just leaving and had locked the door behind him."

"He could have come back afterward and come in—"

"With the door locked?"

Stedman's face relaxed in a tentative smile, and Gittel, too, smiled and nodded approvingly.

"But look here"—Adoumi was exasperated—"if the door was locked and no one could come in, there was no point in his arming himself with the bottle. Which means he must have been holding it that way for some other reason."

"Unless it was against someone who was there before the door was locked."

"But that's absurd. There was only the doctor. Why would he arm himself against the doctor?"

"Why not ask the doctor?"

"He's out of the country." Adoumi gnawed on his upper lip in annoyance. Then his face cleared, and he smiled. He came back to his seat. "This is all very interesting, but entirely beside the point. You always find baffling little angles in every case of this kind. The point is that the man was killed by a bomb—"

"How do you know?" the rabbi interjected quickly. "That picture shows that he was struck on the head, on the temple. He could have been pushed and struck his head—on the corner of that same mantelpiece."

"Yes, and precisely the same thing could have happened from the force of the explosion." Adoumi was once again at ease, the momentary doubts induced by the rabbi's argument now gone. His tone as he continued, disinterested, even ironic. "Or are you suggesting that after he fought with the doctor, or whatever happened, that someone came along and planted a bomb on his windowsill? That would be a pretty remarkable coincidence you'll have to admit. What's more," he added triumphantly, "it's the bomb we are primarily concerned with, and you haven't demonstrated that your young man could not have come back and planted it, locked door or no."

"As you say, it would be a remarkable coincidence and so not very likely," the rabbi admitted. "The likelihood would be that if Memavet were killed by a blow on the head, then the killer would have been the one who planted the bomb."

"Why? Why would he want to bomb him if he had already killed him?"

"Why?" the rabbi echoed. "Because anyone can kill with a blow on the head, and so anyone can be suspected of it. But a bomb implies terrorists, and they are usually obliging enough to claim the credit for it."

"But you have suggested that it was Dr. Ben Ami who did the killing. Where would the doctor get a bomb? Do you think doctors carry them around in their bags?"

The rabbi was troubled and his face showed it. "I am relatively new here, so I don't know what is possible and what isn't. But the country is at war and has been for some time. I thought perhaps a bomb, or at least explosives, might not be hard to come by. Gittel had mentioned that Dr. Ben Ami got you this apartment, so I thought that perhaps he was connected with the contractor in some way—"

"He's his brother; he's Phil Resnik's brother," Adoumi interjected. "So what?"

"Well, contractors do a lot of blasting," the rabbi went on doggedly, "and I thought—"

"You thought he could just go to his brother and ask for a few sticks of dynamite?" asked Adoumi jocularly. He laughed. "Was it your idea that Phil Resnik gave his brother some dynamite to experiment with," he went on, his voice dripping with sarcasm, "or did Dr. Ben Ami run down to see him at home after he killed Memavet, get the dynamite, wire it up, maybe rig a timing device to it, and run back here to set it?" His eyes flicked at Stedman and Gittel and saw that they were squirming in embarrassment. His tone changed, and he went on, not unkindly, "It is a good effort, Rabbi, even ingenious, but the fact of the matter is that it wasn't that kind of bomb at all. It was a special type that the terrorists have used before. It looks like a small plastic radio. We have run descriptions of it in the press. . . ." His voice trailed off as he realized that the rabbi was not listening. Instead, he was staring up at the ceiling.

"Resnik, Resnik," the rabbi murmured. "It must be." He leaned forward. "When we went to see Memavet, Dan and his son and I, he told us a long story about a terrible injury he had received at the hands of a certain Dr. Rasnikov."

"That's right," said Stedman. "I remember. Rasnikov was the name of the doctor who assigned him to the Forestry Detail."

"We were perfect strangers to him, mind you," the rabbi went on. "But he told us just the same. It was obviously an *idée fixe* with him, and the chances are he told it to many people."

The rabbi got up and began to pace the floor, the eyes of the others following him. "Rasnikov, Resnik— it's the same name. I don't know any Russian, but I know that the 'ov' is a common suffix in Russian and means 'son of.' I don't know what Resnik means—"

"Shohet," said Gittel promptly, "a *resnik* is a shohet, a ritual slaughterer."

"Is that so? Well, it's the same name—shohet or son of a shohet. The one who went to America, the contractor—Phil, did you say?—shortened Rasnikov to Resnik because it had a more American sound just as the family called itself Rasnikov in Russia because it had a more Russian sound. And the one who came here chose an Israeli name because—because many people do and the state encourages it—"

"You fill out a form and you pay a lira," said Gittel.

"Precisely. And although a shohet is a dignified and honorable profession with us, he did not take the name of Shohet or Ben Shohet or Bar Shohet, I suppose because it has unfortunate connotations for someone in the medical profession. Instead, he took the common name of Ben Ami. And Memavet had no way of knowing that Ben Ami was Rasnikov and so did not hesitate to call him when he needed a doctor. That is a coincidence, if you like, but one that is quite likely to happen in this country because it is small both in area and population and because Jews from all parts of the world feel drawn to it. Sooner or later, you are apt to meet the most unexpected Jews. I met one when I had been here less than a week. I would have sworn it was the last place I would see him, but he had come here and settled. After meeting Willard Abbot at the Wall, I do not think it so unlikely that the doctor whom Memavet called should turn out to be his old enemy, Dr. Rasnikov."

"And you think they recognized each other when he came in?"

"If all there is to the story is what Memavet told us, then I doubt if the doctor recognized him," said the rabbi. "It's possible, but not likely. The doctor had only seen him a couple of times very briefly. There was no reason why he should remember him. But Memavet would remember the doctor. His face was photographed on his mind. I suppose he called him by his old name—"

"And the doctor remembered him and they fought?"

"More likely, Memavet came at him with the bottle, and the doctor pushed him away violently, and he struck his head on the shelf."

There was silence, and all eyes were on Adoumi as he gnawed on his lower lip to induce cerebration. "It's possible," he said at last, "but the bomb, how could he get hold of a bomb?"

"He probably couldn't get hold of one if he tried," said the rabbi, "but after the publicity you gave it, and the picture of it you ran in the papers, he'd recognize one when he saw it."

"What do you mean?"

"There was no car on Mazel Tov Street, no car parked in front of Memavet's house. Roy was explicit about that. Which meant the doctor must have come on foot. Where could he have come from? In his statement to the press he said he sandwiched in his visit to Memavet before another call. So he must have come here to see your wife. Anywhere else, even in the immediate vicinity, he would have got into his car. But if he had come here first, rather than get back into his car and turn around in this narrow muddy street, he would walk down the alley that connects the two streets. So he must have come from here."

"Well, that's true enough because he phoned me at my office and asked when I'd be home, that there was something important he had to tell me."

"He put it that way?" asked the rabbi curiously. "That there was something important he had to tell you?"

"Why, yes."

"I mean in those very words?" the rabbi persisted.

Adoumi pursed his lips and stared up at the ceiling. Then he faced the rabbi and nodded. " 'I have something important to tell you.' That's what he said. I'm sure because I naturally assumed he had just seen Sarah and there had been some sudden change. But he told me he hadn't seen her yet. The house was dark, you see, so he knew I hadn't got home yet. Or maybe he noticed that my car was not where I usually park it."

"And he knew what your position is, the kind of work you do?"

"Oh, certainly. Not because he was a friend, you understand, but"—he smiled faintly—"because there was a possibility that my wife's sickness might have some connection with my work. Gittel never tires of telling me that if I want my wife to get well, I should give up my job."

Gittel nodded vigorously. "And you should, Avner."

Before Adoumi could retort, the rabbi said, "It explains things, doesn't it?"

"What does it explain?" demanded Adoumi.

"It explains why he did not notify the police when he found the bomb," said the rabbi triumphantly.

"What bomb? What are you talking about?" Adoumi was exasperated.

Stedman and Gittel were equally mystified, but they remained silent.

"Look here. Dr. Ben Ami comes here and parks his car in front of your door. Then he realizes that you are probably not at home because the apartment is dark. Some doctors are reluctant to see a married woman alone, or the women are, or the husbands. Whatever the reason, he decides to see his other patient first. He probably knows you'll be along shortly, and he can see your wife after he's seen his other patient. But the other patient is in the corresponding apartment on the next block, and there is an alley between the two streets. So he takes his bag and walks down the alley." He got up and walked over to the window and stood looking out into the alley between the house and the embankment. "It was a cloudy night, misty. Later it began to rain, if you remember. So probably he used his flashlight to light his way along the alley, which must have been pretty dark at the time. My guess is that he saw the bomb on the sill of this window which can't be seen too easily from the street."

"This window? You are suggesting it was on my window?"

The rabbi nodded. "I would think so. Gittel claimed all along it was you they were after. I think she's right. She has said that you have a very important position in the government."

"Of course, I was right," said Gittel smugly. "Why would the terrorists be interested in this old used car dealer? I've said from the beginning it was you they were after, Avner." To the rabbi she said, "Avner has a very important position. Why, in Tel Aviv, before he came here—"

"*Sha*, Gittel. You talk too much," said Adoumi. "So you think the bomb was on my windowsill, Rabbi? And Ben Ami saw it?"

"I would say so." He leaned back so that he was sitting on the edge of the windowsill. "I don't know what I'd do if I came across a bomb as Dr. Ben Ami did. I'd be scared to death, I suppose. It was armed and could go off at any moment. What could he do? Run? Try to hurl it away? He had no way of knowing how long it had been there and when it was due to go off. I'd say he acted very sensibly. He remembered that the stories in the newspapers carried instructions on how to disarm it—by pushing in the plunger. Then normally, he would have called the police, and they would have come in several cars and searched the area and frightened your wife out of her wits in the bargain. So instead, he called you because he knew, I suppose, that the terrorists and their activities were even more your concern than they were the concern of the police. In any case, he knew you'd know what to do. He called you and said that he had something important to tell you."

Adoumi nodded slowly.

"And what did he tell you when he saw you?"

"Only that after he examined her, he said he thought she ought to come into the hospital for observation and some more tests."

"But he phoned you *before* he had examined her."

"Well, I suppose he had been thinking of it—"

"Then wouldn't he have said there was something he wanted to discuss with you or talk over with you rather than that he had something important to tell you?"

"I get what you're driving at," said Adoumi. "He goes down the alley and sees the bomb. He disarms it by pushing in the plunger and then calls me. Then instead of waiting around for me to come home, he goes to see Memavet first. No reason why he shouldn't. He wouldn't just stand there. But even if I accept your account of what happened between him and Memavet, I don't understand why he would then reactivate the bomb. You said it was to make the killing look like a terrorist crime, but why did he have to? He could have said he rang Memavet's bell and there was no answer—"

"Because Roy was there!" the rabbi exclaimed.

"When he opened the door to leave, there was Roy. To be sure, the death was accidental, but it was the result of violence. There would have been an investigation, and would everyone have believed it had been purely accidental? He had established himself here in Israel and was liked and respected. Would that continue after the police started digging? And if he did nothing, the body would be found, the next day perhaps, and Roy would come forward to say that he had seen the doctor leaving the apartment and closing the door behind him. But then he thought of the bomb and realized he could make it appear a terrorist act—and he knew they would immediately claim the credit for it because they always do. And of course, they did plant the bomb originally. So he reactivated it and placed it on the corresponding window of Memavet's apartment."

"But Sarah, he was endangering her," Gittel objected.

"Was he, Mr. Adoumi?" asked the rabbi. "In the newspaper description of the bomb, it said that it was of limited range and power."

"That's right," said Adoumi. "The noise and the shock, of course—but he gave her a sleeping pill. She awoke but went right to sleep again. Poor devil—I can't help feeling sorry for him." He got up from his chair and began pacing the floor while all three of his visitors sat silent, following him with their eyes. "Maybe we haven't got anywhere with Abdul because we've been harping on the connection with Memavet," he mused, seemingly oblivious of his guests. "Maybe if we change our line of questioning—" He broke off to turn to Stedman. "I—I am sorry," he said awkwardly. "Sometimes, mistakes are made—you understand—it is the safety of the state—"

"I understand," said Stedman. "I have no hard feelings toward you."

"Thank you." Adoumi smiled sheepishly. "And he *was* responsible for the bombing, you know—just by being there." He looked from one to the other of his guests uncertainly. "Rabbi, I want to thank you, and you too, Gittel, for bringing them here—I—"

"You should have known, Avner," she scolded, "that the son of a man like Mr. Stedman would not be mixed up with terrorists—or a friend of a nephew of mine."

"I—I should have known."

She looked sharply at him and then at her nephew and his friend, who were both grinning. "Men!" she exclaimed, striding to the door. "Well, are we to spend the whole afternoon here and Miriam at home wondering what happened to us?"

Meekly, Stedman and the rabbi followed her to the car.

50

"THEY'VE got a flight out Monday," said the rabbi. "Dan said he'd try to drop by sometime tomorrow to say good-bye."

"But why can't Roy finish the year?" asked Miriam.

They were alone in the apartment, Gittel having taken Jonathan to the park. The rabbi shrugged and didn't answer immediately. He went to the stove and poured himself a cup of tea, looked questioningly at her, and poured another.

He brought both cups to the table. "It's probably best," he said only after he had sipped cautiously at the cup. "The boy got off on the wrong foot. And then he suffered a pretty traumatic experience. I don't think he'd be able to do much in the way of studying the rest of the year. Besides, there might be some danger— from Abdul's Arab friends, who wouldn't know what had happened except that they had gone off together, he and Abdul, and he is free while Abdul is in custody."

"And Dan?"

"Under the circumstances, he couldn't very well just ship him off alone."

"But his book—"

"So he'll come back a little later. Or maybe he's got enough material now to sit down and write it." He drained his cup. "At the end of next week, we will have been here three months. We ought to begin thinking—"

"Oh, but Gittel said she had seen Mrs. Klopchuk and she was quite agreeable to our staying on for a while if we wanted to."

"No, I didn't mean just this apartment," said the rabbi. "I meant that we ought to begin thinking of going back to the States."

"Oh?" She controlled her surprise, waiting for him to go on.

He was embarrassed. "The last thing they need here in Israel is another rabbi. It's outside that they need them. Don't you understand? A doctor goes where there's sickness, and a rabbi, too, goes where he's needed."

"But your idea was to give up the rabbinate if you stayed on."

"I know," he said sadly. "That's a kind of daydream that occurs every now and then to anyone whose work carries with it responsibility for others. But it's only a daydream, and sooner or later you have to come back to reality and pick up where you left off."

"Was it this business with Roy. . . ."

"I suppose it helped trigger my decision, but I imagine I came to it a long time ago. I've been wrestling with the problem for some time you know, even before we came here."

"But when you broached the idea to me—"

"I was half hoping you'd object. It would have made it so much easier. But I'm glad you didn't because, of course, it's something I had to decide for myself."

There was a pounding on the door, and she got up to open to Jonathan and Gittel.

"I played football," Jonathan shouted. "Didn't I, Gittel? Tell them. There were some kids, and they started to play, so I played, too."

"Why, that's wonderful," said his father.

"He's quite a kicker," said Gittel.

The rabbi looked at his watch. "It's later than I thought. It's time to go to the synagogue for *Havdalah*. Do you want to come, Jonathan? You'll have to change your clothes."

"All right. It won't take me long. You'll wait for me, won't you? Will you help me with my jersey, Gittel?"

"Sure. Come along, Jonathan."

The rabbi leafed through his pocket diary and said to Miriam, "If we take off a week from Monday, we will get home three months to the day. I'd like that. Maybe you could call the airline tomorrow and see if we can get a flight."

When the rabbi and his son had left, Gittel said, "You know, Miriam, I didn't have time to tell you before, and I didn't like to say it in front of him, but Avner Adoumi was very impressed with your David, and—and, so was I. He did a fine thing for the Stedmans, but also it was very good for Israel."

"But not so good for Dr. Ben Ami," said Miriam, "and I feel sorry for him. The one time you took me to see him, I was in something of a state, and he was kind and gentle and very helpful. I wonder what will happen to him?"

"Dr. Ben Ami? Nothing will happen to him."

"Nothing?"

"Of course not. Adoumi is not police. The Shin Bet work largely on their own, I imagine. And if he does have to report to a superior, it would probably be merely to tell him that he is satisfied that Roy had no connection with the terrorists, and that will end it."

"But he can't simply ignore what Ben Ami did."

"What terrible thing did he do? That business in Russia? There is no proof of that, only Memavet's story. Always, when you make an administrative decision, the person affected thinks you had it in for him personally. In any case, what happened in Russia years ago is no business of Adoumi's."

"But he killed Memavet," Miriam protested.

"Yes, but your David proved that it was an accident and that Ben Ami was acting in self-defense. It must have been something like that because Ben Ami wouldn't recognize one former prisoner out of the thousands he dealt with, but Memavet would remember *him*. So what else? He didn't report finding the bomb? He tried to; he disarmed it and called Adoumi to tell him about it."

"But then he rearmed it and exploded it."

"True, but essentially without doing any harm, because Memavet was already dead. He damaged the building, to be sure, but it's his brother's building. I doubt if *he* would want to lodge a complaint even if he were to find out about it. No, I'm sure by the time Ben Ami gets back, that's the way Adoumi will think of it, and take no action against him, or even say anything to him. You'll see, when Ben Ami gets back, he will probably go right on treating Sarah."

"I won't be here to see, Gittel. We're leaving and returning to the States, in a week or so."

For once, Gittel's assurance and poise left her. "But I thought you said——"

"That David wanted to stay on? I'm sure he does, but he knows he has to go back. He knew it all along deep down."

"It has been lonely here with Uri in the Army," said Gittel sadly, "and I hoped that at last I would have a family—to visit, to help. And now you are going away, and Uri will get married, and I will be more alone than ever."

Impulsively Miriam went over to Gittel and sat down and put her arm around her. "Don't be sad,

Gittel, we'll be coming back regularly—to relax, to renew and refresh ourselves."

"I *am* sad," Gittel admitted, "but it is for you. It is sad to think of you returning to the Exile when you could have remained here in the Promised Land. But go in health and return in health. Your David is a smart man. Maybe next time he can arrange to stay."

51

"WHEN I got your cable, I was sure you were bringing home some girl," said Betty Deutch as she maneuvered her car expertly out of the airport and onto the highway that led to Barnard's Crossing and home. "You said, '*We* are arriving' instead of just 'Arriving.' It seemed an uncharacteristic extravagance to use two extra words, and then I thought it was your way of alerting me that you were coming with a girl you had picked up or who had picked you up."

Stedman laughed. "That was shrewd of you, Bet, but it wasn't a girl; it was Roy. I thought we'd come here for a week or so; but Laura met the plane at Kennedy, and Roy decided to go home with her first."

"Oh, I would have loved to have him down for a while. You know how I feel about him, Dan."

"Well, he's your only nephew—"

"When you have no children of your own, a nephew becomes something more than a nephew, even more than an only nephew."

"Well, he'll come down for a nice long visit after he gets settled," he promised.

"That's wonderful. He must have worked hard to get through so early. He's taken his exams already?"

"Well no," said Dan. "There was some mixup—"

"He's all right, isn't he?" she asked quickly. "He didn't get ill or anything?"

"Oh, no. He's fine. I'll tell you all about it when we get home. No sense in my having to repeat it to Hugo. How is *he*, by the way?"

She would have preferred to talk further about her nephew, but she knew her brother and knew he was not to be drawn. "Well, Hugo is in good health. He's always in good health," she added, "but he can be very aggravating at times."

Although she was intensely loyal to her husband, she was not blind to his faults, and although she would never mention them to an outsider, she did not hesitate to admit them to her brother, who was, after all, family and hence in a sense even closer than spouse.

"It's hard to be married to a rabbi; they're home so much of the time. They're around and underfoot. And then you never can tell when they're going to have to run off to some special meeting, maybe to substitute for a speaker that didn't show up. So you prepare a nice dinner and plan on going to a movie afterward, and there you are eating alone and watching TV afterward instead. Or it might be some youngster who is in trouble, or thinks he's in trouble, and has come to talk about it. And of course, it has to be right then and there because otherwise he'll run away from home or commit suicide or elope with someone quite unsuitable, and you sit and wait while the dinner gets spoiled, wondering whether to go ahead and eat by yourself or wait while you listen to the murmur of voices in the study and try to guess from the sound whether they're finishing up or will go on for a while."

Stedman laughed. "But surely you ought to be used to that by now."

"Some things you never get used to. When the roast is overdone, it doesn't help to remember that it was overdone last week, too. But what I was going to say is that all that is nothing compared to living with a rabbi who is not actually holding a pulpit. When Hugo retired, he was full of ambition; he was going to edit his sermons and publish them in book form; then another book was going to be worked up from his notes on counseling; and another was a book on the Jewish holidays. He was full of ambition, full of the wonderful things he was going to do now that he finally had the necessary time. He had his typewriter over-hauled and he laid in a supply of paper and carbons and an extra typewriter ribbon and a special kind of paper that made it unnecessary to erase if you made a mistake. And for just three days he went to his study right after breakfast and stayed there for a couple of hours. Then the next day he decided to take a walk first. I went into his study, not to spy, you understand, just to clean up and dust. And all there was were a few sheets of paper on which he had typed things like 'the quick brown fox' and 'Four score and seven years ago'—that kind of thing."

"Well, sometimes it's a little hard to get started."

"He never did get started, Dan," she said softly.

"I suppose all people who retire have to take a little time to adjust."

"But it's much worse for a rabbi," she insisted. "There is so much that he can't do. He has a certain image in the community that he has to live up to. Other people, when they retire, can play golf every day and cards every evening. They can go to the movies or read detective stories. But a rabbi is supposed to be on a higher plane; at least he thinks he is. It's all right to play golf occasionally, but if he's seen on the links every day, people will begin to wonder. We used to walk over to the library because it was a mile or so away from our house. It was a good distance for a nice brisk walk, and it gave us a destination of sorts. And we'd walk along the shelves and look at the books and every now and then he would point to a detective story and ask me to take it out on my card. The poor man didn't want the librarian to know he was reading something light. He'd take out books on sociology and comparative religion, that sort of thing, on his own card. But it was the books he had me take out that he read."

Her brother laughed. "What difference did it make to you what he read? It kept him busy, didn't it?"

"Oh, I didn't mind that," she said. "I just mentioned it to show you that it is different for a rabbi. But he couldn't read all day long. As a matter of fact, Hugo never was much of a reader. It was just that having nothing to do, the poor man would follow me around all day long. When I was making the beds, he was right there. And when I was in the kitchen, he was there, offering to do things, ready to hand me things I didn't want. You know, a woman develops a certain rhythm in her work. If she's used to walking over to the cabinet to get the pepper, it doesn't help her when she finds it at her elbow. It throws her off. I tell you, if this job hadn't come along, I would have gone out of my mind."

"But it did come along," Dan said.

"Yes, and it's really very pleasant here. And Hugo is very well liked by the congregation. As for the board, they just can't do enough to show how much they appreciate his coming. And Hugo loves it here, a lot better than his old congregation where he spent thirty years. He's had no quarrel with the board since he's come; everything is completely agreeable. From that point of view it's the easiest job he's ever had. And it's not as though he's an old man, you know. I mean, a rabbi at sixty-five is really at the height of his powers. After all, he doesn't dig ditches. And then he has all his old sermons that he can give, and of course, they're new to these people."

"But then it's only temporary," Stedman observed.

"Well, it needn't be. If Hugo weren't so indecisive about things and downright impractical, he could stay on here as long as he liked. I'm sure he'll discuss it with you. I've been talking to him, and I think I've about convinced him!"

She flashed her turn signal and made the corner. "This is our street." She brought the car to a halt at the curb, and simultaneously Rabbi Deutch appeared on the veranda to wave to them.

When Dan got out of the car, he was greeted effusively by his brother-in-law.

"It's good to see you, Dan. You're going to stay with us for a while, aren't you? Here, let me take your bag." Over his brother-in-law's protest he grabbed the larger of the two bags Dan had unloaded on the sidewalk and headed for the house.

"Life here must agree with him," said Dan to his sister. "Hugo seems a lot peppier, a lot more vital somehow than when I last saw him."

"Oh, he is. It's this new job here. He's really enjoying it. You must help me persuade him to stay on."

Stedman looked at his sister and pursed his lips. "We'll talk about it," he said enigmatically.

52

IT had been agreed between them that Raymond was to do the talking, not only because he was the president, but because he was a lawyer and was presumably smoother in negotiations.

"You tend to jump the gun, Marty. With high-class people like the Deutches you have to be easy and relaxed. You know it's not like a couple who lost the rent money at the races and come to you for a loan."

"All right, all right, so you do the talking, but get that contract signed tonight."

"You keep saying we should get it signed tonight, but as far as I'm concerned if he just says he'll stay,

I don't mind when he signs the contract. For all I know he might want to have his lawyer look it over—"

"Yeah? Well, let me tell you, Bert, so long as we don't have his signature on paper, we got nothing. I know he's a high-class guy, and maybe his word is as good as his bond, but me, I've been in too many deals where everybody agrees and shakes hands and then later they say you misunderstood them or conditions had changed. You think we're the only ones who are after him? Maybe we are, and then again, maybe after he'd been here a couple of weeks and decided he liked working better than loafing, he sent some letters out to congregations where the rabbis were going on sabbatical, saying, 'I have been informed that your spiritual leader, Rabbi Zilch, will be absent on a sabbatical leave, ta-da, ta-da, ta-da . . . so I would like to inform you that I am willing to consider helping you out— ta-da, ta-da, ta-da. Yours truly, Hugo Deutch, Rabbi-Emeritus.' "

"C'mon, Marty!"

"Believe me, it wouldn't surprise me. Look, he was retired for only a few months. Right? And we came along and offered him a job. Right? Now why did he take it if he was retired? I can see where he might to help out some rabbi pal of his who got sick or wanted to go on sabbatical. But he didn't know Small. So I'll tell you why he took it. It was because he was tired of sitting around on his rabbinical fanny doing nothing. Retirement ain't everybody's dish of tea, you know. But he knows the job is only for three months. So if he liked being back in harness again, wouldn't he start contacting other congregations?"

"Well—"

"So that's why I want his signature on a contract. Besides, when Small comes home, and it's only a few days now, he's going to act like he went away on an ordinary vacation and is back now ready to go to work."

"So we tell him we figured he resigned and we made other plans."

Marty Drexler shook his head vehemently. "Unh-unh. It's my opinion Rabbi Deutch would bow out immediately."

"So how does it change things if we have Rabbi Deutch's signature on a contract?"

"Then he's committed, and he can't back out. So it would be Rabbi Small who would bow out."

"How do you know he wouldn't make a fight for it?"

"Because he's a proud bastard and wouldn't give us the satisfaction of admitting he'd been kicked out. He'd act like he wasn't planning to come back anyway."

"I seem to recall he's fought for his job in the past. There were a couple of times—"

"No, Bert, those times were different. There was some special principle he was fighting for, not just his job. You trust old Marty. You want Rabbi Deutch? Get his signature on the contract."

Nevertheless, in spite of the sense of urgency that Marty Drexler had inspired in him, when they arrived at the Deutch home and were seated in the living room with the rabbi and his wife, Bert Raymond employed the easy, relaxed approach he preferred. He talked about the weather and how nice Barnard's Crossing was in the summer. He inquired about Mrs. Deutch's famous brother and what news he had brought back from Israel. It was only when he noticed that Marty was getting restive that he said, "We came over to finalize the matter we discussed last week, Rabbi."

"You have heard from Rabbi Small?" asked Rabbi Deutch.

"Well, no, Rabbi, not directly."

"So you don't know his attitude in regard to the position here."

"Well, not in so many words, but I'm sure he's not interested. I mean, from the whole history of our negotiations with him, the board feels that he is not interested in coming back. We want to make sure we have a continuity, so we'd like to get this matter settled tonight by getting your signature on a contract."

"But Rabbi Small is likely to be home in a few days. Surely we can wait until he arrives before settling the matter."

At this point, Marty Drexler's patience gave out. "Look here, Rabbi, I'm a businessman, and I don't like to pussyfoot about a deal like Bert here. That's the legal mind at work. I'll put it to you straight. We don't want a fight in the congregation. We don't want people taking sides and arguing the pros and cons of which rabbi is better. Personally, I don't think that's dignified," he said virtuously. "Now, if you want to stay, we have a contract right here. You sign it, and that's the end of it. We're pretty sure Rabbi Small wouldn't argue about it, not if he's faced with what Bert here calls a *fait accompli*. See? We sign the contract right here and now and everything is hunky-dory. We wait until Rabbi Small arrives, and there's a hassle."

Rabbi Deutch nodded his head slowly. "I see," he said, and he spoke in his normal rather than in his pulpit voice. "Well, when Rabbi Small comes home, I will talk to him. If he says flatly that he does not want the job and that he had no intention of returning to it, I will then sign your contract. If he is interested in the position, however, even if your board decides you do not want him and vote him down, I will not be interested in staying on."

Mrs. Deutch jerked her head in a decisive little nod as a schoolteacher might when a dull pupil answers correctly in the presence of the supervisor.

"But your wife said—" Marty blurted out.

"That's how I feel about it," said the rabbi decisively, "and that's how Mrs. Deutch feels."

When they had left, the rabbi said to his wife, "I'm glad that's over. My conscience has been troubling me ever since the idea of staying on came into my mind."

"I'm afraid I had something to do with it, Hugo," Mrs. Deutch said ruefully. "But to tell the truth, I really did think that Rabbi Small was not coming back. I mean, not writing to the president—"

"Well, I think I can understand that. He's quite young, and I think they hurt him. So he wouldn't write them. Not even a card saying he was having a good time."

"I suppose so." She hesitated. "Of course after what Dan told us he did for Roy, it was impossible for you to decide anything else. But I don't mind admitting, Hugo, that I'm sorry. I really enjoyed our few months here—"

"Well, I've been thinking about it, and I've come to the conclusion that I've enjoyed being here not because it's this particular temple or congregation, but because it was new to us. And being temporary, everyone treated us exceptionally well."

"That's true, I suppose—"

"But don't you see, Betty?" he went on eagerly. "The trick is to be a guest. If I had accepted the appointment, that would have been over."

"What are you getting at?"

"I think we've gone about this retirement business the wrong way. The whole point of retiring is that you're free and you've got enough money to be free on. That means doing what you want to do."

"But you tried that and you were bored," she said.

"No, I did what other people thought I should do: I did nothing. And that's boring. I'll admit. But if you do what you want to do, that means doing nothing some of the time and then when you feel like it—working. I didn't tell you, but I called the seminary yesterday. I had a long telephone conversation with the placement office and I told them that I'd be interested in temporary jobs, substituting for rabbis taking a sabbatical or for someone who is sick and is likely to be laid up for some time, and that money was a minor consideration. I asked them to keep me in mind. I gathered that I'd have no difficulty getting all the jobs I want."

"You want to go back to work?"

"Only when I want to," he said. "I'd like to travel a little, perhaps to Israel. Maybe we could stay a few

months the way the Smalls have done. Then I'd take
a pulpit for a few months or half a year—if I wanted
to; if I liked the place and the people. That way, where-
ever we went we'd be new—and independent. And if
I say so myself, I do think I'm rather good at running
a congregation."

"Oh, Hugo, one of the best," Betty said with a rush
of excitement. "I do think it will work, too. And perhaps if they ask you to stay on—"

"I'd tell them I was sorry," he said firmly, "that I've
retired and that I'm not interested in a permanent
position."

"I suppose that would be best, dear."

They did not talk as they got into their car, each
immersed in his own private thoughts. But as the car
pulled away from the Deutch residence, Raymond
asked plaintively, "Now what do we do?"

"Hell, what can we do?" Drexler demanded savagely.
"We start planning a welcome home party for the
Smalls."

53

"THE missus tells me you people are due over
at our place tomorrow night," said Chief Lanigan, "but
I happened to be in the vicinity—"

"Of course," said Miriam. "And you'll have a cup of
tea, won't you?"

She got up from sitting on the divan and started
for the kitchen. The chief's eyes flicked at her middle
as she passed, and he said, "Well I see you weren't
idle over there, David. And I don't know but that it

might not justify the trip. But did you find what you went over for?"

"Oh, yes," said the rabbi as he helped Miriam with the tea things. He offered their guest cream and sugar. "It was there all right, and we found it—practically the day we arrived."

"Well, that's fine. Still, it was a mite foolhardy, wasn't it, leaving your job for three months especially where the competition was so good? Although I suppose this welcome home party they gave you proves you knew what you were doing . . ." he added grudgingly.

Was the chief scolding him for risking his job by staying away? The rabbi was touched. "Yes, he's a good man, Rabbi Deutch," he said. "They liked him in the town?"

Lanigan nodded vigorously. "Very impressive. He looks the part for one thing." He eyed the rabbi appraisingly. "You don't, you know."

"I know."

"Well, don't knock it. Impressing people is part of your stock-in-trade. It's not supposed to be the style now, they tell me. There's a fashion in ministers, I guess. But I'm not sure the new style will last. Like we've got a new curate down at the church. He came while you were away. He's the new type of priest. You see him around in blue jeans and a sweater. He sits on the floor with the kids and plays the guitar. Religious songs I'll admit, but they don't sound religious. At least not our kind. So what's the result? When I see him in front of the altar in his vestments celebrating the mass, all I can see is a hippie in blue jeans. And when he preaches, I find myself thinking: Prove it, prove it. I mean, if it's not magic, if it's just everyday argument, then he's got to convince me. And of course he can't."

"And Father Dougherty?"

"You never see him except in a Roman collar and proper black. So he always seems to be in his vestments, and when you see him before the altar, you believe him. Now Mike Dougherty is no great brain, but he doesn't have to be because you feel that it's Somebody talking through him. Maybe there's a lot of hocus-pocus in religion, Rabbi, but it works somehow."

"Well, it's a little different with us," said the rabbi. "The rabbi is not a priest."

"Yes, I know, you've explained it to me, but does your congregation know it or do they feel the need of the hocus-pocus anyway?"

"I guess some of them do," said the rabbi. "Maybe all of them at one time or another."

"Well, that's why Rabbi Deutch was so popular, I suppose. I heard him once when he chaired a meeting. He kind of intoned, if you know what I mean. Very impressive. Now with us the priest wears a uniform, and the vestments are a kind of full-dress uniform. You people don't go in for that, so you've got to get the effect by voice and manner, because a uniform is important. Ask any cop."

The rabbi glanced at the chief's blue cap on the floor beside him and said with a smile, "The chief of police in Jerusalem or at least the inspector wears one of these." And he touched the yarmulke he was wearing.

"Is that so? You mean that's part of his uniform? He wears it in the street?"

"No, he has a cap like yours. It was just while he was in his office—"

"You saw him in his office? Did you get involved with the police over there?"

The rabbi grinned. "Not really. There was a bombing, and I had some knowledge of it and was questioned by the police."

"A bombing! And you were grilled by the police?"

"I suppose you could call it a grilling," said the rabbi, smiling reminiscently. "But it was mostly about my religious views. The inspector doubted my orthodoxy."

The chief shook his head in wonderment. "A policeman questioning your religious orthodoxy? What kind of place is it where a cop would question a rabbi on his religious views? That's police business?"

"It's that kind of place," said the rabbi, "and it is not general. Just this particular cop."

"But you say there was a bombing. Then there *is* danger there—"

"Oh, no."

"Now, look here. The monsignor over in Salem is leading a group to Ireland, Rome, and then the Holy Land. The missus had been making noises about going and I've half a mind to let her. But if there's danger—"

"Oh, there's no danger," said Miriam. "For her," she added. "But for us—"

"What danger was there for you?" the chief demanded.

Miriam looked at her husband. He smiled. "For us," he said, "there's always the danger that we won't come back."